# BEDAZZLED - AN ARRANGED MARRIAGE BRATVA ROMANCE

*Book Two of the Morozov Bratva Saga*

Arianna Fraser

STA, LLC

Copyright © 2023 Arianna Fraser

All rights reserved

The characters and events portrayed in this book are fictitious. Any similarity to real persons, living or dead, is coincidental and not intended by the author.

No part of this book may be reproduced, or stored in a retrieval system, or transmitted in any form or by any means, electronic, mechanical, photocopying, recording, or otherwise, without express written permission of the publisher.

ISBN-13: 9798388694119
ISBN-10: 1477123456

Cover design by: Art Painter
Library of Congress Control Number: 2018675309
Printed in the United States of America

*To my Todd, the best of husbands with the most twisted of plot ideas.*

*And to you...*
*A sincere and whole-hearted thank you to you for reading Bedazzled. Proceeds from this book benefit the two crisis nurseries in my city. The crisis nurseries here are non-profits that help families who are overwhelmed and in desperate need of help. Their little people can be lovingly and safely cared for while their parents are hooked up with services for anything from housing, to employment, to mental health. Thanks to your kindness, I've had the chance to purchase much-needed items, like cases of diapers, industrial-sized boxes of goldfish crackers, books, formula, toys, and more.*

*And socks. Those kiddos can never hold on to a pair of socks.*

# CONTENTS

Title Page
Copyright
Dedication
Free Books!
Spotify Playlist For Bedazzled
Preface
| | |
|---|---|
| Prologue | 1 |
| Chapter One | 7 |
| Chapter Two | 16 |
| Chapter Three | 26 |
| Chapter Four | 37 |
| Chapter Five | 47 |
| Chapter Six | 58 |
| Chapter Seven | 67 |
| Chapter Eight | 78 |
| Chapter Nine | 82 |
| Chapter Ten | 90 |
| Chapter Eleven | 98 |
| Chapter Twelve | 105 |
| Chapter Thirteen | 114 |

| | |
|---|---|
| Chapter Fourteen | 123 |
| Chapter Fifteen | 131 |
| Chapter Sixteen | 141 |
| Chapter Seventeen | 152 |
| Chapter Eighteen | 168 |
| Chapter Nineteen | 175 |
| Chapter Twenty | 184 |
| Chapter Twenty-One | 197 |
| Chapter Twenty-Two | 208 |
| Chapter Twenty-Three | 216 |
| Chapter Twenty-Four | 230 |
| Chapter Twenty-Five | 242 |
| Epilogue | 252 |
| Read the Extended Epilogue! | 255 |
| Afterword | 257 |
| Books By This Author | 259 |
| About The Author | 265 |

# FREE BOOKS!

Join my email list and I'll bribe you shamelessly with a free book! You can download your free copy of The Reluctant Spy here: dl.bookfunnel.com/p5xo4q2kj1

I'm too lazy to spam you, so you'll only see an email pop up when there's giveaways or a new release - like Book Three in the Morozov Bratva Saga - which will be released in May 2023.

# SPOTIFY PLAYLIST FOR BEDAZZLED

Do you get into a story more when there's music to inspire you? Find the Spotify playlist for Bedazzled here: bit.ly/3LS9zzw

# PREFACE

*Bedazzled - An Arranged Marriage Bratva Romance* is set in the brutal world of organized crime. These Russians are not messing around.

As such, there is violence, torture, explicit sex between consenting adult partners, kidnapping, forced marriage and profanity. Oh, so much profanity.

If these things are not to your taste, I thank you for stopping by, but please find something you'll be more comfortable with.

Still here? Excellent! Grab a glass of wine or a bag of Cheetos and let's get started. As always, thank you for reading and supporting my stories.

-Arianna

# PROLOGUE

*In which Yuri and Tania's plans for a romantic evening are shot to hell. Literally.*

**Yuri...**

"So, how big are we talking, babe?"

Tania's voice was at her most sultry, and as always, she turned every sentence into an innuendo. This was a quality about her that I deeply appreciated because those innuendos were traditionally directed at my cock.

"We are talking huge, darling," I assured her, smoothing my tie.

Patrick, the Morozov Bratva's *Obshchak* was sitting across from me in the town car and he rolled his eyes.

"Well, damn! I can hear the BDE loud and clear," she laughed, "hurry up with your voodoo business and bring that bedazzled dick to me."

"I will see you soon," I promised. Tania might be the most unrestrained woman I have ever met, but she had created a code to refer to my family business - the Bratva's business - and had not slipped once.

Patrick shook his head. "I don't know how you handle that one, brother. She's out of control."

"You have no idea," I chuckled. Tapping the divider between the driver's seat and ours, I reminded Ivan, "Do not forget to stop at Bud's."

"*Sovietnik*, you can have this flower arrangement delivered, you know," Patrick persisted.

"True," I agree, "but her appreciation is most enthusiastic when I arrive with a massive bouquet in hand. She calls it 'putting in the work.' We will finish this meeting with Hideo Tanaka as quickly as is polite and I am reserving my evening for Tania."

"You've been seeing her for what, ten, eleven weeks?" Patrick's head tilted curiously. We had known each other for ten years and he knew I rarely saw the same woman twice.

"We met at Maksim and Ella's wedding," I said.

"Wait, she's the one you took up to the honeymoon suite at the Four Seasons?" He started laughing. "The men still talk about the noise complaints from the other guests on that floor."

Shrugging, I checked my phone for any messages from my brother.

"Really," he persisted, "we all expect that behavior from the boss, but you? You're the classy one."

"You're treading dangerous ground, *ginger*," I raised a brow warningly, but Patrick, our Irish *Obshchak* was not finished.

"Did you take a break? From all accounts, there was definitely a spark between you two." He was desperately trying to keep a straight face and I cracked my neck irritably. Perhaps inspiring fear in our men would work better than inspiring respect.

"She was with me at the New Year's Eve shootout." My tone had cooled and his grin faded. "She told me afterward that she did not want to see me again," I shrugged. "That is understandable. We reconnected during Ella's brief separation from Maksim. She helped them reunite."

"The Morozov men, settling down," he rubbed his chin reflectively, "I'll be erasing that from my list of things that will never happen."

The town car pulled up to the florist's; Patrick and two of the men stepped out first, checking the surroundings before he opened my door, nodding to me.

"Three of you?" I murmured as I passed him, "I almost think you care."

Patrick looked stern and deadly in *Obshchak* mode, but his right eye closed in the most subtle of winks.

Bud's Floral always smelled like jasmine. "There you are, sir!" Mrs. Novikoff gently shoved the girl manning the cash register aside. "There is no charge for Mr. Morozov," she hissed.

The cashier - who could not have been older than fifteen or sixteen, looked up at me with wide blue eyes, then blushed and scurried into the back of the store.

"I'm sorry! She has a terrible crush on you," Mrs. Novikoff said, "she is always checking the orders to see if you put one in."

I chuckled politely, "It is not a problem. Do you have my flowers ready?"

Beaming, she nodded, bustling off to get the arrangement. "When you're using the language of flowers, matching personality type to the right blooms can be really fun." She put a beautifully wrapped bouquet of yellow and dark purple sunflowers in front of me.

"I've never seen black sunflowers before," I said.

"The sunflowers represent a cheerful, optimistic personality," she fluffed the satin ribbon a bit. "The purple sunflowers are special- they're bred to be a shade that's so dark that they do look black. Those specialty sunflowers say that the person has hidden depths, passion, and courage." She was blushing a bit, and I raised an eyebrow, leaning across the counter.

"Speaking of hidden depths…"

Mrs. Novikoff giggled, and it was charming on her sweet,

weathered face. "Oh, if only I could get my husband to flirt as well as you do!"

I put five hundred dollars in the tip jar, knowing that while she may refuse to charge me, it is also important to support Russian-owned businesses.

She called after me, "It's too much, Mr. Morozov!" as I waved without looking back.

Back in the car, Patrick dramatically moved over to make room for the flowers. "Daaamn, this is going to block the driver's rearview mirror."

"A short meeting with Tanaka," I reminded him, "and then I cannot be reached for the rest of the evening."

He made a suggestive gesture with two fingers with an inch of space between them. "How short?"

"Stop talking about your dick in such a sad, disrespectful manner," I shook my head sadly. "It cannot help being so tiny."

"*Tá an mac so Éire ar crochadh, a thóin,*" Patrick mumbled and I grinned.

"You, son of Ireland, have nothing to brag about, and you apparently forgot I speak Gaelic."

It was shaping up to be a great day.

"I'm outside your door, darling," I purred into my phone, watching Tania pull aside the curtain in her apartment window.

A luxury, highly-secured apartment that my brother and I insisted on buying for her, Maksim insisted on contributing because she was his wife's best friend. I refused to hear any argument from her because being close to the *Pakhan's* wife and dating his *Sovietnik* made her too tempting as a target. Any number of organized crime outfits would kidnap her to get to us. And one kidnapping she endured was enough.

"That was a short meeting," she said into the phone, waving down at me. "Of course, short is a word I would *never* use about anything having to do with you."

I laughed and bent inside the car to get her flowers and then Patrick roared, "Gun! Across the street!" The gunfire was instant and savage, bullets flying just over where my head had been. "Get in the car, boss!" He was still covering me, but I could see the driver was dead, slumped over the steering wheel and a slash of blood across the windshield meant one of my guards was down, too.

"Tonight!" I roared mindlessly, "You had to do this *tonight?*" Two of their men went down in quick succession, but I lost my other guard. Patrick and I were crouching behind the car, I fired underneath, taking the gunmen down as they raced across the street, chips flying off the granite front of the apartment house and there were screams as windows shattered.

"See if you can make it to the lobby," he shouted, "I'll cover you!"

"That's suicide for you," I shouted back, "keep firing, they're slowing down."

*Tania,* I thought, *please have been smart and stepped away from the window.*

There was another hoarse grunt and Patrick flew past me, shot in the chest. His eyes were open and blank, staring unseeingly at the blue sky. I was thrown back against the car shot in the shoulder I don't have time to fire in the direction of the new shooter before something slammed against the back of my head.

**Tania...**

Damn, that man of mine is *such* a snack. He was standing on the sidewalk, giving me That Look - which I can see even from the sixth floor, thank you - and he was pulling out a giant arrangement of flowers like the world's hottest magician and I was *such* a sure thing tonight!

And then, goddamn gunfire.

I slipped to my knees, rocking back and forth and its New Year's Eve again, and the screams, the gunfire, the shattering glass…

*Get the fuck up, get the fuck up, you idiot! Yuri's out there!*

Popping back up, I looked through the shards of glass left in the window frame and frantically scanned what was left of his town car. A van with tinted windows was tearing down the street and I just knew he was in there. *Please let it be one of his*, I thought, dialing Maksim's number as I ran for the elevator.

"Yes." Maksim's crisp, cold tone was cut off because I have no time to waste.

"Yuri! My apartment!" I was gasping out short chunks of information as fast as they form in my stupid, shell-shocked brain. "Guns! Lots of guns and they took him-"

"Where is Patrick," he enunciates carefully.

"I think he's dead," I was crying because why not? Yuri's gone and a bunch of his people are dead and-

"Tania, do not go outside," his stern voice broke through my hysteria a little, "there may be more. Stay inside!"

I ignored him and slammed through the front doors where the poor doorman was dead I think and dropped to my knees by Patrick. There was an ocean of broken glass around him and I was trying to stop the never-ending flow of blood even though he was probably dead and I stared at my sunflowers. They were crushed and torn and the yellow flowers were nearly as dark as the purple ones because they were stained red with my Yuri's blood.

# CHAPTER ONE

*In which Yuri and Tania experience the better "Meet Cute."*

***Yuri...***

***Maksim and Ella Morozov's wedding: Six months ago...***

"Really Maksim, I must ask this yet again, "Why must you do everything the hard way?"

Being *Pakhan* to the Morozov Bratva is a grim business, but even here, in front of the archbishop and about to marry the world's most unwilling bride, my brother's expression was cold and composed.

"Shut up, Yuri." He refused to look at me, still gazing stoically down the aisle.

I turned slightly so no one could read my lips. "I have seen this woman angry. I have no doubt she will attempt to murder you in your sleep. It is possible," I allowed, "that you deserve it, but…"

"You're betting your personal safety on the fact that we're standing in front of the archbishop and you know I won't beat the hell out of you in front of a man of God," Maksim said, "but you are forgetting that my memory is long, and my reach is longer. It might be five years from now when it amuses me to do it, but I *will* punch your pretty face."

The archbishop was gazing at us sternly, so I struggled to stop laughing before my brother really made good on his promise.

Ella was lovely, I absolutely agreed with that. Tall and elegant, and physically, at least, she was a perfect match for my brother. They made a stunning couple with their black hair and pale eyes. She was walking sedately down the aisle until her steps slowed, and then the girl holding up the wedding gown's silk train behind her discreetly punched her in the back.

*Hmmm… who have we here?*

She might have been petite, but she was balancing on sky-high heels like she did it every day. She looked up, and I noticed her eyes, a spectacular golden color I had not seen before. Her blue dress showed off all kinds of curves and luscious, tanned skin.

I love a woman with a tiny waist, and I caught a glimpse of her shapely, round ass before she turned to face me. My gaze darted up but she was trying to smother a grin. She knew exactly where I had been looking.

It was clear no one had warned her about her role in the ceremony, so when I lifted the golden crown for Maksim, I nodded toward Ella's. She watched me lift it over his head and did the same, though even those four-inch heels were not quite high enough. But she held the crown up and steadily, even though she was doing it on tiptoe. My new sister-in-law glanced at us as her friend winked at me and I grinned back, rolling her eyes at the both of us.

*Tania…*

Was it wrong that I absolutely intended to bag Maksim's brother before this night was over? Yeah, this was the most fucked-up wedding ever and the ballroom of the Four Seasons was filled with bad guys. I mean, *really* bad guys but this Yuri looked like he was a bad, bad boy in all the best ways.

But first; keeping Ella's shit together because my girl was on the edge. We were hiding in the ladies' room, because ever since junior high school, that's where we had all our best conversations.

"You don't really have to pee, huh? Are we hiding from someone?" I rubbed her back and checked my hair in the mirror. Oh, man, the dam broke and she told me about getting threatened at gunpoint by Maksim's psychotic ex - Cat… Kitty… Katana, I don't remember, Sokolov - and Ella's shitty ex-boxer bodyguard was in on it and even though she was marrying into the Bratva this was her first held-at-gunpoint experience and I was ready to shoot this Russian hellhound myself. And to top it off? The bodyguard was getting a blowski as we passed by on the way to the bathroom! That was one shitty work ethic, dude.

Poor Ella's face was crumpling and I panicked and grabbed tissues and threw them at her like confetti.

"Okay, okay," I babbled and waved my hands around a little. "Okay, listen here, little missy! You just suck it up, do you hear me!" I knew she would laugh because that's what my mother used to tell us.

Her bodyguard had zero sense of timing and pounded on the door like his bladder was about to detonate and this was the last toilet left in Manhattan.

"Mrs. Morozov, they are calling for you."

"She'll be out in a minute!" I shouted, "Look, get through this shitshow, eat some cake - oh, and make sure you take a giant chunk home because that looks delicious - and then tell Maksim-"

"Mrs. Morozov, you will come out now."

"In a minute!" Ella and I shouted together and I tried to refocus. "Tell Maksim later so he knows how to handle the Sokolov's who are clearly seriously fucked up. Okay?"

"Okay," she wiped her eyes before the mascara smeared because we did not want to know what the wedding planner would do to her if her makeup turned out all smudged.

All in all, the wedding wasn't too bad. No one got shot, Ella seemed to chill out as she and Maksim left and the ballroom was emptying when I stomped over to that tall, cool drink of Russian vodka standing by the bar.

"Hey, you're Yuri, Maksim's brother, right?"

"I am." He was looking down at me from his towering height and I was sorry I didn't wear my six-inch heels. He had to be, what - 6"6? He was kind of the light to his brother's dark, with his blonde hair and his blue eyes that were vivid, not like his brother's creepy pale ones. This gorgeous bastard was going to be *mine.*

As soon as we cleared a few things up.

"Ella tells me you're the diplomatic one in the family, so I figured you would be the one to handle this." I leaned in and pointed a finger into his amused face. "Ella got held at gunpoint this morning-"

His genial expression was gone. "Where?" Yuri asked sharply.

"Outside that hellspa! It was Maksim's ex. Lurch was supposed to be guarding her and that punch-drunk fuckboy left my girl in the SUV with this psycho bitch and her gun issues! This is extremely indifferent security, Yuri!"

Oh, now he was paying attention, his gorgeous face was cold and he grabbed my arm. "Who," he enunciated, "is Lurch?"

Craning my neck, I found the giant asshole standing sullenly by the door to the kitchen. *Probably hoping he can finish up with that banquet server,* I thought angrily. "That douche over there who looks like an ex-boxer."

"He'll be disciplined severely for allowing Ella to be in danger, but why do you think he was acting on behalf of the Sokolov woman?"

"Because Lurch has the IQ of a Fig Newton and when Ella asked how he didn't see the woman holding her at gunpoint, he actually said, 'I did not see Miss Sokolov,' I mean, are you kidding me?"

Yuri rubbed his forehead. "I have no answer for this level of stupidity. I will take care of it," he took one step away and halted. "You will stay here? I have so many questions to ask you." He looked me up and down like he was a starving tourist and I was the prime rib buffet at Jersey Steve's down by the shore.

"You fix Lurch," I smiled alluringly, it might have been more of a smirk but whatever. "I'm planning on getting drunk tonight because this booze is some top-shelf shit. And you, my friend, are the hottest man in this ballroom. It's time to find out if you Russians can really hold your liquor."

His pretty blue eyes were taking a slow circuit up and down my body and I was completely comfortable being objectified. With a slight sigh, he straightened his tuxedo jacket and took off.

Getting comfortable on a barstool, I swiped a glass of champagne from a passing waiter.

Oh, hell yes this was going to be the best night of that man's life.

*Yuri…*

"Take Lurch - I meant - Oleg out quietly. Send him to the warehouse and alert Bogdan that we will have need of his services in the morning." I was giving orders to Patrick, but I could not take my eyes off that luscious little Tania, who had convinced the bartender to line up a tidy row of shots.

Patrick was all business. "Oleg? How serious is this?"

"He left the new Mrs. Morozov in an SUV with Katya Sokolov

today," I snarled.

"That thick-headed gobshite," he said, "I'm on it. Do you need anything else tonight?"

"Not from you," I assured him.

He shook his head sadly, "And yet another perfectly nice lass will be ruined for all other men," Patrick sighed before he headed toward a group of guards.

"I certainly hope so," I murmured, straightening my tie.

**Later at the Four Seasons...**

"Okay, so you have to agree this is the worst 'meet-cute' in history, Maksim chases my poor girl through the woods?" Tania's hands were waving, champagne slopping over the side of her glass. "That's some primal shit right there you have to admit it."

I was fascinated by her. Women in our circles were careful, well-behaved, or at least terrified of the Morozov Bratva and anyone in it. It could not be more clear that Tania did not care. At all. None of this impressed her, aside from the drinks.

"Wait, what is a meet-cute?"

She tapped another shot glass against mine. "One, two- oh, my god that one's harsh!" Tania wheezed, laughing a little.

"Akvavit," I explained, "very popular with our Norwegian associates."

"Oh hell, that is lighter fluid! I have got to get this taste out of my mouth," she gasped, blindly reaching for the tray of hors d'oeuvres I'd had sent over.

"So, meet-cute?" I prompted.

Tania popped a tiny lobster puff in her mouth, "Meet-cute, the story of how a couple meets," she explained, "you know, you're at a party and someone's showing off their engagement ring and then you're all, 'Oh, that's gorgeous! How did you two meet?' And they tell you a story of how they both reached for the same Frappuccino at Starbucks or whatever and the rest is history."

I nodded. Maksim mistaking Ella for a traitor who had stolen our arms stash, then drugging and kidnapping her was not at all a 'meet-cute.' Holding up another shot glass, I smiled devilishly. "Now, darling I have saved the best for last, are you ready?"

She cocked her head, watching the light gleam through the crystalline liquid in the shot glass. "What is it?"

"The Eye of the Dragon," I said, gently tilting the glass. "This was not served at the wedding, it is from my private stock. I had planned to toast the wedding with Maksim, but they are gone and I think I would rather share it with you."

Propping up her chin on her hand, Tania raised her brow. "And what makes this magical mystery fluid so special?"

"The Eye of the Dragon is a vodka filtered through diamonds, the finest winter rye distilled five times. Only ten bottles have ever been sold."

"Yeah? If this has been filtered through diamonds..." Her golden-brown eyes widened. "How much did this bottle set you back?"

Handing Tania her glass, I leaned in to whisper, "Five and a half million dollars."

"Woah! I don't... are you shitting me?" She gently placed the glass on the bar.

"I am not... shitting you, darling," I ran my knuckles up her smooth arm. "Try it with me. Sip."

"My hand's shaking," she whined, "I don't think I can-"

I picked up her glass and held it to her lips, "A sip." Watching her lush, red lips pucker on the edge of the glass made me instantly hard. With a silent groan, I moved subtly, trying to stop my cock from breaking through the zipper of my tuxedo pants.

Tania sipped, swallowed, and groaned in a way so sexual that I nearly threw her on the bar to take her right then. "That is... oh, my god Yuri! I hate you for introducing me to this because everything else is going to taste like rubbing alcohol for the rest of my life!"

The hotel banquet staff were carefully moving around us, trying to clean up as quietly as possible.

"You know," I whispered in her ear, "Maksim had booked the honeymoon suite here, but they left for their honeymoon before they could make use of it. I want to take you up there, pull that pretty blue dress off you and bury my cock in you until you're crying and begging me to let you come again. Will you join me?"

Her eyes were wide, her pupils swallowing up the golden iris. "Well, you know. Waste not, want not, right? It would be a shame to let all those chocolate-covered strawberries go uneaten."

I moved slowly, letting her pull back if she wanted to, but Tania was still, watching me with her pretty mouth slightly open and still wet from the drink. Pressing my lips on hers, my tongue slid out to taste her and the vodka.

Groaning, I pulled her off the barstool, heading for the elevator. When she nearly tripped, trying to keep up, I swung her up in my arms and pushed the elevator button with my elbow.

*Current day...*

*Tania...*

"What do you mean, they don't know who took him!"

Ella put her arms around me, squeezing gently. "Tan, you know Maksim's got every one of his men within five states out looking for answers." Her eyes were red, too. We had both been crying on and off for a while.

"Well, don't- don't-" I stuttered, "don't gangsters make ransom demands? Why isn't Maksim getting a proof-of-life picture of Yuri and a demand for a billion dollars or something?"

"Honey, sometimes they don't…" she started crying again, "sometimes it's not for a ransom or for keeping a high-level hostage. Sometimes…"

For a second, I couldn't draw in air, like someone had punched me in the solar plexus. "No! That's not it, Ella! So just, you know, just don't talk like that because that's not…" Now I'm sobbing, too. "Just don't talk like that!"

Maksim walked into their bedroom, where we were huddled on the bed. He looked like shit. I knew he hadn't slept for two days because neither had I. Ella sprinted off the bed to hug him. He allowed it, but his hands were loose, just hanging down.

"Do you…" I didn't know what to ask for. "Is there any good news?"

Running a hand down his haggard, unshaven face, Maksim said, "We have our Bratva, the men from the Turgenev group, the Toscano *famiglia-* everyone is searching. There is nothing. The shooters had no identifying marks, no dental record, no fingerprints. We can't tie them to any of our enemies."

Ella sat next to me on the bed again, taking my hand. "What do we do now?"

"We keep looking," he said, his voice like frostbite. "We kill and torture and tear this city apart until we find him."

# CHAPTER TWO

*In which Tania discovers why Yuri is so popular with the ladies*

**Yuri…**

**Current day…**

"Let's take his arm off!"

I could hear the chainsaw starting up, but it was muffled like everything else. This was not the first time I'd been tortured, it started when I was ten when my father decided my brother and I would be tortured to "toughen us up."

There was no happier day for me than the one when Maksim killed that *zloy ublyudok,* but after a childhood of unspeakable pain and a couple of episodes of bad luck in my twenties, I knew how to send myself away from the agony. I could mute it, at least enough that they could not break me.

I chuckled a little, blood dripping from my mouth. But maybe this would be the exception.

Tania.

She was always there on the edge of my consciousness. She was the lynchpin that kept me from flying off into hell.

**Six months ago - The Four Seasons Honeymoon Suite…**

Pinning Tania between me and the door, I fumbled for the keycard while she was biting my neck. When I felt her quick little hands go for my zipper, I groaned and pushed her harder against the door. "This is not helping my concentration."

She couldn't stop laughing until I finally got the door open and we tumbled inside. We landed on a soft oriental rug, and I braced myself above her, my forearms framing her lovely face. Her eyes were molten gold, and she was still laughing breathlessly.

"Do you know, darling, that you have this beautiful red flush that starts on your chest…" I kissed her there, between her breasts. "…moves up your throat…" The tip of my tongue ran up the throbbing vein in her neck. "…and lights your face so sweetly? It makes your lips fuller, redder…" Putting my mouth back over hers, I tangled my tongue with hers for a minute, tasting the sharp vodka we'd just had.

"L- look at you, sweet talker," Tania was trying to stop laughing, but I'd moved and was kissing along her sensitive neck again.

Her laughter had cut off when I stood up with her legs still wrapped around me like a particularly aggressive strain of ivy. Pulling her harder against my cock, I rubbed against her. "Do you feel that? I'm going to be inside you so deep that you'll never draw a full breath again."

She arched one wicked eyebrow and thrust her hips up against me, making me groan. "Damn, honey, you are a *bad* idea. On steroids. And I am 100% here for it."

I have never been so turned on and yet laughing at the same time. I staggered into the bedroom and dumped Tania on the bed. As her legs flew up, I grabbed them against my chest. My hands slid up to hold her ankles, and I parted them wide to look down at her wet center. "Your panties are ruined," I said with faux sympathy. "We should take those off before you catch a cold."

Tania began giggling helplessly. "I don't think my pussy can catch a cold, big man." Her giggles cut off and she yelped when I ripped her undies off, appreciating the wet silk before I put them in my pocket. "Let us not take any chances," I murmured, my eyes still on that perfect little cunt. She was shaved bare, and her pink lips were swelling so invitingly as I lightly circled her clit with my thumb, and dipped my finger inside her.

"Take off your dress," I ordered, pulling my hand away. I put my finger in my mouth, tasting her. "I knew you'd be sweet."

Sitting up, Tania wiggled her dress off and kicked away her heels. I rubbed the front of my dress pants, trying to stop my cock from tearing loose from the fabric. That tiny waist made an appearance again, and silky breasts with taut, brown nipples. I slid my hands up her rib cage and under her breasts, cupping them and squeezing. "Gorgeous," I groaned, sucking one nipple into my mouth, then the other.

"Hey! Time for the grand unveiling, Yuri. I wanna see." She put her hands over mine on her chest, giving me a sly little smile and running her foot up my thigh and brushing it over my painfully hard cock.

"Oh, do you want this?" I inquired pleasantly, rubbing her little foot over it.

"Yes!" Tania laughed, curling her finger in a 'come hither' motion.

"You can't have it yet," I grinned, turning my head to bite her calf, then the thin skin of her inner thigh, and running my tongue up the delicate crease where her thigh met her pussy.

**Tania... *The Four Seasons Honeymoon Suite...***

*I can't have it? Oh, this Russian fuckboy is about to learn who he's dealing wi-*

"Ow! You dick, that hurt!"

Yuri's ridiculously broad shoulders shook while he smothered his laugh in my center, rubbing his nose against my clit while that stubbled chin of his dug in to my softest parts and I forgot all about those bites because sweet baby Jesus this man knew what he was doing.

Most guys would give me that, 'Oh, yeah baby you're gonna *love* this' face when they were going down on me, but their work south of the border? Not great. But damn, this beefy sweetheart was settling in like he'd packed a lunch and was staying the day in my pussy.

Which I was not against. But I had seen that epic bulge in his pants and it was going to be mine.

Yuri's thumbs were holding me open while his lips, teeth, and tongue were attacking me, there were little bites, licking, sucking, nibbling again and it took less than two rounds of this torture to put me right on the edge and so damn ready to fall over and-

"Hey!" I stared sternly up at this smirking bastard. "Why did you stop?"

He slid a knuckle up and down between my lower lips, nudging my clit on each pass. "You do not come until I say you can come." I tried to tighten my thighs around his head and Yuri had the nerve to laugh, wedging his shoulders between my knees and holding me open. "Keep your eyes on me, darling."

He had the audacity to leisurely make another round in my pussy before arching one evil brow. His white, even teeth very gently took my poor, swollen clit between them and I sucked in a breath so fast that I started coughing. His tongue started batting it back and forth, still held between his teeth and I collapsed onto my back, my hands were reaching mindlessly for his hair and-

"Okay goddamnit, Yuri! Again?" I was ready to put my fingers to work and show this sadistic sex fiend just exactly who owned my orgasms when he lightly slapped my center. A shock of heat and a flash tingled through me and I could have come from that if he would just-

"Ah, ah," he shook his finger at me, still wet from being inside me. "Put your hands under the pillow and keep them there. I would hate to have to tie you up. This early in the evening, at any rate."

"Are you a punishment for something I did in a past life?" I whined, "Because I haven't done anything evil enough in this one to deserve- ah!" He slapped my pussy! Again! I was so wet that it stung but it only made the ache worse. "I swear to god, Yuri…"

"I wonder," he said in that arrogant, smirking, dumb, hot way, "If I just blew on this poor, wet cunt, do you think you would come?"

"Try it and see," I said sweetly, wanting to just grab that thick blond hair of his hand and push his face back to work on my girl parts because this was mean. No orgasm? No cock? "Hey, do you do the torturing thing for your Bratva?"

That got him to look up at me, all stern and sexy. "I do not."

"Are you sure?" My thighs were futilely trying to tighten and get some stimulation and his monster shoulders were in the way. "Because this shit must be illegal under international law. Even political prisoners get to come, you know!"

That spiteful son of a bitch just laughed and lowered his head, wrapping his muscled arms around me to keep my lower half still, and *did it all again!*

After a few more minutes of, *Am I gonna let you come? I'll bet this time I'll let you come - psych!* Yuri abruptly pulled away from me, standing at the foot of the bed to pull off his jacket and shirt. His chest was… he had an eight-pack? Seriously? And biceps possibly bigger than my thighs and ink everywhere; intricate stars on his shoulders, a snarling wolf on his left side, a silver dagger on one forearm… his entire upper half was a tapestry of sleek, dark images coiled around each other.

I was so busy admiring his stupidly gorgeous chest that I almost missed him unzipping his pants - *finally*! - and one hand stroking his cock which was, frankly, more than I'd bargained for. Thick, with a shiny, circumcised head and I didn't get to see much more which was very unfair because Yuri put one knee and then the other on the bed, sitting back, heels on his perfect ass, and abruptly pulled me by the waist until my lower half was resting on those gorgeously muscled thighs and his thumbs were spreading me open again.

"I want you to come as I push my cock up into you," he said, "I want to hear you moan and feel you come all over me."

"Well, maybe I don't want to anymore," I tried to give a credible sneer but I was shaking with anticipation. I could feel the broad, hot head of his cock notching into me gently, then a swift, hard thrust of his hips and he was showing my pussy who was in charge here. "Oh, holy shit!" I wheezed. I was wet enough to be a slip-and-slide but I was not prepared for his size. No human body was prepared for his size. Oh dammit, he was right! I gripped his arms and I let out a yelp which was not attractive but an orgasm was searing its way up my spine and then radiating back down again to my pussy, his outrageous, porn star style cock was striking sparks and setting everything inside me on fire.

Yuri's pretty blue eyes were focused on where he was currently splitting me into two pieces and his jaw was set.

"So slick," he groaned, "and yet I can still barely get inside you."

Well, that just made me come again.

Okay, it took me a few minutes to come back from this and Yuri was lazily circling his hips, moving his magical dick side to side inside me to loosen me up. And when I was capable of noticing more than the fact that my pussy would never be the same again,

I felt it, a long row of- something? Hard somethings rubbing against the front of my channel, against my G-spot, rippling through me and no wonder I came so fast!

I managed to draw in enough breath for a full sentence, "Hey, wait- hold up gorgeous, just… gimme a minute… just pull out for a minute."

Slowly, he moved his hips back and I felt it again; that ripple inside me that nearly made me come again.

Bracing my hands behind me, my stomach contracted when Yuri - and it took a while because he was gigantic - pulled out of me, resting it between my legs. There were six circular bumps on the top of his dick.

"What *are* those?" I demanded, instantly enchanted with whatever these were.

Running his thumb along the bumps, he explained, "I have six pearls inserted under the skin of my cock."

Scrambling off his lap, I leaned down, tracing them with my tongue. Below the smooth skin, the bumps rolled slightly against my lips and I circled the silky head of his cock before sucking him into my mouth, feeling each pearl against my tongue.

A groan distracted me, and looking up, I saw Yuri's manly, square jaw tighten. Slowly pulling him out of my mouth- *bump… bump… bump…* I grin. "Can you come like this?"

His brow rose, "I am barely keeping from coming right now. I am thinking about our old housekeeper in her underwear and it is not going to be enough if you keep playing with them with your tongue."

Cupping his balls in one hand, I open wide and go back in.

**Yuri…**

***Much later, in the Four Seasons Honeymoon Suite...***

"So, explain the pearls."

Tania was lying halfway on, halfway off the bed, apparently too exhausted to decide which direction to take. I gently pulled her back up, put a pillow behind her and handed her a bottle of water.

"Drink that."

She held the glass to her lips with a challenging grin. "Just as soon as you start talking, you Slavic sexy pants."

I burst into laughter. "Slavic what?"

"Slavic sexy pants," she corrected, "talk to me."

Shrugging, I sat next to her. "Pearls have always been popular with Russian nobility. Royalty in particular for centuries would adorn themselves in pearls; jewelry, clothing, crowns, even furniture, and art. But there was one ruler - Tsar Alexis - who had the royal physician sew pearls under the skin of his cock. He was known as Tsar Alexis, the Quietest."

Tania began her hoarse little chuckle again. "Oh, hell yes. That's because his dick did all the talking. I'll bet he had one happy wife."

"Hmm," I tried to remember my history, "I believe he outlived four wives."

"Of course, he did," she scoffed, "he killed them with his magical bedazzled cock. How many women have you sent six feet under with a smile on their faces?"

"Bedazzled?"

"Bedazzled, you know." Tania took the plate of cookies I had put on the side table and shoved half of one in her mouth. "You never saw the infomercials?"

I shook my head when she offered me the plate. "I don't believe so."

She was trying to laugh and keep the cookie in her mouth at the same time, so it took a moment. "The infomercial used to be all over TV, but now you can just get them on Amazon. It's like a wand and you stick the crystals in it and *whap!*" She slapped her knee for emphasis, "It punches a hole and you can embed crystals and beads and shit in your clothes, or... I dunno, stuffed animals..." She nods at my cock, which is still half-hard, "Bedazzled."

"That sounds..." I shake my head, chuckling, "horrific."

"Oh, dude," Tania rolls her eyes, "you're the *Sovietnik* of the biggest Bratva organization in the US and you think that's horrific? Please."

"That is not something you should be talking about," I said coldly. This was the second time she had casually thrown out something about the Bratva. These things were never spoken of.

She shrugs, unperturbed. "Do you think I'm some little farm girl who just blew into the big city with the egg money? I'm not a moron. But since your brother wouldn't let her have her phone - super controlling, dude, and it reeks of desperation - until right before the wedding I had to do the research. My only role in this shit show is as Ella's like, emotional support animal. Now that I know what she's dealing with, I'm not going to make it harder for her."

Settling more comfortably against the pillows, I put my arm behind my head. "So even knowing what I am, you were still willing to come up here with me?"

Tania took another bite of her cookie, putting her bare foot carefully against my cock, which was now moving past half-hard and into a full-blown state of skin splitting off it if I did not get back inside this woman immediately.

"I told you. I was going to get drunk tonight - well last night now, I guess - and you were the hottest guy in the room." Her foot moved a little, pushing into my cock, which was now hard enough to push back. "You were the only one with a sense of humor and you totally had this crazy BDE energy." She gave me a sly smile, "I had a feeling about you Morozov men."

*zloy ublyudok* - evil bastard

# CHAPTER THREE

*In which Tania fights her completely understandable addiction to Yuri's bedazzled body part.*

**Tania…**

**The day after the wedding, Four Seasons Hotel…**

We were in bed. Again. I was still panting as Yuri gently lifted my legs down from the pretzel shape he'd had them in. *Thank god for yoga, huh?* I thought.

We both groaned as his cock slipped free.

"I'm going to miss you, little fella," I said, giving a soft kiss to the source of so much pleasure over the last twenty-four hours.

"Little fella?" Yuri chuckled, sitting up with a groan, "I do not believe that was how you were addressing him twenty minutes ago. As I recall, your words were, "Get that monster dick out of me, I can't come anymore.""

"Well, you proved me wrong, didn't you?" I admitted, rolling my eyes. "I have to shower and get dressed, babe."

Yuri gracefully (of course) rolled from the bed and put his boxer briefs on, an action I viewed with regret. "Of course, darling. Would you like to shower together? Conserve water?"

Laughing, I leaned weakly against the bathroom door because I didn't have the energy to stand up without assistance at that point. "Yeah, that's what you said last night. And this morning. Nothing got clean."

"Now, that is not true," Yuri was looming over me. Sexy looming. Because he was gigantic. And he had the nerve to look hurt. "I washed you clean." He took a step closer, "Made you a very dirty girl…" another step and I was pinned between him and the door, "and bathed you clean all over again."

"Nooo," I groaned. "I really have to go." Not that I actually wanted to leave, but no matter how many bottles of water and tasty bits of food Yuri had urged on me, I didn't think I had any fluids left in my body. It was bad enough that I was going to be walking bowlegged for the next month.

He kissed my hand lingeringly, "I understand," he said. "Go have your shower, I'll have them send up brunch-" he looked at the clock, "lunch."

"More like dinner, hot stuff," I laughed. It had only been twenty-four hours but damn, I wish we could stay in this suite for another week. How could anyone get sick of quality cock like his? I turned on the shower, groaning in relief as the hot water hit my shaky muscles.

It wasn't just that magical bedazzled dick, the guy attached to it was pretty amazing. Yuri might be a gangster, but I have only seen the sweet, sexy as fuck Yuri. Who had a massive cock. And knew how to use it.

*Great,* I thought, *even for me this is a terrible level of dick obsession.*

When I emerged from the shower, there was a dark red dress hanging next to my poor, wrinkled bridesmaid gown, a shiny black box with lingerie, and a pair of six-inch Louboutin's.

*Oh, yeah. This man understands me.*

"You're beautiful," Yuri said, looking me up and down when I emerged from the bathroom.

"Well, thank you for the outfit," I smiled a little awkwardly. Gifts? Expensive gifts? The kind of guys I dated didn't give gifts.

Really. I think the closest I ever got to a gift was a two-for-one coupon Mikal once gave me for a dinner out.

A dinner I paid for.

"It is a lovely color for you," he was still giving me a really thorough visual examination.

Dinner was hosted by charming, attentive Yuri and I was enjoying each facet of his personality as he revealed them to me. "So, how come you're not as constipated as your brother?"

He broke into quick, shocked laughter for a moment before sobering. "I would suggest you never use that term to describe my brother again. Particularly where he could hear you."

"But you know what I mean." I'm a persistent little shit when I have to be. "I mean, you're all up in the family business too, and you're so…" I waved my hands around, "you know. Charming. Debonair. Great sense of humor. I can't picture you snatching up some poor, innocent girl out of your nightclub and then making her marry you."

"If I had seen you there," his eyes flashed and for a minute, I could see dangerous Yuri, "I might have been tempted, darling."

"Hmmm…" I finished my Mimosa. "Don't you get all dark and sexy on me." Letting out a sigh, I stood up. "Time for me to go." He insisted on being all gallant and escorted me to the lobby.

"This is my driver, Timur," he said, nodding at a scary-looking guy in a black suit, "he'll take you home." Yuri kisses my hand. "I would like to see you again, Tania."

His mouth was so warm, and the perverted little shit touched the tip of his tongue to my skin, making me shiver.

"Don't take this personally, gorgeous, but I have terrible taste in boyfriends. I do not think we want to get into this."

His elegant brow rose again. "Bold of you to assume I was looking for something so serious," but he was smiling, damn him.

"Bold of you to assume you wouldn't be begging to be my boyfriend after just one more date," I sassed. Sobering a bit, I kissed him on the cheek. "This has been the most spectacular twenty-four hours of my life and given my past, that is saying something. Thank you."

Something flickered in his pretty blue eyes, but Yuri nodded and kissed me one last time. "Thank you, Tania. You are quite unforgettable."

"I know." I blew him a kiss and sauntered out, even though a good 83% of me wanted to turn around and take him up on that date offer.

*You suck at boyfriends,* I reminded myself with a sigh.


"Hey, Timur, my address is-"

The driver's voice sounded like he was gargling with gravel. "I know, Miss."

I shake my head. Of course, he does. He was driving at the correct speed, hands at two and ten on the steering wheel. "Timur."

"Yes, Miss."

"Those X tattoos on your hand, what do they mean?" I asked, "There's like forty of them."

"They're for..." the poor man hesitated, his hands loosening and tightening on the steering wheel.

Light dawns. "Oh, they're for kills, right?" There was a strangled sound from the front seat. I am freaking out by this revelation because I'm sitting in a car with a guy who immortalized his kills via tattoo and that is so fucked up. As always when I'm trying to not completely lose my shit, I chatter. Mindlessly.

"Well, it does seem like a high number, given how young you are.

But in your line of work, maybe that's not so unusual. Is there a quota you need to meet, or something?"

He stares at me bleakly in the rearview mirror, like I'm draining him of his will to live.

***Two weeks later…***

That damn bedazzled dick and the gorgeous man attached to it have ruined me. I have tried everything to get off without him. I have worn out the batteries in my favorite vibrator and… nothing. I'm still turned on, day and night and this sucks.

Maybe if Yuri would stop doing annoying shit like sending me flowers every day, it would help me forget him. And all those orgasms. And the laughing. And the talking. And the pretty dress and shoes.

"Tania, what's your thought on the Jensen-Smith merger?"

*Oh, shit.*

I blink and try to form a serious, interested expression so that my boss on the Zoom call doesn't realize that only my physical body has been present for this meeting.

"According to the federal tax report, they're claiming less than half their value on their tax returns, which puts them in an unsuitable category for risk."

He scowls, which usually makes everyone else quake in terror but I already know that Ezio Papachristodoulopoulos is a pussycat with the longest last name on the planet. "Take another look at their energy holdings and double-check if anything's been put under another LLC."

"Yeah, okay," I agreed absently, even though this deal screamed of galactic stupidity and poor life choices on the part of everyone involved.

"We're done here," Ezio ordered, "Tania, hang on for a moment."

I stifled a groan. I appreciated him for hiring me immediately while the Feds were confiscating everything at my old company for insider trading, but he never stopped asking me out. When I reminded him that this could be considered inappropriate workplace behavior, he protested that he was Greek and that he would lose his manhood and cultural identity if he didn't ask out a beautiful woman like me.

Blah, blah, blah.

"Tania, we have an important corporate event this Friday," he said, shuffling some papers to attempt to look like his mind was totally focused on business. "I'll need you to join me."

Sighing inwardly, I asked, "Is this corporate even an after-hours party?"

"Yes," he blustered, "and there will be key players from the Vladelets Real Estate group there. I'll need you on board."

"Just as work associates, Ezio," I warned.

"Of course!" He had the nerve to look insulted.

"What are you doing tonight?"

I was talking to Ella on my way downtown. "Ezio's making me go to an 'important corporate function' tonight," I said, imitating his nasally voice. "He swears there are key players from some real estate group that he's been romancing."

She laughed, such a supportive friend. "Is that like that time he told you there was a corporate retreat in the Poconos and when you got there you and he were the only ones?"

"Probably," I groaned, "he's such an assface. I charged him for the Uber drive back to the city for that little stunt. I think it was like $1,200 bucks."

"Good," Ella said, "he deserved that. Give me a call if you need to be rescued tonight."

"Like the blind date 911 texts we used to send each other?"

"Exactly! But hey, it might be fun," she said.

"How about you, Els? Have you spoken to Maksim since you got back from St. Johns?"

There was silence for a moment. "No."

"That man is such as dick," I snarled. "Why couldn't he have been all sweet and charming like his brother?"

"You still have a thing for Yuri, don't you?" Ella teased.

"No!" I lied, "It's just that magical bedazzled dick of his. It's supernatural. It cast a spell on me."

"We're not talking about my brother-in-law's junk," she said.

"Swear to god, Els! Yuri's dick could be seen from space, like the Great Wall of China! It's the Eighth Wonder of the World! I think he moved my intestines three inches to the left, his dick is-"

"I'm hanging up, Tania."

"I'm telling you there is no getting over that bedazzled dick, and-"

There was a sigh, then the call disconnected. Whatever. She couldn't handle the truth.

"You're here! Good," Ezio bustled up to me the minute I made it through the door of Le Bernardin. This place was one of the most expensive restaurants in Manhattan, and apparently, the Vladelets Real Estate group was big enough to buy out the place for the evening.

Taking my elbow, he started steering me toward the center of the room. "Now, I want you to be at your best tonight, Tania, this could be our biggest client in ten years and-"

Planting my feet, I stopped dead. "Are you expecting me to sleep with him, or something? Because that shit is not happening. And this whole conversation requires a drink." His mouth opened and I held up a warning finger.

Stopping a wandering server, I took one of the square glasses from her tray. The drink was a pretty yellow color. "What is this?" I asked, lifting the glass to the light.

"Our signature cocktail for the Vladelets Group," she said. She was either sincerely excited about this drink or a stage actress getting by with server gigs. "It is infused with the aroma of tangy citrus spice, made with Grey Goose VX Vodka, with bitter orange and cardamon accents."

I took a sip, it was as good as her drink narrative. "Super tasty, thanks!" She smiled brightly and moved on as my boss's sweaty paw latched onto my arm again.

"This is important, Tania!" He's breathing heavily in my ear and I'm already wishing I didn't give up religion years ago because now would be a good time to ask God to just kill me and put me out of my misery.

"I can listen if you let go of my arm," I snarled.

"Is this man bothering you?"

I close my eyes in defeat. It was Yuri. Of course, it is.

Throwing back the rest of my drink in one go, I sucked in a deep breath and turn to face him. Oh, yeah, I forgot that I had to look up until my neck cracked to look this gorgeous giant in the face.

Yuri looks smugly delighted, "Hello, darling. How are you?" He leans down to give me the Russian social kissing thing, kiss on the left cheek, the right, then the left again. "But back to my earlier question, is this man bothering you?"

I looked at my boss, whose expression is a sad mix of terror and hope. "You know Mr. Morozov, Tania?"

"Yuri, this is my boss, Ezio Papachristodoulopoulos of the Papachristodoulopoulos Equities Group. He is very interested in your *real estate* venture." I try to imitate his haughty raising of the eyebrow thing but it just gave me a look of perpetual surprise. "You're a man of many talents, aren't you, Yuri?"

He has the nerve to smile at me innocently. "Yes, Morozov Holdings has multiple business ventures."

I seize another drink off the tray of a passing server.


One hour later, Yuri's limo was cruising slowly around Central Park while I straddled the man and rode him like he was in the lead at the Kentucky Derby.

"*YA skuchal po etoy ideal'noy zadnitse,*" he grunted. His fingers were digging into my ass and thrusting me harder against him.

"Tr- tr- translation, please?" I gasped.

He pushed me down, burying his cock high enough to puncture a lung. "I said, I have missed your perfect ass," he said, kissing me greedily.

"Trust me, it's my pussy that has missed you," I laughed breathlessly.

Yuri gently pushed me back with a hand on my breasts, making my spine arch. Running the heel of his hand against my stomach, he groaned. "Feel this." He put my hand under his and I could feel the solid bulge of his cock under my skin.

"Oh, my- fuck! Yuri! Fuck!" I'm not super articulate when I come.

Another hour later and the poor driver was still cruising Central Park. I was lying on top of Yuri, his magical bedazzled cock finally softening inside me and I was boneless.

"Would this count as a date?" Yuri finally said, and I laughed weakly until I felt his cock getting hard again.

"No! No more of that right now! Look, Cockmaster General, I can't think straight when you're doing that." I feebly tried to move away before he could start his pearl-encrusted mojo on me again. He relented and lifted me easily off his most prized possession. Or maybe it's *my* most prized of his possessions, I was on the comfortable leather seat again and after he tidied me with his pocket square, monogrammed, of course, Yuri gently pulled my undies back up.

"Drink, darling." He offered me a chilled bottle of water from the bar.

"Do you have anything stronger in that fancy limo bar, babe?" I angled to sit on my right butt cheek because my pussy was too sore. Unfortunately, he noticed and cupped my stinging girl parts with one huge, warm hand.

"Are you all right?" It was so adorable; this big Russian gangster actually looks concerned.

"Yeah, I just need a way to put all the parts of my pussy back together," I was trying to make a little joke and he was not amused.

"I should have spent more time getting you ready," Yuri said, deep recrimination in his tone.

"Oh, my god, you're so sweet you're making the fillings in my teeth hurt! I'm good, I promise." Heaving a little sigh, I rest my head on his lovely, broad shoulder, *"Really* good."

"You did not answer my question," he said, barely keeping the Smug out of his tone, "does this count as a date?"

I sat up to take a glass of champagne from him. "Why is that important?"

"Because if this was a date," he said patiently, "I believe it went rather well. So, you should have no reason to refuse another?"

"Just because we were doing squat thrusts in the cucumber patch doesn't mean this was a date, Yuri!" I was trying to think of something more articulate to say but my IQ apparently ran off with my orgasms.

He choked on his drink so it took him a minute to respond. "I am impressed by your extensive gift for metaphors. But I do believe this-" he made a circular gesture indicating the backseat of sin, "does show we share a certain spark. Join me on a proper date."

"Yuri, I told you. I have the worst taste in boyfriends…" I wanted to. I really wanted to date this guy because Yuri was a god among men. "Breaking up with some loser because he wanted a threesome with my cousin-"

"I will break both his legs," Yuri interrupted me.

"No! No, Yuri, we don't do that in polite society! We like, hack their Con Ed account and get their gas turned off in the middle of winter or something. But what I'm trying to say is, dumping that troll didn't give me a second of heartache. But ending it with a man like you…" My stupid throat closed up.

He took my hand, kissing it gently. "Why not use your legendary courage and just… see how you feel after a date or two. No pressure, yes?"

When I was a kid, we'd go down to the Houdaille Quarry in New Jersey to go swimming and I would climb to the top of those sheer stone walls to jump. I couldn't look down, I had to run full out and jump or I'd never do it. Looking at Yuri, I remembered how it felt, screaming all the way down and plunging into the cool, dark water.

"Okay. One date, Yuri. One."

# CHAPTER FOUR

*In which Yuri is lost, and Yuri is found.*

*Tania...*
*Present day...*

I have circled every room in the palatial Morozov penthouse maybe nineteen times in the last hour. Maksim got a call that gave him the first, actual emotion I had seen on his face since Yuri was taken, hope mixed with terror.

"We've found him," he was striding down the hall while Ella and I were trotting after him.

"Let me come, please!" I begged, "I've already been in a shoot-out, you know I'm good for it, Maksim please!"

He turned to look at me just before the elevator doors closed. "I will call you as soon as I..." he swallowed, "as soon as I know."

I turned to Ella, who had been crying for the last day and a half. "He means as soon as he knows if Yuri is dead, doesn't he?" My knees turned into water and I sat down abruptly on the entryway floor. She sat down next to me and we hugged and cried and waited for news.

Ivan, Ella's personal bodyguard and substitute father, hurried over to us a couple of hours later. "Come, I'll take you to him." I was already off the floor and hauling Ella up by the arm before he finished the sentence.

"C'mon c'mon c'mon…" I chanted, rocking back and forth in the back seat of one of the Morozov bulletproof SUVs.

"He's alive," Ella whispered, rubbing my back, "he's alive, that's good. That's okay."

I did not know that there was a VIP entrance at New York Presbyterian Hospital but apparently so because the bodyguards hustled us out of the car and into an elevator. I raced out as the doors opened ignoring Ivan, who yelled at me to slow down and I skidded to a stop when I saw Maksim.

"Wh- is he-" An ugly, convulsive sob broke loose and I slapped my hand over my mouth. The legendary *Pakhan* of the Morozov Bratva had blood all over his face and shirt.

"He's in surgery," Maksim said, "but they'll be bringing him back here, so why don't you both just sit down for a moment?"

I always joke with Ella that the Morozov family own everything in the tri-state area, and that must include New York Presbyterian because the entire floor looks deserted. There's a lounge with dimmed lights and a spread of food on a table nearby.

"You catered your brother's surgery?"

Maksim just stares at me, lips pinned tightly together.

"Hey, Tan, come sit down," Ella saves me from a stare-down with her husband. "Ivan, could you get us some coffee, please? Tania takes hers with half coffee and half sugar."

His sad, pit bull face lightened for half a second before settling into a droop again. "Of course, Mrs. Morozov."

"God, Ivan! Just call me Ella."

He walked down the hall but I still heard a faint, "No." She looked pissed off at his insubordination.

"Ella honey, are you focusing on your tedious battle to get Ivan to call you by your first name so you won't think about…" I take a deep breath but it is not at all cleansing in the way my yoga instructor always insists it will be.

She puts her arm around me, "Are you trying to psychoanalyze me so you don't cry until you throw up?" I just slumped against her, and we gave up trying to distract each other.

About two hours later, I looked at the clock on the wall. "He's been under for a really long time," I whispered to Ella. "That's a good sign, right? That he's still fighting?"

"I think so," she whispered back.

Ella?"

"Hmmm?"

"Do they…" I take a deep, shuddering breath. "Do they know what happened to him?"

"I don't know," she murmured, "but…"

"What?" I whispered hoarsely.

"It was the Irish, they're so…" Tears poured down her cheeks. "They're the monsters my brother was with."

I stuffed her hand with tissues and bent over, clutching my midsection. Ella's shitty brother bought his way back into the O'Connell mob with her inheritance. When she was kidnapped, he stood there and watched them torture her. That fucker wanted to make sure she'd end up in a whorehouse somewhere to "shame" Maksim and weaken his Bratva. The piece of shit was dead, but the rest of the "family" was apparently even worse.

I could so vividly remember seeing Yuri standing there on the sidewalk with my flowers, smiling up at me with his devilish grin. The sun was shining on him like he was the brightest thing on the block. What have they taken from my Yuri? What had they left?

Another hour passed before the elevator doors opened and a clot of medical personnel surrounding his gurney hurried Yuri to his room. All I could see was the outline of his body under the sheet and I surged forward.

Maksim caught my arm. "Hang on," he said, not unkindly. He fixed the poor surgeon with a murderous stare. "Tell us."

The woman looked exhausted, there was blood on her scrubs and I nearly threw up when I realized it was Yuri's. She pulled off her scrub cap, and rubbed the back of her neck. "Mr. Morozov has lost his spleen and part of his liver. Several ribs were broken. One of the broken ribs punctured his right lung. There are multiple cuts and contusions and a laceration on his left deltoid that nearly severed the muscle."

Black spots were clouding my vision and I closed my eyes for a minute, biting the inside of my cheek. *You do not get to faint. This is about Yuri.*

Ella squeezed my arm. Hard. "What about nerve damage under the deltoid muscle? Were you able to successfully reattach the *Supraspinus* and *Teres Minor* tendons?"

"Yes," she nodded, clearly happy to offer some good news, "there is minimal damage in the underlying tissue and tendons."

Maksim spoke, his voice was completely emotionless. "What else?"

She pulled in a long breath of air and released it slowly. "The most severe laceration was on his face, it required nearly one hundred stitches to close. He has a serious concussion, and he's lost two fingernails and three toenails."

*Oh, Yuri. Oh, god sweetheart, this life is so fucking cruel to you.*

"Where is the laceration on his face?" Ella's voice was so steady. She was going to be an amazing doctor one day.

"Upper quadrant, right side," the surgeon clarified.

"What is his condition?" Maksim was still using his emotionless robot voice. Knowing him a bit better now, I suspected he did it because if he lost his shit right now, this hospital would be nothing but rubble.

"Your brother," the surgeon shook her head, "is the toughest individual I have ever worked on. His injuries were so severe… At any rate, his condition is critical, but stable for now. We had to put him in a medical coma. We'll monitor his vitals and if he can stay in stable condition for forty-eight hours, we'll bring him out, and we'll have a better idea of what his recovery will entail."

I looked at Maksim pleadingly, and he turned back to the surgeon. "Can we see him?"

She nodded, "One at a time, sterile conditions."

Maksim, naturally, went first. He was his brother. Of course, he should. I also wish he would hurry the fuck up. Oh, damn it. Yuri and Ella are really close. She would go next. She should. She's family.

"Tania?"

Oh, she has been talking to me? "Yeah?"

"Why don't you go in next."

My eyes were wet again and my nose was running. "Um, are you sure?"

Ella's so fucking sweet. "Yeah," she hugged me hard, "go in and remind him that he's got your hot ass to live for."

That choked a laugh out of me. "You're so weird sometimes."

"I know." She tilted her head in the direction of his room. "Go."

The room was darkened, the machines surrounding Yuri were the only light, beeping their messages about his pulse and blood oxygenation rate, his blood pressure but none of them told me if the man I love was going to live.

I tried to scooch the chair closer to the bed and winced as the metal legs screech across the tile.

*Smooth, girl.*

"Hey, sweetheart. You scared the shit out of me, just so you know."

My beautiful gangster's body was littered with tubes and wires and bandages. One eye was covered and I prayed that didn't mean the cut the surgeon mentioned went over-

*Stop it. This is not helping.*

Yuri had always had an almost offensively good color, like he'd just come back from a relaxing weekend in Ibiza or something. He was so pale now, almost as white as the sheets.

"You know, when I first came in, I was going to do something like pull back the covers and make sure your bedazzled dick remained uninjured. But I can't imagine anything I could do that would make you laugh right now. Instead, I just keep thinking of how gorgeous you were on the sidewalk under my window, smiling up at me, holding those amazing sunflowers. But since I did not get my bouquet or my evening alone with you, you owe me."

His hand that was closest to me was terribly bruised, and bandages on two fingers stopped me from trying to hold it. Instead, I dusted my fingertips over his skin, feeling the veins and corded muscles in his forearm.

"When my *abuela* was lying in state, as she called it, she told me that a life well-lived was seeing loved ones on both sides of her bed. Family on one side, friends on the other. Babe, your bedside is packed with loved ones. Your room would be stuffed with the people who love and count on you. Probably spilling out into the hallway. Maybe covering the top floor of this hospital, which by the way, I think your brother cleared, just for you. We're all here, sweetheart, just waiting for you to wake up."

*Two days later...*

The medical dramas on TV always made the loved ones who hover over the patient look like cast members from The Living Dead. We had set up camp on the top floor of New York Presbyterian and I suspected the hospital administrators were getting worried that we would never leave.

Maksim's arrangements meant there was a bathroom and shower reserved for our use, a couple of empty rooms where we could switch off with each other and sleep, the catering table stuffed full of food every day which still seemed oddly hilarious to me and helpful "associates" who brought clean clothing and essentials. We could last for years here with this setup.

Ella spent hours reading the surgery notes and going through his chart. After I begged her to give me something to study, something to understand how Yuri was going to possibly recover from this level of brutality, she gave me a long reading list, and we exchanged notes on what we learned.

She had always wanted to be a doctor for as long as I'd known her, but after four years of med school, she found out her scumbag brother had stolen their parent's inheritance, and she got her Ph.D. in pharmaceutical research instead, because Big Pharma made sure there were millions and millions of dollars in grants available in that field.

After they got married - the second time - Maksim hired some top-shelf physicians to tutor her privately and she was working toward her medical degree. How he pulled this off... Only the uber rich can get away with shit like this.

"Hey Doc, today's the day, right?"

Dr. Gulianos gave me a tired smile. "Today's the day, Tania." She was apparently the best trauma surgeon on the East Coast so she was always exhausted from the constant demands for her expertise. But this afternoon she was all ours.

"Did you ever try those ginseng capsules I gave you?"

She cleared her throat, "Well…"

I laughed, "You sent them to the lab to see if I was giving you fentanyl or something, didn't you?"

A flush crept up the poor woman's neck, "Well no, I just-"

"Oh, I get it. Random person handing you random pills. I get them from a custom compounder in Chinatown- Mr. Li Jie Chang? He does a lot of medicinal herbs. The ginseng supplements give you mad energy. This is from a woman who used to drink coffee until I was vibrating for most of the day."

She gave me a relieved smile. "That's kind of you, thank you. I'll have to try them out."

"Yeah, the ingredients are on the bottle, no extra fentanyl."

Maksim turned around with a frown as Dr. Gulianos and I stopped at Yuri's door. "What are you talking about?"

"Ginseng."

I should probably explain what that means to him but a fist was twisting my stomach in half.

It had hit me that this is the moment. What if Yuri didn't wake up? What if he has brain damage? I have spent the last forty-eight hours reading about every possible complication with his injuries. But his healing abilities must have been supernatural. All the scars on that poor man? This wasn't the first time that he should have died.

She was speaking in low tones with the other medical personnel including Ella, all clustered around the bed, monitoring his vitals while Maksim and I stood in the corner. I shifted from foot to foot, whispering "Please please please please please…" until

Maksim told me to be quiet.

When Dr. Guilanos looked up at us, she smiled. "You can come over. This is not an instantaneous event; it may take him a while. But the sensory stimulation of having you close can help him."

We clustered around the bed, Maksim and Ella on one side, me on the other. Like my *abuela* had said, loved ones on both sides.

"Come back to us *moya dusha*," Maksim murmurs.

I sat on Yuri's left side, where his poor hand did not have any fingernails torn off. I slipped my fingers under his lax ones and just waited. For what, I didn't know exactly, but I wasn't moving until he opened his eyes.

"Moya…" I tried to remember my Russian lessons. "My soul? Is that what you called him?"

"Yes." Maksim sounded like he was choking. "He has always been the soul of the family. A better man than me."

"That's not true," whispered Ella, kissing his cheek, "and you are the heart of the family. A lion's heart."

"*Solnyshko*," he murmured back, and I tuned out the rest. I just wanted to see Yuri wake up. I wanted to see the light come back into his beautiful eyes.

*Please, please please please please please…*

Three hours later, I got my wish. There was a jump in his vital signs on the monitor and then Yuri was just… there. His eyes were clear and he looked up at the ceiling for a moment, confused, and then to us.

Maksim kissed his forehead, speaking quickly in Russian and he gave a pained grunt.

"Hey, sweetheart, do you want some water?" I wanted to cry. I wanted to scream with excitement and the best I could come up with was, "Do you want some water?"

But Yuri smiled at me and mouthed 'yes,' and I knew he had come back to me.

# CHAPTER FIVE

*In which there is French food, epic insults, and Rico Sauve-looking mobsters.*

**Yuri...**

**Two weeks later...**

"Oh, babe let me do that for you."

I closed my eyes and took a deep breath to keep from brushing Tania away, who was trying to help me dress.

She quickly buttoned the stiff, starched cuffs on my dress shirt, the one I was going to burn when I took it off tonight. When did Gucci start making a dress shirt that takes hours to button? I had learned to work around the two fingers without fingernails that the fucking Irish had torn out. But I moved so slowly, like an old man.

Like a weakling.

"All done," Tania said, she looked up and gave me the smirk that meant she wanted a kiss, so I forced a smile and gave it to her. For a moment, the howling in my brain quieted, her lips and her sweet tongue playing with mine. As I slid my hand up into her hair, a lightning bolt from my left shoulder seared down my arm. Gritting my teeth, I pulled back.

"Are you okay?" She looked at me anxiously.

"I'm fine." I was lying, but I would say anything to stop the endless questions. "Are you ready for dinner?"

"Yep," she said, "Els and Maksim are boozing it up in the living room, if we don't hurry, I'm not sure they're going to make it to the restaurant."

I nodded and escorted her down the hall. Maksim and Ella were adamant that I stay with them during "my recovery." I had reached my limit of the fussing and catering to me and the endless, concerned glances. This would be my last night here.

The Fortress was the place to be seen in the organized crime world. Philippe-Alain's food was superb, but that was not why everyone went there. The heads of every major criminal enterprise on the planet had come through its doors at one point or another. No gunfights broke out, no one would dare. The shame of being denied access for a full year after an infraction was a serious loss of face.

"Holy shit, is this a castle?" Tania cackled with delight as the Maserati made a turn up the long driveway. The huge stone building, flanked by two towers rose majestically over the trees and marble statuary surrounding it.

"It was a castle," I corrected, "now, it's a private club and a restaurant."

"A private club?" She made a little face. "Sooo, who belongs to this private club?"

I put her hand on my thigh, squeezing it gently. "People like us."

"Oh, you mean hot as hell sexy people?"

Ella laughed, "Definitely not. Most of them are mean and old and smoke cigars."

Maksim grunted, which could have meant disapproval, amusement, or a warning.

The conversation felt good, normal. Nothing about physical

therapy or recovery or - good god - wound care.

"Tell me again, brother," I used the innocent, sincere tone that I knew drove him mad, "why you traded in your Maserati MC20 for a Levante Trofeo? A Maserati *SUV*? Are you turning into a family man?" I smothered a chuckle as his eyes narrowed warningly at me in the rearview mirror.

"This *family car*," Maksim growled, "goes from zero to sixty in three point eight seconds and has a top speed of 187 miles per hour."

"Yeah, and you could put a car seat back here, huh?" Tania chimed in. There was nothing she enjoyed more than taunting my brother.

As the uniformed guards moved to open Tania's door, I put up my hand and they halted. "Before we go in, you need to know most of these people are utter bastards. No matter what you hear, no matter what anyone says, do not engage them. It is important." Her lovely golden eyes were wide, but she nodded.

"I get it," she said, "you need to be seen here, don't you? To show how invincible you are?"

I drew in a breath and let it out slowly. "Yes."

Her hand on my thigh tightened, "I wish it didn't have to be so soon. It's only been two weeks-"

"Stop." I didn't mean to sound so harsh; Tania pressed her lips together and nodded.

The warm lighting inside the club mellowed the chill of the stone walls, and antique oriental rugs covered the intricate design of the granite and marble floors. Tania stared at the huge, sweeping staircase leading to the second floor, overlooking the restaurant.

"Where does that go?" she whispered.

"The private, *private* dining room," I whispered back. "We keep a table there."

She gave me her mysterious Mona Lisa smile. "Ooo, we're so bleedin' posh!" She affected a terrible cocky accent that made me chuckle and I instantly regretted it. I grit my teeth against the flare of agony in my abdomen, which set off corresponding pulses in my shoulder. Dr. Gulianos had done a masterful job of reattaching my deltoid muscle, but every movement felt like it was tearing it loose again.

**Earlier that evening...**

"We don't have to go tonight."

Maksim was watching me make a drink in his office, lounging behind his huge mahogany desk.

"Yes, we do," I poured two fingers of vodka into the glass, shrugged, and filled it to the brim. Holding it up, I asked, "Do you want one?"

"No thanks," he said, "you know if Ella smells vodka on your breath, she's going to follow you around, nagging you about mixing pain meds and alcohol."

I smiled bitterly. "Is that what you are doing, brother?"

"No," he sighed, "you're an adult, you make your own choices."

"I threw the pain meds away yesterday," I added, closing my eyes to enjoy the soothing bite of the alcohol hitting my throat. "They made me slow. Stupid."

Maksim laughed, "There's nothing on this planet that could make you slow. Stupid? Well, you have always been that."

"I can see six items on your desk alone that I could use to stab you," I returned pleasantly, but I was grateful that my brother still treated me the same as he had before the fucking O'Connell's had... Well, before then.

"We found out how the Irish tracked you that day. They had someone working at the flower shop- a girl. When you picked up the flowers, they knew they had time to set up the ambush at Tania's."

Remembering the wide-eyed girl at Bud's, my jaw tightened. "Mrs. Novikoff claimed the girl had a crush on me since she was so interested in my orders."

"Yes, we questioned the Novikoff's very closely about how they could have been so sloppy in their hiring practices," Maksim's jaw was tight enough to crack a tooth. "The wife told us the girl didn't come back to work that day after leaving for her lunch break."

"Don't hurt them," I said, "they're under our protection."

"That agreement no longer exists when their sloppiness allowed my brother to be taken," he hissed. "I told them to leave the city quietly and if I ever saw their faces again, they would get the same treatment you did."

I picture Mrs. Novikoff's open, cheerful expression and how she refused to ever let me pay for the flowers. A memory of those men cutting into my shoulder blurs out her face. "That is fine. Have you found the girl?"

Maksim met my gaze steadily. "We will." He rubbed his eyes and stood, "Two weeks isn't enough time, brother. You have nothing to prove."

"I am fine," I did not mean to speak as harshly as I did, but he did not seem to take offense. "We need to be seen there, together."

*Currently...*

"The Morozov men have come to see us again! Such a pleasure!" Philippe-Alain bustled over, his ruddy, round face beaming as if he was truly happy to see us. His gaze went to Tania and Ella and he gave a little bow. "And you have brought *such* delightful company with you."

"This is Maksim's lovely bride, Ella Morozov, and my beautiful companion is Tania Hernandez."

"Ladies!" He placed extravagant kisses on their hands and beamed at us all. "Come, let's make you comfortable."

*"Merci Monsieur,"* Tania said, *"J'ai tellement entendu parler de votre nourriture."*

"You have heard of our simple meals here?" Philippe-Alain gasped, pretending to be humble. "I will bring you something special, *mon cherie.*"

He settled us at our table with a great deal of fussing and noise, and then withdrew gracefully. He was a master at reading the room; when a guest needed more attention, or when it was time to absent himself as quickly as possible.

Maksim looked at Tania, brow raised, "I didn't know you spoke French."

"Oh, she's good with languages," Ella said proudly.

Tania shrugged, giving her 'I'm so modest and demure smile,' and then leaned into me a bit, whispering, "So, the couple by the balcony…" She nodded at an older couple, ignoring each other as they both flirted with the waitstaff. "He's a male fashion influencer, super famous for modeling fur coats over his naked body, which has so much hair it is indistinguishable from the actual coat."

I suppressed a smile. This was Tania's favorite game when we were out on a date. But here, there could be no backstory she could possibly imagine that would be as shocking or outrageous as the reality. She was speculating about Bujar Toska, head of the Albanian Mafia, best known for dipping his victims - slowly - into vats of acid.

An excruciatingly vivid memory surfaced from when I had been tied to that table, covered in blood, and praying that they had not severed my arm. As they powered down the chainsaw, they discussed acid as the next atrocity they had planned for me.

I took a long swallow of my drink and forced a smile. "And he recreates the pose of lying naked on a bearskin rug in front of a roaring fire, because…"

"…No one can tell he's naked," she whispered back, trying to keep her hoarse little chuckle low. "Now, his lovely companion…" She tapped her chin thoughtfully. The woman in question was younger by twenty years than Bujar, but still quite a bit older than I knew he preferred.

"She is actually the first woman astronaut, Valentina Tereshkova…" Tania drew the name out slowly, using her best Russian accent. "But, the Vostok 6 went through a mysterious solar flare which altered her DNA and made her *immortal*." She leaned closer, really getting into the tall tale she was spinning for me. "But! Every ten years she turns into a-"

"Yuri Morozov, I wouldn't have expected to see you out so soon!"

"Julio Ortega," Maksim said coldly, "we thought business in Mexico kept you busy?"

Ortega had just inherited control over the Sangre cartel, by killing his father. He was young, but vicious and cunning. And a sadistic bastard.

He made a dismissive gesture, "Hey, Maksim, well, I have to make time to visit all my friends here on the East Coast. Like you two, huh? I'm opening up new lines of distribution that you should take a look at before they're all spoken for." His eyes darted between Ella and then Tania, who was blessedly silent but eyeing him like she was trying to assign a species to him.

A white-hot stab of agony tore through my shoulder when he patted it heavily, his hand slapping down hard. "And how about you? How you doing, Yuri? I heard those *pinche pendejos* cut you into pieces, huh?"

"As you can see, Ortega, I'm still here, alive and well." There was not the slightest hint of the pain I was feeling in my voice. Our father trained that out of us early.

He was avidly searching me for wounds, though the long scar that ran across my forehead and down my left cheekbone was enough to catch his attention, searingly red and still swollen.

Tania touched my thigh gently. "Hey, honey, our food's arrived, but I think the waiters are too nervous about interrupting this?"

I loved this woman.

I knew she was dying to make some scathing remark to Ortega, but she kept her promise while still giving me an opening to get rid of him. She smiled at me innocently and I kissed her hand.

"You'll have to excuse us, Ortega, these ladies have never enjoyed Philippe-Alain's food before."

"Yeah, his food is worth the trip, just for dinner…" He was still lingering, his eyes went back to Tania, surveying her thoughtfully.

"If you'll excuse us?" Maksim's voice made it clear the conversation was over.

Tania squeezed my leg. "That fucker," she hissed as he walked away, "patting you on the left shoulder?"

"Right?" Ella's lip curled, "What a prick. That was no pat. That was a punch."

I kissed Tania's cheek. "Nothing to worry about, darling." There were still flames of agony from the burning ache in my shoulder traveling down my arm, but I picked up my drink, trying not to drain it in one gulp.

*Tania…*

Dinner was spectacular, aside from that Rico Suave-looking asshole who smacked Yuri on the shoulder. Prick. I was still thinking about the Coquilles St. Jacques and duck confit with some serious appreciation when I bumped into someone on the way to the ladies' room.

"Oh, excuse me-"

He caught my elbow, pretending to steady me. "Are you all right, gorgeous?"

Great, speak of the devil. Ortega was trying to loom over me but in my epic new Louboutin's, we were the same height. He was attempting to give me a sexy grin. Ugh.

"Glad I ran into you," he leered, "I didn't catch your name at the table?"

*Oh, it's too late to smile at me,* I thought, *I've seen the swamp troll you're trying to hide under the human skin suit you're wearing.*

"Yeah, that's because we weren't introduced," I pulled loose from his grip on my arm. "So, excuse me and everything-"

"Hey, hey honey," he stepped in front of me and tried to touch me again, "wait a minute. I want to get to know you. You can't want to stick with Morozov," he scoffed, "that fucker is roadkill. He's just meat, and he knows it."

"I'd tell you to go to hell, you asshole, but it's not like it would be a burn since that's your hometown," I snarled, "but *you*- you are an infinitesimal speck of hair pomade compared to Yuri."

"Miss, if you'll come with me, I'll show you the way to the ladies' room." It was Ivan, who moved gracefully between me and Mr. Murder Britches, whose nostrils were flaring and chest was heaving.

"Thanks, Ivan. You're a gentleman and a scholar." I looped my arm with his, even though I knew his soul was curdling at the wildly inappropriate lack of distance between said bodyguard and bodyguard's client's friend.

Deftly leading me in the opposite direction and down a long hall, he murmured urgently, "That is not a man you ever want to offend. Or speak to. Or even look at."

"It's not my fault!" I protested, "The asshole deliberately bumped into me and was trying to ooze his charm all over me like a slime bath."

Ivan waited outside the bathroom while I speedily got business done, washed my hands and checked for lipstick on my teeth. But it wasn't fast enough.

I could hear the shouting from the private dining room the minute I walked out the bathroom door, and Ivan and I raced back down the hall, my heels slipping and sliding on the marble floor.

"You fuckin' think you're better than me?"

It was Ortega, screaming at Yuri, who had kept control of himself. He stood up and towered over the screamer, making him look even more ridiculous, like one of those little yappy dogs barking at a massive Doberman.

"You should turn around right now, Ortega. Walk the out that door and never come near me again. I will not tolerate your disrespect."

My Yuri's standing perfectly straight, no sign of the suffering I know his broken ribs and all the stitches must be causing him.

"Fuck you, man!" I can hear the loud sniff from here and I know that jackhole took some of his own product. And where's Philippe-Alain's legendary security? Because right now there's a bristling wall of bodyguards and bad guys - ours and Ortega's - on either side of the table and I know they're armed.

It was so quick that I had to replay it in my head later to get the sequence straight. Yuri's fist lashed out and crushed Ortega's nose. The blood flew away from his face in gruesome splatters and I could see his nose, flat against his face as he fell backward and hit the floor before his men could catch him.

"Oh, god…" I whispered it, terrified to distract Yuri because now the guns are out and pointing at everyone.

"This will stop immediately!"

Oh, *now* the Frenchman was charging up the hill - or the stairs in this case - surrounded by his guards.

"Nice timing, *pal*," I mumbled as they passed us. Ivan still had a death grip on my arm and I was straining to see if Yuri was okay. Ella tried to go to him and Maksim was holding on to her, too.

Then I could see why. There was a red stain, spreading across his white dress shirt and I know he had popped some stitches. God, there were so many stitches, especially around the area Dr. Guilanos had to take part of his liver and his hand was swelling too, more blood tingeing the tips of the two fingers where his nails were torn out. But he was still standing tall, his beautiful face stone cold and composed.

I knew he would still think this was a display of weakness to all these grotesque thugs and made men, and fuck them all, sitting there watching like it was all a show for their entertainment. Of course, for these assholes, it was the best kind of entertainment. Pain, blood, brutality… they must have been squirming in their seats.

The Morozov security surrounded Maksim, Ella, and Yuri as they headed for the stairs. "Not the stairs!" I moaned, "That's going to make this so much worse on his injuries."

"Shhh," Ivan hissed, "do not let him hear you, let's go."

Yuri reached his hand out for mine and I took it, squeezing his cold fingers gently. I would have given my own liver if he would have just let me put my arms around him and made him lean on me, let me help him out to the car.

Instead, I followed him past the staring dregs of humanity in their $5,000 suits out to the waiting Maserati at the curb.

# CHAPTER SIX

*In which Yuri finds that helplessness is the worst torture of all.*

**Tania...**

"Wait, when did Yuri move out?"

I was having lunch with Ella at our favorite coffee place at the back of an independent bookstore, one happy to close off the coffee area for three or four thousand dollars stuffed in the tip jar when we stopped by. We didn't ask them to close down the bookstore itself. We're not animals.

"The morning after that terrible dinner at Philippe-Alain's. Because Yuri just had to be all stoic about it, he wouldn't let me stitch him back up until he sent you home."

"You look so tired, girlie, all those private hospital rounds wearing you out?" I loved that Ella was indeed going to be the doctor she'd always wanted to be, even though I had no idea how she was keeping up with current events.

"Not as much as my incredibly, stupidly stubborn brother-in-law," she sighed. "I asked him if he would rather have Dr. Guilanos dragging her exhausted self in to check him every day or would he prefer to have me handle the wound care? He rather sullenly agreed that if anyone had to see him, I was his choice, but he hates accepting help."

"Accepting help? Gee, not a Morozov man," I rolled my eyes. "Can't tarnish that shiny alpha glow, huh?"

"When did you last see him?" Ella was turning her tea mug

around and around, making little tan rings on the napkin.

Sighing, I tried to smooth my hair with my fingers, which was useless. I had my father's hair, coarse, thick, and dark brown. My mother brushed it into a ponytail all through elementary school because otherwise, I'd get it caught on things - tree branches, swing sets, a dumpster lid after I threw a sixth grader in there for bugging Ella - and age has not improved its ability to behave. Anyway, personal grooming wasn't exactly at the top of my list right now since Yuri stopped taking my calls.

"I haven't, not since that night," I admitted. "I called him first thing in the morning and he said that he had a meeting to attend with Maksim. It's been four days since we talked."

"That's definitely not Yuri," she fretted, "Maksim used to be merciless with him because he was always on the phone with you."

"There's a phrase for men who leave a relationship after a trauma," I said miserably, "they develop avoidant attachment style. I looked this up today." Pulling up the link on my phone, I read, *"Still charming, these men look like they've got their lives in order. A relationship with an attachment-avoidant can be fun and easy-going, until you get too close. They will pull away from any intimacy that might allow a partner to see the trauma."*

Slumping in my chair, I admitted, "I know this comes as no surprise to you, bestie, but we bonded through sex. We bonded our asses off. It was-"

"Wait," Ella was trying not to laugh, "you bonded your asses off? Like, do you mean anal or something?"

"Oh, yeah, of course," I agreed, absently stirring my tea. "We had to work up a lot of plug sizes for sure, though." I looked over and she was trying to hide her laughter by putting a napkin over her face. "Oh, whatever, Little Miss Sheltered, like Maksim hasn't turned you ass-up more than once."

The nice barista with the man bun bringing us our cake stumbled for a second before putting down our plates and whisking himself away like some English butler.

"That's not what I meant, though. Sex connected us when talking couldn't. When he couldn't tell me where he'd been or why there was blood on his shoes or under his fingernails, but whenever he got his bedazzled dick back in me, it felt like a reset, you know?"

At least she'd stopped laughing and actually looked a little guilty.

"He's pulling away, Els. And I don't know what I can do about it."

*Yuri…*

*They were laughing, running the blade of a KA-Bar knife over my forehead, down my cheekbone, and pressing the tip to my eye.*

*"I want to pop it out," hissed one, "let me take his eyes and I'll hang them from my rearview mirror like those assholes do with the fuzzy dice."*

*Three of them, splattered with my blood, leaning over and laughing, stinking of smoke and booze and whatever they'd pulled from me.*

*Iisus Khristos not my eyes…*

I shot up in bed, groaning. Every muscle in my abdomen felt like it had been dipped in gasoline and set on fire. Sitting on the edge of the bed, I pressed the heels of my hands over my eyes.

"It is not real. I am not on that table. I will tear each one of those bastards apart." I repeated the same three sentences, over and over, rocking slightly. I felt weak, disgusted with myself to have allowed those memories from when I lay chained down, suffering for their amusement to take root in me. The phone buzzed on my bedside table with Tania's ringtone, 'I Will Show You Mine,' which never failed to make me grin. Until now.

"It is not real," I whispered, "those *cykas* didn't break me." I pushed my hands harder against my eyes, trying to wipe away the images seared into my memory. My phone buzzed again and was finally silent.

"Let's see if you can keep these stitches in, okay?" Ella had her doctor's coat on and the attitude to match. "I can't wrap you for any extra stability because of your broken ribs. How did you pop the stitches this time?"

The vision of stabbing one of the O'Connell captains until his chest was hamburger meat during a raid last night came to mind. "I am not certain," I shrugged painfully. "I must have bumped something."

"Like a shotgun?" Ella smoothed the surgical tape over my chest, "Flamethrower? Surface to air missile?"

"Why sister, I am hurt by your implications. I have been a model patient and followed every one of your exacting, unreasonable demands." I opened my eyes wide to show my sincerity, and she laughed as I hoped she would.

"Yeah, model patient. I think your picture is listed under the definition in the dictionary. Right next to the 'I am so full of shit' entry." My sister-in-law's smile faded as she cut another piece of tape. "Tania's worried sick about you."

"There's no need," I said coldly.

"Ah, ah! You do not get to try the patented Maksim Polar Chill Move on me, mister!" She was frowning at me, attempting to look stern. "You are the charming, kind Morozov brother, remember? You communicate?"

"Tania said you always mentally put your long, extravagant phrases in capital letters," I said. My smile faded as I realized I had said her name.

Ella looked up at me, her pale green eyes were wide and sincere. "She can help you heal."

Exasperated, I sighed, "There's nothing to heal."

"Oh my god do you hear yourself? Yes! Yes, Yuri, you *do* have many things - physical *and* emotional - to heal. But facing them together will make you stronger. Both of you." She had her gaze intensely fixed on mine.

"You look like you are attempting to drill into my subconscious," I said.

"I own your braaainn…" She attempted to look sinister, "You must bend to my willll…"

I could not keep a straight face, but the second I started laughing, I regretted it.

"I'm sorry! I'm sorry!" Ella cried, patting me gingerly on my good arm.

"You have a terrible bedside manner, Dr. Morozov," I groaned.

"This could be true," she agreed, "but will you please call Tania? For me? Please?"

Dropping my head, I took as deep a breath as I could with my broken ribs. "If I do this sister, you may not ask me for another favor. You will not interfere with my personal life."

"That's… a little more final than I expected, but okay," she said. "There are some things a doctor can't heal, but a loved one can."
I narrowed my eyes. "I'm done! I promise!" Ella threw up her hands defensively, then gathered her medical supplies and made a quick exit.

Cradling my aching head in my hands, I heard the drill again. The laughter. The cigarettes put out on my skin.

*Tania…*

It had been a week since Yuri ghosted me, so I actually yelped when his ringtone blared from my phone. It was "Sixty Minute Man," an oldie but a goodie and damn, did it fit that man's style in bed.

Maybe I was too suspicious. Maybe I was too paranoid but for a moment, I backed away from my phone. Was this goodbye?

Finally, *Oh for hell's sake, you chickenshit! Answer the phone!*

"Hello?" I tried to sound cool like I hadn't even noticed he was pulling away from me.

"Hello, darling."

I could hear him breathing, a little fast, a little hoarse. *Probably from the screaming all the screaming he must have done when they tortured him. Shut up brain!*

Clearing my throat, I said, "What's up?"

There was a low chuckle that set everything south of my waist to a low simmer. "I would like to say me, but I suspect you would slap me for it, based on my recent behavior."

"You would be correct. What happened to my man who used to make *me* - ugh! - communicate?"

There was silence and my heart twinged. *Smooth, girl. Real subtle.*

"He would like to see you and apologize."

I let out a shaky sigh of relief that I hoped he didn't hear. "I'd like that too."

I paced in front of the huge window in the living room. The same window where I had seen Yuri for one sweet moment before those Irish fucks started shooting at him and poor Patrick.

Looking away, I said, "Alexa, put on the Yuri playlist." He loved Abel Korzeniowski, a composer who created mournful - and wildly beautiful - violin music. Hearing it always made me wish I hadn't given up playing. However, since my mother *wanted* me to play the violin, naturally I stopped the minute I was old enough to refuse. The music was too sweet. Too refined, or something. It gave me a rash. Though on nights like these, waiting for him to show up and know he was safe, my hands would twitch in the familiar positions, and I wanted to feel the strings press under my fingertips again.

*The doorbell made me jump. Jumpy, much?* I lectured myself. *Relax, you big baby.*

I opened the door and there he was. Yuri, tall and blond and so damn beautiful. Leaning against the frame, I looked him up and down. "You here to deliver my groceries?"

*Not the devilish grin! Don't you dare try to charm me, you dick!*

"I'm not that kind of delivery man," he smiled charmingly. "I deliver orgasms." He watched my eyes narrow and pulled out the huge bouquet from behind his back with a flourish. "And apologies."

"Good save," I said, taking the flowers. "You brought me my sunflowers." I touched them with reverent fingertips, the brilliant yellows blending in with the dark, dark purples. Almost black. For one horrible second, the vision of his blood splattered against the yellow flowers hit me and I shuddered.

"Was it the wrong choice?" Yuri's expression fell and he tried to take them back.

"No, I want them," I stepped back, letting him in. "When I was talking to you in the hospital, when you were in your coma? I told you that I didn't get my night with you or my sunflowers, so you had to make it up to me."

He bent down, carefully placing his forehead against mine. "I want to make it up to you."

I hugged him as hard as I dared, crushing the flowers between us. "You already did. You woke up."

He made a noise that sounded a lot like pain and kissed me, his plush lips pressing hard against mine. My Yuri playlist shifted to "Satin Birds."

"Will you dance with me?" He put the flowers on my hall table and pulled me into the living room with a dark little smile. The piano notes made a gentle, orderly rhythm to move my feet to while the mournful violin pulled painfully at my shoulders and back, swaying me back and forth in his arms.

We had danced so many times in this huge, fancy living room. He taught me the box step as I stood on his feet, laughing. The Waltz. Swing dancing, the Tango, the Paso Doble, the Foxtrot, and on one drunken evening, the Hornpipe. We had laughed so hard we fell over and he pushed inside me right there on the floor.

"What are you thinking about?" Yuri murmured.

"Dancing the Hornpipe."

His chest moved in that new, careful way that meant he was laughing without moving enough to hurt his slowly healing ribs. "That was quite the evening."

"I had rug burns on my ass, babe. I couldn't sit down for like three days," I was laughing, too. "Not that it wasn't worth it."

His huge hand cupped my cheek, his thumb rubbing against my lips. "I have never met a woman filled with more light than you. How you can always make me laugh?"

This tenderness was flustering me, so I scoffed, "It's because you Russians are so stoic. I don't think I ever saw your brother smile unless he was shitfaced."

"He smiles for Ella," he said.

*Like I smile for you.* I heard it, even if he didn't say it out loud.

# CHAPTER SEVEN

*In which Yuri struggles to overcome the horror of his captivity and JUST LIKE A MAN, will allow no one to help him.*

**Yuri...**

The song drifted away into silence, but Tania and I moved together gracefully like the sad violin was still propelling us across the floor.

Drawing the tip of my nose up her throat, I groaned. I had always loved her scent. Sharp, like rosemary, maybe, with a bit of a bite. Something like jasmine too, sweet, it made me want to lick and bite her. She moaned, dropping her head back to give me more room.

"I've missed you," she breathed the words out like a sigh.

"I know, I am sorry. Trying to put everything back together has..." I pulled her a little closer, her warmth and softness had always calmed all the noise in my head.

Tania rested her chin on my chest, looking up at me. "I can't fix it, I know that. But I can listen if you want to talk. Or, I don't know, we can just sit and you can read to me and I'll run my fingers through your hair the way you like." She placed a line of kisses up my shirt. "Just please don't pull away, okay? You don't have to be perfect with me. It's okay if you're actually a human." She smiled mischievously. "I won't tell anyone that you're not a supermodel cyborg like your brother, okay?"

Burying my face in her huge cloud of hair, I breathed in deeply.

Rosemary. Jasmine.

"Take off your dress."

I was sitting in a comfortable chair in Tania's bedroom. A large, sturdy chair, capable of handling anything. We had proved that more than once. Running a finger over my lower lip, I grinned when she widened her eyes, looking at me innocently.

"Gee, mister. I don't know. I'm awful shy."

I nearly choked on my drink.

Her ability to keep up the act was impressive, particularly when she sling-shotted her undies at me. I plucked them from where they landed on my chest and tucked them into my jacket pocket. Curling two fingers, I said, "Come here, darling."

Sauntering over with one hand on her hip, she looked me up and down appreciatively. "Well, aren't you a fine piece of man candy."

I fought down another chuckle. This woman was going to kill me. "Thank you. Unzip me."

Kneeling gracefully, she did as I asked, then ran her thumb along the top of my cock, bumping each pearl. Swallowing down a groan, I watched her mouth open. Tania hummed happily as she spread her lips around my cock and I slipped my fingers into her hair, enjoying her warm mouth for a moment before pulling lightly.

"Come here." She did, arching her back and rubbing those lovely, round breasts against me all the way up.

"I'll kiss you if you let me take off your tie," she whispered, sucking on my earlobe. "And unbutton two buttons on your shirt. Just two!"

Groaning, I reached between her legs and squeezed her. "Already so wet?" Stroking my middle fingers between her silky lips, I warned, "Just two." No lower. She will see the wreckage of my chest, still blooming violent purples and yellows on my skin.

My tie was tossed over the arm of the chair in seconds and her lips were latched onto my Adam's apple, sucking lightly. I slid my hands over her plush ass and squeezed, lifting her and angling her against my cock.

This was the first time we had been together since the kidnapping. My fingers flexed and tightened on her perfect, plump cheeks and my heart started thudding in my chest.

"Shhh…" Tania whispered, "kiss me, my beautiful man." She slid down my cock, slowly, rotating her hips. I bit into her neck, fighting down a groan.

It was heaven being back inside her, the only place in my life where everything else disappeared. The way she clutched and squeezed me, the heat of her. "So beautiful, *moye serdtse*," I said and slipped my hand behind her neck to bring her closer, kissing her lush mouth. My other hand moved to her hip, helping her lift up and drop down again.

She laughed breathlessly, tapping between her breasts, "I think your bedazzled dick ended up somewhere about here with that last thrust." Her thighs tensed as she moved with me. "So good, Yuri," she moaned drunkenly.

Moving her hands behind her, I helped her brace them on my thighs. This arched her back and pushed her breasts closer and I sucked one nipple to a tight, hard peak and then nipped the other.

*I can do this,* I thought, feeling the cold sweat beading on my forehead, *I can be normal with my woman, I can have sex with her. I can keep it together.*

*I am fine.*

Tania surged forward, wrapping her arms around me, and burying her face in my neck. "I love you," she whispered, "thank you for coming back to me. Thank you for surviving."

I froze, holding her as tightly as I could, feeling her breasts heave against me as she fought tears. "Shh…" I murmured, "Hush, sweet girl." It was too much. My chest was tightening and the anguish was surging up like a toxic tide. Her tenderness was unbearable, it made the pain and grief tear through me. I can't be soft… I am not strong enough to handle this.

"Ride me, show me you've missed me."

She does, slowly at first but I slapped her hard on the ass and she yelps pleasurably.

*This cannot be slow, it's too much we have to finish before I break…*

I slapped her again, and again, feeling her tighten against my cock. "Faster," I said hoarsely, trying to move ahead of the pain and grabbing her ass, bouncing her up and down as quickly as I could. Her warm hands go to my shoulders, trying to hold on. Trying to slow me down.

"Shh," she whispered, "stay with me. We can do fast and hard later. Just kiss me, okay?"

She was too close to me, too warm and soft. I wanted to stay buried inside her where I did not have to be strong. I did not have to think.

My hips moved faster. *I cannot be weak. I cannot break.*

We were getting closer, I know her breathing, how her eyes dilate and how she gasped.

*Faster, faster get ahead of it.*

My eyes are wet. I cannot be crying. I have not cried since I was a boy, I cannot.

*Make her come. Hurry, do not let her see this hurry hurry…*

I did the thing I knew would set my Tania off, and pushed the heel of my hand hard against her abdomen, right where my cock was pressing against her from deep inside.

She gasped, contracting so tightly against me that it was

impossible to move inside her. She took my face between her hands, looking into my eyes and she was weeping. When she shuddered against me, I came too, shocked, moaning into her mouth as it hit me out of nowhere, making me shake and push deeper inside her.

Tania's hands did not move from my jaw as she put her lips against the scar on my face tenderly, making soft kisses along its long, ugly slash against my skin. We gazed at each other, our cheeks wet and I pulled her against me, wrapping my arms around her.

We finally climbed into bed, where we were fused together, one organism with two hearts, hers wide open and mine shredded and useless. "I love you, too, *moye serdtse*," I whisper, "my heart."

Tania sighs contentedly, resting against me as I stare across the room, finally dry-eyed.

I cannot stay. I cannot be here or I will break into too many pieces to put together again.

I have to go home. To St. Petersburg.

I watched as the sky's purple shade faded to violet, to pink and then, shades of orange and yellow.

Rising heavily, I gritted my teeth against the red flare of pain in my chest and got dressed. Seating myself at her desk, I pulled out a piece of paper and started writing.

*My beloved Tania,*

*I cannot stay here. I am returning to St. Petersburg to take over the family's business there.*

*Our time together has been the best of my life. I am sorry I must say goodbye. But I must.*

*Yuri*

*Tania…*

My hand holding the paper is shaking. That son of a bitch.

I was naked and sitting at my desk and I was trembling hard enough to make my teeth chatter. That heartless bastard.

We could not have been closer last night without actually crawling inside each other. When we came together, I'd seen his soul in his eyes, I saw that reservoir of pain and anguish I'd always known he held there, and I thought we felt it together.

Would it have always played out like this? Even if he hadn't been kidnapped and tortured? Eventually, would Yuri have just smiled his pretty smile and told me I was no longer necessary via my purloined stationery? Because I wasn't important enough to him to talk to in person, not important enough to be honest?

All my insecurities flared like a nuclear bomb strike, obliterating everything I'd worked for. Not rich enough to go to Ivy League schools. Not tall enough. Not pretty enough. The little girl with the unmanageable hair and cheap clothes. Not deserving enough for a man to treat me like a human being with a heart and feelings.

I'd told Yuri the truth. Dumping those other guys wasn't hard. I wasn't even surprised when they turned out to be assholes. But I knew he was going to tear a strip off my heart and leave me bleeding out, and I *still* said yes to one more date.

I ran and jumped off the cliff, but this time, there was concrete greeting me at the bottom instead of the cool, dark water.

*Two days later…*

"What the hell are you doing?"

Ella was standing in the middle of my living room between piles of boxes and haphazard stacks of my clothes and all the sports gear I bought and never used.

"I'm moving," I skirted around her to dump another box on the floor.

"Yeah, I see that, thank you. But you can't move, you know that place has the best security-"

"I don't care!" I shouted and she stepped back in shock. Picking up the tape, I angrily secured the flaps on the box. "I don't need the Morozov family charity, I am done with this mobster circus of bullshit."

"It's not charity," she tried to argue, "those idiots owe it to you for putting you in danger and anyway you pay rent every month-"

"I pay rent for what I could afford for my one-bedroom in Queens," I scoffed. "They probably use my rent payments to buy like, bullets. No, that would be too expensive. For gum? Rich people lip balm?"

Moving a stack of files over, she sat on the couch. "Is this why you haven't been answering my texts or calls for the last two days?"

"Did Yuri tell you?" Oh, for fuck's sake my voice was quivering.

*Get it together! Suck it up!* My mom's stern, no-nonsense voice was so clear and I laughed a little.

"I didn't know he was leaving until today. Maksim finally told me." Her eyes were narrowed and I knew he was going to pay for that little oversight.

"Oh, well, here's how I found out," I took the letter back out of my trash bin and handed it to her. "After the most emotional, intimate night we've ever had where we both cried and said we loved each other and shit, I found this."

Oh, my girl was *pissed*. Ella's lips thinned to near invisibility and when she looked up, she had the crazy rage eyes going. "I'm going to set his Aston Martin on fire. I'm going to burn all his Italian suits. That chicken-hearted-"

"Yeah." I pulled a bottle of Yuri's expensive wine out of the cooler and held it up. "Cocktail? And don't bother telling me what time it is."

Two bottles later, we drunkenly decided to go out to dinner.

Ivan had the audacity to attempt a smile as he helped us into the SUV.

"Ivan?"

"Yes, Miss Tania."

"No pity smiles. Be the grim Russian bulldog you've always been. Smiling is beneath you."

"I'm Ukrainian, Miss Tania."

"Be the grim Ukrainian bulldog you've always been, Ivan."

"Understood, Miss Tania."

"Where are we going?" I looked out the darkened window while Ella tapped furiously on her phone.

"Marcel's. Yes, I know it's a Morozov property but we're going to burn through the wine cellar and make it hurt Maksim and Yuri where it counts." She smiled grimly and I have never loved that girl more.

The driver stopped in front of the restaurant and after getting out of the SUV and taking a deep breath, I nodded. I could do this. We linked arms and headed for the door while she went through the wine list on her phone so we could pick the rarest and most expensive bottle.

"I might even make them use it to cook our Coq au Vin…" she said before looking up from her phone. Her eyes widened like a cartoon cat's. "Hey, Tan, I forgot something in the car, let's go back for a minute, c'mon-"

"What's going on with you?" I pulled my arm loose, "Just send one of the guys for it…" My gaze went to the entrance and my breath left me in a gasp, like someone just punched me in the heart.

Yuri was leaving the restaurant with a blonde girl. Tall and sleek like him. Crazy expensive dress. Crazy expensive nose job. She was clinging to his arm like it was a life preserver on the Titanic. And giggling. There was only the slightest hitch in his step when he looked up to see Ella and me, mouths open. There was only one second where the heartless bastard looked me in the eye, then turned back to his date, guiding her past us. They were speaking Russian to each other. How fucking sweet is that?

"Hey! Yuri Mikail Morozov! Are you serious right now?"

His steps slowed and he finally turned around, looking at me just… bristling at him with my hands on my hips and Ella whispering, "Hey, maybe not right now, hon?"

His beautiful, disgusting face was totally composed, and his little date was looking from him to me, adorably confused.

"I beg your pardon?" Yuri inquired politely.

Well, this was some awkward shit. Ella's security and his security were looking confused. There was no one to take down as an active threat unless they counted me.

"Oh, look, and here I thought you were just a pretty face with a forked tongue. You're also a fabulous actor! How did I not know this about you?" I was on fire, so angry that I was stuttering which was much better than crying, which would have been so pathetic that I would be required by my own code to throw myself in front of a bus.

"I mean, you were so sweet when you fucked me - what, two days ago? Well, until you blocked my number the next day. You were actually going to dump me without a word and then pass by me like I'm badgering you for spare change on the street? Are you for fucking real?"

Yuri nodded to a bodyguard, "Please help Miss Lenkov into the car."

Hanging on to his arm, she said, "*Milyy* Yuri, is she… safe? Are you sure?"

"Oh, my god…" I shook my head. *Oh, honey, it's not like you can be any more obvious. Just lift your leg and spray him already.*

"I will be fine," he smiled down at her politely. "Go with Boris, please."

She followed the man obediently, her large curious eyes looking me over as she passed by.

Then, we were alone on the sidewalk. Everyone here had a strong sense of self-preservation and backed *way* off.

I sucked in a deep breath of air. "Yuri. Is this…" I glanced away from him, I couldn't look into his eyes right now. "You really want to be this person?"

"I am Bratva. I am nothing else. And I have always been this person," he said. Not a flicker of emotion. Maybe polite disinterest, like I was trying to sell him fake Gucci wallets or a timeshare.

"No," I said sadly. "You were so much more. And so much better than this."

We were both silent for a moment, the sounds of the passing cars seemed muted, too. Finally, Yuri sighed. It was exhaustion. It was sadness. But worse, I knew it was goodbye. "Have a good life, Tania," he murmured, trying to kiss my cheek.

I stepped back. "You gave up on us. You're a coward, and you don't get to touch me."

Turning around awkwardly, I looked for Ella. "Els?" I whispered. She was right there, putting her arm around me and leading me away, after sending Yuri a glare that should have left him a pile of ash on the sidewalk.

# CHAPTER EIGHT

*In which Tania discovers that it is possible to re-break a heart that is already broken.*

**Yuri...**

"How did the dinner meeting go with Lenkov last night?" Maksim offered me a drink, calmly but firmly shutting the door on his assistant Alina and two of his captains.

"I am sure you already know that he did not come. He sent his daughter Mila." I put the cold glass against my forehead, relishing the chill. The scar there had been throbbing painfully since last night. "I had Boris drop her off at home after dinner. She pouted. I believe she thought it was adorable."

"Why does it feel like someone shot off a starter pistol when word got out you were moving back to St. Petersburg?" He pinched the bridge of his nose between his thumb and forefinger. "Every single Bratva princess is suddenly finding reasons to call Mariya and Ekaterina. To meet for lunch, you understand."

"It looks like we are both cursed with headaches," I noted, draining half my glass.

"The largest one would be my wife," he admitted.

"Why brother, I am *shocked.* The mighty *Pakhan,* terrified of his wife?"

"Don't think I won't punch your pretty face in before you escape to St. Petersburg," he said, pointing a finger at me.

"Not so pretty anymore," I said, shocked and a little embarrassed at how bitter it sounded.

"What was the phrase Tania always used when one of the bodyguards got injured?" He smiled, "Chicks-"

"-dig scars, glory is forever, babe." I finished. "I heard one of the captains made a sign with the quote and posted it over the surgical suite in the safe house."

"Yuri," he sighed. "I never thought there would come a day I'd ask you if you really wanted to walk away from Tania, but…"

"Stop." I put down my glass and stood up, buttoning my jacket. "I still have a lot of work to finish before I leave tomorrow."

"*Sovietnik!*" The word came out harshly, and I turned to Maksim. "Do not turn your back on me."

"What do you require, *Pakhan?*" I tried to stir up some anger, but there was nothing. The words were as lifeless as I was.

He walked around the desk and stood in front of me, putting his hand on my uninjured shoulder. "I say this as your brother and your *Pakhan.* I find Tania…" he scowled as he tried to find the right words, "irritating. Exasperating. Infuriating. But I have also seen how good she is for you. How happy you are together. Walking away from her…" He shook his head, clearly confused. "We both endured a childhood of torture. We always understood each other. But I don't understand this. This woman loves you, despite being Bratva, not because of it. Just like Ella, and me."

I smiled. My brother, the powerful Maksim, trying to talk to me about true love and happy endings. I was happy for him that he found his, there was not one for me.

"Is there anything specific you need me to handle before I leave for St. Petersburg?"

Maksim's mouth thinned in disappointment before he squeezed

my shoulder and stepped back. "You already have too much on your plate. Let me know how the meeting with the Manolos Cartel goes."

*Tania…*

"So, he's insane," Ella said emphatically. "Yuri's so traumatized by what happened to him that he's just, what, giving up?"

"Not giving up on the gangster life," I said bitterly, taking another gulp of wine. "Just giving up on me."

We were still sitting in the wreckage of my living room because I hadn't found a place to move to yet. As much as I wanted to put the Morozov brothers and their unwanted charity behind me, the specter of getting kidnapped by the lunatic head of the Sokolov Bratva to force Ella to trade her life for mine, made me never feel really safe again. It was always on the edge of my consciousness that another van could pull up, someone could yank me inside and this time it could be game over.

"I can't stay here, Els," I stood up, walking over to the huge window and looking out over the street. "Between the shooting and seeing Yuri in every corner of this place, I just… I'll find something else."

"Look, of all the things Maksim owes to you, my beloved emotional support animal, he owes you safety. If you don't want to be here, we'll find you another super safe apartment instead, okay?" She came over, putting her arm around me. "Although, are you really sure you want to move? Look at that guy across the street! What the hell size weights is that man lifting?"

"Right?" I agreed. "He works out in his living room, I think he converted it to a gym. You should see him on butt and leg day. It's better than Pornhub, I swear." She cracked up, just like I knew she would, and we finished our wine, watching the hot guy across the street bench press his body weight.

*Two days later…*

I woke up around midnight, gasping. My heart was trying to pound its way out of my chest and I was dripping sweat. I dreamt that Yuri was lounging on his private jet, just taking off from JFK Airport. And then the jet exploded in a giant fireball, flaming pieces of torn metal falling to the ground.

Checking my phone, I sucked in a shaky breath. Ella had told me he was leaving for St. Petersburg tonight.

He was really gone.

# CHAPTER NINE

*In which a mysterious and exceptionally spiteful billionaire delivers the final blow.*

**Tania...**

**Three months later...**

"...So, if you take a look at the data, you'll see why I think MacGown Oil is an excellent prospect."

"Great presentation, Tania, thank you," Ezio beamed at me from the head of the conference table. "Ladies and gentlemen, please take a look at the spreadsheet, I'm sure we can answer any questions."

As everyone filed out, my boss walked over grinning at me. "That was a masterful PowerPoint, really. You have really been on fire for the last few months."

I smiled weakly. Sure. I didn't have anything else in my life, so there was always work. It was so much easier to plunge into the numbers instead of lying on the floor of my new apartment, drinking and crying my eyes out. Ella came over every chance she got - she knew I didn't want to see anything Morozov-related so I wouldn't go to her fancy penthouse - but between her medical training and her *Pakhan's* wifey responsibilities, there wasn't much time.

The only upside of Yuri being in St. Petersburg was there was less fodder for the gossip sites, so I could keep away from any painful, accidental sightings popping up when I was scrolling around on my phone.

There was one time about two weeks ago when an article about some rich people's event in Paris looked interesting, I clicked on it, and there was Yuri, gorgeous and in a tux. He was smiling down at a striking redhead.

I knew that smile, it was the 'I am so bored and this means nothing' smile, but the girl with him didn't seem to care, her hand was on his arm, leaning in just a bit.

I stared at the picture, tracing the lines of his face with my finger. He looked as tall and bulky as ever, but his face was thinner. Then I clicked out of the site and drank myself to sleep.

"...do you think, Tania?"

I blinked and tried to focus. Ezio was looking at me expectantly.

"Uh, that seems good." I nodded as if I had the slightest idea of what the hell he had been talking about.

"Excellent!" He clapped his hands together. "I'll let the board members know we're meeting the clients tonight at Bar Hugo."

Clients. And the Papachristodoulopoulos Board of Directors. The biggest group of obscenely wealthy and utterly useless assholes in the tri-state area. It would be a night in hell.

*Please,* I lectured myself, *it's not like you had anything else to do.*

Even after making it home for a quick shower, my good black dress, and an extremely non-motivating pep talk, the evening forced me to question many of my life choices, including having given up drinking for a week or two to dry myself out.

"Are you sure I can't get you something stronger?" The super hot bartender was flirting shamelessly with me, which would ordinarily make my evening because it would mean free drinks and giving him my number if he managed to stay charming and hot all night. But now… eh.

"No thanks, I'm pretty sure my blood could be used as lighter fluid at this point," I smiled to make it sound less weird. "Just doing a little detox."

"Oh! Which detox are you doing?" An excitable brunette bounced up to me in a dress so tight that I could count each of her ribs. I think her name was… Lana? She was here as the date of Ezio's biggest investor on this new project.

"Because I just got finished with this amazing new plan that Giselle Bundchen uses?" She said eagerly, "You mix kelp and…"

Maybe I should have taken the hot bartender up on the offer of that drink.

"…and then you'll poop out your body weight for like three days, but at the end, your colon is squeaky clean."

"So clean you could eat off it, huh?"

Lana nods enthusiastically for a moment then frowns at me, confused.

"I'm sorry," I really was. "I have a terrible sense of humor."

"That is not what I've heard. Tania, right?" Speak of the devil.

I spun around. "Oh, hello, Mr. O'Rourke, how are you enjoying your evening?"

"It's good so far," he smiled, "and call me Nolan, please."

Nolan O'Rourke was one of those men unfairly gifted with shrewd intelligence, a bulging bank account, and a level of supermodel hotness that - even in his early forties - really didn't exist outside of New York Fashion Week.

His warm brown eyes focused on Lana for a moment. "My darling, would you mind getting me another drink?"

"No problem, babe." She gave a little giggle when he lifted her hand and kissed the back of it lingeringly.

I watched her walk away, smiling at him over her shoulder and nearly knocking over one of the waiters. Not that I could blame her. His charm was lethal.

"You really kept me on my toes with all those financing questions today," I said. "Ezio's very happy you're sharing his vision on this project."

He ran his hand through his perfectly sculpted hair, blond and sun-kissed with the slightest bit of a curl. "Well, you had an answer for everything, you were the one really sold the project," he said with a slight, elegant Irish accent. "They're lucky to have you at Papachristo… dou…"

"It's rhythmic," I waved my hand like I was leading music, "Papa. Christo. Doulo. Poulos."

"It sounds like one of his ancestors lost a bet and had to use the surname as some kind of eternal punishment for his family," he said wryly.

It had been so long since someone had made me laugh like this. *That used to be Yuri's job…* I thought.

"It's entirely plausible," I agreed, smothering the last of my laughter in my club soda.

"I must admit," he said, "I can see why Yuri was so taken with you."

There were alarm bells clanging in my head, "Do you do business with the Morozov's?"

"Word is that he was very fond of you," he continued, ignoring my question, "but they always go back to their own kind, don't they?"

I opened my mouth to snarl at him then paused. Wait, did he mean to be xenophobic toward Yuri, or was he being classist to me, or…

"It's a shame," O'Rourke continued, "I wouldn't have let you go, even if I did have to make an advantageous marriage."

I frowned, equal parts concerned, weirded out, and horrified that he brought up Yuri at all. He smiled at my confusion.

"Oh, you didn't know?"

"Know what?" I asked sharply because I was done with this game-playing rich boy.

"Yuri Morozov's getting married," he said, watching me closely. "A sweet young thing from the Balabanov Brat- oh, excuse me, the Balabanov *family* in Moscow. Sometime next month." He accepted the fresh drink from Lana, grinning at my stunned expression, his perfectly straight, white teeth gleaming. "You really didn't know, did you? Ouch."

"Did you know?"

"Know what? Are you okay?" Ella's voice went from cheerful to concerned.

I was huddled in the back seat of my Uber, sobbing hard enough that my phone was getting wet.

"About Yuri. That he's getting married."

"WHAT?" She screamed, loud enough that my driver looked up, alarmed.

"I guess that's a no," I would like to say something scathing so it doesn't sound like I'm crying blood, but that's sure what it feels like.

"How- where did you hear this?" I could hear her heels clacking down the marble hallway of her penthouse and I was pretty sure she was breaching the sanctity of Maksim's office.

"One of the asshole investors in the new Papachristodoulopoulos real estate project told me tonight. He was all kinds of thrilled to deliver the news," I sniffled.

"This can't- there's no way- Maksim, I really need to talk to you!" There was muted grumbling in Russian and I knew the room was clearing in a hurry. "Look honey," she said, "I'll call you back, okay?"

"Okay, thanks."

I looked at my driver, who was still watching me in his rearview mirror, wide-eyed. "Just let me out here, please."

"You sure?" But he was already pulling over to the curb. "Hey," he said as I clumsily got out, "whoever he is, that asshole does not deserve you, sister."

I nodded, giving a weak, polite laugh. "Yeah, men are trash, huh?"

He nodded back, solemnly. "Men *are* trash."


While walking the last forty-six blocks home in high heels was, as my mom says, "punishing no one but me," it gave me a chance to almost convince myself that O'Rourke was completely full of shit.

Until Ella called me back.

"What did Maksim say?" There was a moment of silence, and it was all I needed. "That heartless dick is getting married."

She was crying, "He told me he'd only known for a couple of days and he was trying to get Yuri to change his mind. Maksim thinks he's punishing himself for living. Survivor's guilt?"

I laughed. It was not a nice laugh. "He's working through his survivor's guilt by marrying a hot little Bratva princess after skipping town? Yeah, that's definitely a sound therapeutic approach. Unbelievable."

"I'm coming over," she said fiercely, "we'll talk and work this out."

Rubbing my eyes, I shook my head. "No, it's past midnight and knowing you, you have clinical rounds in the morning. I'm going to go home and process this by breaking some shit."

"I don't care! I need to be with you." I have not heard Ella this furious in forever. I was not sure Maksim was going to be keeping his nuts after this little revelation.

"Let's talk tomorrow, I'm just turning down my street now," I said. "Maybe you'll have more information and maybe I won't feel like setting Yuri on fire."

"Tan, honey. You know I will come right now," she promised.

"I know, and I love you for it. Can you come over tomorrow night instead?"

"Yes. Absolutely. But text me in the morning so I know you didn't fly to St. Petersburg and beat the hell out of him, okay? Or if you do want to go to St. Petersburg and beat the hell out of him, I want to be there to watch." This was why Ella had always been my best friend.

"I know you would," I managed to laugh. "Thanks. Talk tomorrow. I love your guts."

"Love your guts," she said. "Tomorrow. We'll fix this."

Ending the call, I stared at my phone. Clicking the contacts, I selected Yuri, blocked his number, and deleted the contact. How long had I waited for him to come to his senses and call me?

"There's no fixing this one," I whispered.


The following month passed by in a stumbling kind of mental

fog. Instead of drinking myself unconscious every night, I tried running with Ella in Central Park. That sucked.

I tried hot yoga.

Yoga with goats in the park.

Weight training until I broke my big toe after dropping a weight on my foot.

I went to the book club in my building.

I tried salsa dancing lessons but they reminded me of dancing with Yuri in my living room and I left halfway through the lesson but promised the instructor I would give him a really good Yelp review because he looked so disappointed.

And then I just… didn't do anything. I went to work. Came home.

Until my doorbell rang one night and when I opened the door, Patrick was standing there, back from the dead.

# CHAPTER TEN

*In which a terribly ill-conceived rescue plan is made.*

**Tania...**

*"Patrick!"* I half screamed it and he stared at me like I just farted in church.

"Keep it down, will ya?" He took me by the arm and hustled me back through the door, shutting it behind us.

"Wha- dude, I thought you were gone!" I swallowed down a lump in my throat. I was not going to cry even if this insane Irish ginger rose from the dead to knock on my door. No more tears. "How are you here? Where have you been?"

He ran a hand down his face, chuckling. "What a greeting! I almost think you like me."

"Are you kidding me right now?" I was patting him gently, like the world's most awkward frisking. "I- I saw you die! I was trying to stop the bleeding and there was so much how-"

"Are you patting me down for weapons or something?" Patrick asked, looking adorably confused.

"No, I'm just trying to make sure you're real and not some sad figment of my imagination. I have enough of those," I muttered.

Looking up at him, I cringed. He looked all kind and sympathetic - like I didn't get enough of that shit these days. But the boy was raggedy-looking. Pale, and a lot thinner than his usual bulky self.

"Look, just- here, come sit down. You want a drink? A smoothie?"

He started laughing, heading for the couch. "A smoothie? Who are you talking to? Is Maksim here?"

Rubbing my forehead, I laughed too. Everyone in the Morozov circle found Maksim's "healthy" smoothies acutely disgusting. They always looked and smelled like ground-up lizard. "Oh, shut up! I do have some whisky here… yeah, Johnny Walker Blue Label."

"Perfect."

I eyed the half-empty wine bottle. I'd told myself I wasn't drinking anymore tonight, but… what the hell, I had a guest. Filling my glass and grabbing his, I joined him back on the couch. "You get to finish half your drink and then I want answers."

Shaking his head with a grin, he lightly tapped his glass to mine. *"Sláinte."*

"Right back atcha, pal."

We drank in silence for a moment before he settled back with a sigh. "I like your new place."

"Yeah? Thanks. I didn't want to stay… anyway, thanks," I looked down at my glass for a moment. "Okay, spill. And don't leave out anything because I thought you were dead and right now I want to kick you in the nuts or something. I was so pissed off at Yuri and Maksim because you didn't get a funeral!"

He pointed a stern finger at me. "No kicking the family jewels. I'm lucky I still have 'em. First thing. I've been waiting to say thank you since I came to, all wired up in that ICU bed. You saved my life by stopping the bleeding long enough for the paramedics to get there."

"So where the hell did you go?" I smacked him on his shoulder instead of the family jewels which he still deserved for letting me think he was dead.

He finished his whiskey, rolling the tumbler between his palms. "Just me being here goes against everything the Pakhan would want, you have to know that."

Frowning, I said, "I have never spoken about the Morozov Brat-tastic lifestyle. I'm not starting now, especially if it means risking your life. Again."

"Brat-tastic…" Patrick was chuckling again. "Okay. Since everyone thought I was dead, the boss knew this was a once-in-a-lifetime chance for me to poke around Dublin and Belfast and infiltrate the O'Connell Mob."

"And risking your life just when you got off your deathbed. Nice." I said sourly.

"Ah," he shook his head at me, "he also offered me the chance to leave the life for good. Take my money and go find a tropical island, buy a bar, die of skin cancer because I will never tan…"

"And you still chose the Bratva."

"They're my family," he said simply. "But back to why I'm here. I picked up enough valuable intel and it was getting too risky, so the boss brought me back home. With my fancy, elevated status as his *Obshchak*, he wanted me to move into Yuri's penthouse.

"Apparently," he cleared his throat awkwardly, "he doesn't intend to return to New York enough to keep it."

I flushed, finished my wine, and stood up. "You want another one?"

"Aye, of course," he said. "So I was walking through the place yesterday and looking around, and I checked the safe. It was clear he hadn't opened it because there was dust all over the painting in front of it."

I nodded; it was the one in his bedroom.

He blew out a long breath. "I can't believe I'm doing this. This is against everything I swore an oath to, but I have to believe my duty to Yuri is still in keeping with that. I found this in the safe."

He pulled out a letter with my name scrawled across it in Yuri's bold handwriting and a velvet jewelry box. A little one.

The kind you would use for a ring.

I scooted away to the far end of the couch. "I don't... I don't want that. It wasn't for me anyway. I don't know if they're keeping you up on current events pal, but that heartless dick is getting married this week."

"Please." He pushed it at me. "Please just read it."

Swallowing that stupid lump that would not stop moving up into my throat, I opened the letter.

*Moye serdtse...*

"My heart?" I said bitterly, "That's a laugh in English *and* Russian."

"Keep reading," Patrick sighed.

*Moye serdtse...*

*If all goes to plan, I will be giving you this ring tonight.*

*I am not sure why I am writing this, but I wanted to tell you how much I love you in case I am unfortunate enough to forget everything I want to say to you this evening when I propose, and it ends up as an incomprehensible string of Russian instead.*

*You fly in the face of everything I am used to. You are nothing like the women in my world. You are the only woman I've ever been with who truly did not care who I was and in fact, consider my wealth and status as somewhat of an inconvenience. You insist on paying rent for an apartment that is yours. You refuse to allow me to buy you all the things that I want to give you.*

*But I hope you will not refuse this ring. I know our life is strange and* sometimes terrifying. But Ella has found a place within our family, and I wish above all things that you would as well. You are the only one that silences all the noise in my head and allows me to feel - even if it is for a short time - human.

My love, my heart, my soul are yours, Yuri

Numbly, I smoothed the creases in the paper.

"Open the box," Patrick urged.

"It wasn't meant for me after all," I said sadly.

"Lass! Just… c'mon."

"Fine!" I snapped, opening the little velvet box and *oh my god sweet baby Jesus what is this?*

"I was with him when he was searching for your ring. It was extremely boring, I'm not gonna lie. But when the family jeweler brought this one to him Yuri said, 'This is the one. The precise color of her eyes.' It's called the Golden Empress. Well, the actual Golden Empress is around 132 carats and wouldn't be much fun to drag around. This here is the satellite diamond. There's not another like it in the world." Patrick held the box up to my eyes and compared them.

"I'll be damned, he was right." Shutting the box, he placed it in my lap.

"Look… this is really sweet and it was… nice, I guess, to see this. But Yuri does not love me. He sleazed out of town without a goodbye. He wrote me a fucking note! If Ella and I hadn't bumped into him outside that restaurant I never would have seen him again and oh, for the record, it took him a mere forty-eight hours to get over his heartbreak and sorrow and to get a leg over some Russian daddy's girl! So, *no* Patrick, this-"

His hand went over my mouth. "Can you just hold off for a minute?" I narrowed my eyes and licked the palm of his hand. "Really now?" Patrick sighed, wiping his hand on his jeans.

"Please hear me out. What happened to Yuri is about as bad as it gets. Being powerless, strapped down, and tortured for days… I asked him once how he did it, how could he have held on that long? He said it was you. Yuri said in his mind he was with you and you saved him."

I drew my knees up, resting my forehead against them. I was overwhelmed and heartbroken and I knew my pathetic emotions were bleeding all over my face and I couldn't look at him.

"That's something that does not go away, a love that gives the strength to endure all things." He got up and fetched the roll of paper towels from the kitchen and handed it to me.

After wiping my face, I took a few deep cleansing breaths to give me a couple of seconds to think. "Even if this is true, it still doesn't change that Yuri chose to leave. And he's getting married. Are you telling me this to cheer me up and convince me I'm the love of his life or some-"

"That's exactly what I'm trying to tell you!" Patrick interrupted me. "Yuri has closed himself off. He does nothing but work, and then works out to build his strength up again. He's marrying this girl because it's a useful Bratva alliance. The boss didn't even ask him to do it."

"Knowing Maksim has arranged marriages for both of his sisters, this is a shocker," I said with more than a bit of snark.

"The point here," bless him, poor Patrick was really trying to keep this conversation on track. "The point is that he needs you. He loves you like no one else in the world, and I know you love him. But here's the reason I am risking my position and possibly my life by telling you this. Without you, Yuri may as well be dead. When I talk to him, it's like he's…" He thinks about it. "He's not even there anymore."

I was clutching the ring box in one hand and the letter in the other. "You know, if this was a rom-com you would totally be cast as the sassy best friend."

"Really? This is as far as my sentimental Irish self can go - especially after that wisecrack - so I'll be taking my leave, thank you very much," Patrick says sourly. "I'm gonna let you think about this. You only have seventy-two hours to decide what you want to do about it." He held up a card with his name and number and put it on top of the letter. "I'll be around for the next day or so if you need my help."

I stared at the door after he closed it behind him.

I tried to work for the rest of the night, but after going back over the fact sheet I was putting together for a merger and realizing half of it was wrong, I gave up.

I should call Ella, she'd help me figure this out. But… is it right to put her in this position? Knowing Patrick blabbed to me in a completely non-*Obshchak* way? And what was I going to do with this information?

The one thing I knew that was absolute and irrevocable in the Bratva was that once you married, you were married for life. Not that it stopped any of the men - most of those misogynistic assholes just took on a stable of escorts and mistresses, but no such thing as divorce. Ever.

If I'm going to talk to Yuri, it has to be before he did this completely irrevocable thing. Was it already too late? Could he even get out of this engagement? What could I even say that would possibly make a difference?

All my doubts, my self-hatred, the shame of never being enough broke through the walls I thought I'd constructed so well to keep it all in. Everything that surged over me the night he left me came oozing back.

Why would he break his engagement to a Mafia princess for a girl from New Jersey?

Patrick's words came back to me: *"That's something that does not go away, a love that gives the strength to endure all things."*

"I can't believe I'm doing this," I said, knocking my head lightly against the wall. "I am *so* going to make Yuri grovel for forgiveness when this shit is over."

Grabbing my phone, I picked up Patrick's card and dialed.

"I thought you'd have called sooner, but…"

"Stop gloating, ginger," I snarled, "I need a plan and you're the most cunning guy I've got in my corner right now."

His voice is warm and a touch relieved. "I'm here. Let's plot this out."

# CHAPTER ELEVEN

*In which Tania's audacious plan – which is a complete clusterfuck – does not turn out as expected. At all.*

**Yuri…**

"You don't have to do this."

I straightened my bow tie again, irritated that Maksim would not give up. "No, *Pakhan*, I do have to do this. I have made an alliance with the Balabanov Bratva. Moscow has always been our white whale. Now, we have an in."

"Literary allusion noted," he said, still pacing the room.

"Gentlemen, we are thirty minutes away." Yulia, the wedding planner tapped deferentially on the door. I found it entertaining since I had heard her screaming at the catering group earlier. But she was Ksenia's choice. I left everything regarding the wedding to her and her voraciously greedy mother. I was footing the bill, and I suspected it was going to be one of the most expensive weddings in recent history.

"Thank you," Maksim said in a tone better suited to 'get out or I will kill you and everyone you love.'

She took the hint and disappeared.

I downed my drink and winced at the burn. My gut was already churning and another one wouldn't make it any worse. I held the glass out to him with a raised brow and pulled on my tuxedo jacket.

When he handed it back to me, full to slopping over the edge, I raised it. "To new alliances."

I downed mine in three gulps. Maksim didn't drink, setting his aside.

"I am going to say this, and then I'll accept whatever you want to do." Rubbing the back of his neck, he stared out the window.

"When I decided to marry, it never occurred to me that it would make me happy. It was merely advantageous. I never expected to feel much of anything with Ella. But what we have..." Maksim turned me by the shoulder, forcing me to look at him.

"If a heartless, clueless fool like me could find a life that was shared with this incredible woman, so can you. And you had a love like that."

"*Pakhan* Maksim Morozov, talking about love?" I was mocking him, but it was half-hearted.

"Yuri..." he put his hands on my shoulders and shook me. "We were raised to believe there was nothing else for us than the life that father - the old bastard - demanded. I want you to believe that there is more for you. You can live *both* the life we are forced to lead, and the one you are meant to live with Tania. Don't throw this away."

"You expect me to abandon the only daughter of the Balabanov Bratva at the altar?" I was so angry- I wanted to punch Maksim hard enough to rearrange his face, I wanted to get married with bloody knuckles knowing my wife-to-be would ignore them because nothing mattered in her pretty little world but my net worth. I wanted him to stop talking.

"You are *Pakhan* and yet *I* must be the one to remind you how these alliances work? You want open warfare between one of the biggest Bratvas in Moscow and us because... because you want me to live my best life?" I laughed harshly and grabbed the bottle of vodka by the neck, taking a drink. "This is reality, brother.

Maybe you are strong enough to be soft and still survive. I am not!" I shouted the last in his face and waited for him to hit me. A bloody nose and a black eye for the wedding. Ksenia's mother would change the wedding colors from peach and gold to black and blue before the archbishop even blessed us.

Outside, the noise from the wedding preparations got louder and louder, but in this room, it was silent as he stared at me.

"You are wrong. You are so much stronger than you're willing to see. But you are my brother and I will support your decision, even if Ella can't."

We made an identical wince, recalling Ella's heartbreak and fury the night before.

"Yuri, you can't do this. You really want to be miserable for the rest of your life?"

"Sister, this has nothing to do with you. This is Bratva business," I'd never spoken so sharply to my - usually - sweet sister-in-law, but the scar on my face was throbbing and the searing ache in my damaged shoulder that never really went away was increasing every minute I spent arguing with her.

*Blyat'!* I realized, *I just told Ella something is not her business. She is seconds away from stabbing me with the fireplace poker...*

"That is bullshit!" She was shouting, her face red and her eyes teary. "This is you being a coward! Tania was there for you - she was always there for you and you're throwing her away for some twenty-year-old Bratva princess?"

She was pacing in front of me and stopped to jab a finger in my chest. "You just want to suffer? Fine. Go put on your hair shirt and give yourself a thousand lashes or whatever. Suffer! Because you're not only killing your heart, you're crushing Tania's, too."

Her chest was heaving and she stared at me, waiting for... what? I couldn't withdraw my offer for Ksenia without starting a war between our families. I gave her a kiss on the cheek and walked away.

"Gentlemen, it's time?"

The wedding planner clearly felt the tension in the air and looked like she would rather be anywhere else, it ended the standoff between Maksim and me and I nodded to her. "We will be out in a moment."

He straightened my lapels and forced out a smile. "I'm by your side, Yuri."

I nodded my thanks and we walked out of the room, our men falling in behind us.

The Kazan Cathedral was packed full, and representatives from nearly every organized crime group in the world were here to pay their respects. Chikao Nakamura from the Japanese Yakuza, Thomas and Lauren Williams representing The Corporation, Dario and Giovanni of the Toscano Mafia, Alexi and Lucya Turgenev, our closest Russian allies, and a hundred more.

I took my place with Maksim and scanned the crowd, a grim sort of resignation hardening in my chest. Ksenia Balabanov was approaching the altar and it was time to forget everything else if I wanted to get through this ceremony.

*Goodbye, Tania.*

It was during the betrothal ceremony when the Archbishop's droning voice was interrupted.

"I object!"

**Tania...**

Patrick was extremely helpful in many ways; having the Morozov *Obshchak* in my corner was definitely making the most suicidal, irrational rescue plan ever devised take shape.

"You're going to be taken into the back of the cathedral in a weapons container-"

"Seriously? You guys are bringing Kalashnikovs into God's house? Wow. Eternal damnation. I mean-"

He leveled me with a glare. "My corner suite in hell is already spoken for. Now shut up and pay attention."

It turns out that the Morozov Empire has no less than four private jets, and Patrick and I are on one of them. He had me all dressed up and in a wig and a bunch of other stuff to confuse the flight crew into thinking I was his date for the wedding. But now that we were landing in St. Petersburg, the complete dumbassedness of what I was about to do hit me,

"Um, would your guys or the Balabanov guys actually shoot me in the cathedral?"

"No," he said absently, poring over the schematics, "they'd drag you outside first." Glancing up to see my expression, he grabbed my hand. "No one's going to hurt you. I give you my word. If the worst happens, I will get you out of there."

I squared my shoulders. "Then let's do this. Yuri is going to kiss my feet for the rest of our lives together to make up for his ridiculous beliefs and his overdeveloped need for self-sacrifice."

"*Ar fheabhas!*" Patrick rubbed his hands together. "Excellent! Let's go."

I would have thought infiltrating a huge Bratva wedding wouldn't have been so easy, but Patrick didn't make *Obshchak* without deserving it, thanks to his attention to detail and a level of sneakiness I could not help but admire.

Once in, I walked into the restroom dressed as a groundskeeper and walked out as a wedding guest, wrapping a scarf over my hair the way I'd seen Ella do at church.

The iconostasis of the Kazan Cathedral made the word 'majestic' seem too feeble to explain it. The massive gold arch guarded the doors to the Sanctuary, and exquisite, centuries-old paintings of religious icons covered the walls. A gargantuan chandelier lit the room, reflecting off every gilded surface.

Wedding guests were streaming in through the four massive bronze doors, passing under the dome. For a minute, I let myself stand under it, looking up as expensively dressed people moved around me like a stone in a stream. The dome soared up twenty-one stories high, and it felt like it reached high enough to catch the attention of the Almighty. I said a small prayer, hoping that being Catholic wouldn't make the Russian Orthodox God strike me down with a bolt of lightning.

I made my way to the far left of the women's section behind the icon of the Virgin, planting my feet every time someone tried to get me to move over.

"Weak bladder," I said to one extremely pushy lady in broken Russian, "you really don't want to be between me and a bathroom."

No one bothered me after that.

When Yuri took his place by the altar, escorted down the right side by Maksim as per tradition, my heart nearly turned inside out from needing him. If anything, he was broader and more muscled than before the kidnapping as if he could protect himself from another attempt by sheer muscle mass.

He looked incredible in that tux, I knew it had to be custom-made because no designer built a formal jacket for shoulders the size of Yuri's.

The bride walked in on the left. She was really pretty in that tall, well-bred, "I went to private schools in Switzerland all my life," way. Blonde. Her head was tilted at the weirdest angle, and it took me a minute to realize she was trying to position her chin for the best profile picture.

My heart was pounding hard enough to punch out of my chest if I didn't get it under control. This was such a stupid idea. Why was I doing this? These people are going to cut me up into little pieces and-

Maybe if someone didn't know Yuri very well, they might have missed it, but as the bride walked toward him at the altar, he looked terribly sad. Just for a moment, but I saw it. That's why I was insane enough to raise my hand and shout, "I object!"

# CHAPTER TWELVE

*In which Tania discovers "I object!" in the Bratva means sudden death.*

**Tania...**

I hadn't seen pandemonium like this since the After-Christmas sale at Sak's Fifth Avenue.

I was sitting in the corner of some kind of magnificent, high-ceilinged receiving room after being hustled through a nearly invisible door behind the altar. There were two beautiful statues flanking the wooden bench where they seated me and I really hoped they weren't martyrs who would be predicting my fate. Maybe they would make a statue of me and my horrific end.

Yeah. Saint Tania. That would never be happening.

The room was so grand and regal that it made the angry men, pounding on the table and the crying women seem even more surreal, like nothing as mundane as human heartbreak had any place here.

The bride - Ksenia Balabanov, I learned - spent the first ten minutes screaming in my face until her father yelled at her to shut up. Maksim directed three of his men to form some kind of impenetrable bodyguard wall around me when she tried to poke one of my eyes out with her terrifying, pointy fingernails.

It's not like I could hold it against her.

Ella played her *Pakhan's* wifey role and spoke with the furious Mama Balabanov and the bride, who was now wailing loudly with mascara running down her cheeks.

By the time she'd calmed them down a bit, Maksim was in my face.

"Did Ella help you with this? Do you understand what you have done?"

"No, Ella didn't help me. I would never put her in that position." I was scared shitless but I was not going to show it.

My eyes darted to Yuri, who was still speaking with Daddy Balabanov, who was at least not shouting anymore. The one glance he had sent my way was petrifying. He looked me over like I was an insect, far less than human and certainly not worth anything more than a bullet in the back of my head.

"Tania!" Maksim snapped, "This is very, very bad. I'm not sure I can save your life. The father of the bride is demanding your death as part of retribution for your actions."

"Oh, that is *not* happening!" Ella hissed, trying to keep her voice down. "Write him a check, add some extra zeros but they are not getting Tania!"

He looked at her, his furious expression softened just slightly. "Did you know about this?"

"No," she shook her head, "but I wish I'd thought of it."

"*Solnyshko*, you have no idea how bad this is," he groaned. "This is not about money. This is about honor. And Tania spat in their faces. She could not have insulted the Balabanov family more."

"It was two words!" I protested weakly, "I mean, I wasn't objecting to *her*. Sure, she tried to pop my eye out like the last grape in a fruit assortment but I understand."

He rounded on me in such a fury that even Ella jumped. "What did you think would happen here, you stupid girl? You have started a war between our families. Men will die for your grand gesture. Do you understand now?"

Yeah, I did. And it was not Patrick's fault. He's a romantic Irishman at heart but I should have known better.

"I can't even apologize for being an idiot," I said, even though my lips were kind of numb now and my ears were buzzing. "It would never be enough, would it?" Looking between his furious face and Ella's anguished one, I took a shaky breath, trying not to vomit. "If giving me up will… you know, clean up this mess then do it. No one should be dying for me." My courage cracked wide open like a chocolate egg. "But will you do it? M- make it quick?"

Ella wrapped her arms around me, "No, no no no! No, Tania, that is not going to happen! We'll figure this out."

"If it's me or a bunch of dead guys, Els, I just…" Oh, fuck I have never been so scared. That shootout at King's New Year's Eve party is a fond memory compared to this. I am going to die. I probably deserve to after everything I've done… I'm so terrified that my teeth are chattering.

"That will not be necessary." Yuri was standing next to Maksim, his hands folded in front of him, and his expression… No, there was no expression, his face was completely blank. Like he'd never met me before. "*Pakhan,* can you join me? There have been some new developments."

Ella and I looked at each other.

The blue, cream and gold meeting room was so large that I couldn't really see all the men clustered around the long marble-topped table in the far corner. I knew Yuri and Maksim were there, along with Balabanov and a couple of his guys. There was a freaked-out-looking woman serving drinks - later, I decided that Maksim didn't have time to cater his brother's crashed wedding, but at that moment, I was too terrified to even find that funny.

The bride and her mother settled in the opposite corner on some beautiful silk-covered chairs, but not without giving me the death stare. Once again, I couldn't hold it against them.

The group of men shifted a little and I spotted… "Is that Patrick?"

"Yeah," Ella whispered back, "Maksim had him undercover because everyone thought he died in the-"

"I know," I interrupted, watching Patrick hand a folder to both parties. Yuri opened his, and the only thing he did was raise one brow slightly. The father of the bride was not so subtle. A bear-like roar came out of him that would terrify Bigfoot.

"These are lies!" Balabanov shouted, "How dare you try to blame my Ksenia for this whore's actions!"

"Oh, he did *not* just call me a-"

"Tania, shut up," Ella hissed. "Not a word."

"There is apparently someone prepared to offer testimony," Maksim said.

The door opened as one of Yuri's guards ushered in another man. I squinted. Was that…?

"You have got to be shitting me," I hissed to Ella. "I know that guy!"

"What?" She looked from me to him and back to me. "How?"

"He's the main investor in our company's new development," I whispered, "he was the one who told me Yuri was getting married. He was a total prick about it, too. He was really enjoying the fact that I didn't know."

She frowned, "What's his name?"

"Nolan O'Rourke."

We watched as the bride turned sheet white when he smiled and waved at her like we were all having a lovely time at a cocktail party.

"What the hell is happening right now?" I whispered.

"I do not know," Ella shook her head, a little dazed. "Nothing is ever simple with the Bratva."

Now the poor girl was wailing loudly and waving her hands and her father was striding furiously in her direction until Yuri stepped in front of him.

*Of course, he would protect her*, I thought, hating that I found this beautiful. *Yuri's just like that.*

He spoke quietly with Balabanov for some time and then the man nodded to his wife who took Ksenia out of the room, still sobbing loudly.

I watched O'Rourke shake Maksim's hand, then Yuri's. He held out his hand to Balabanov, who refused it. Strolling over to me, he put his hand to his chest and gave a courtly little bow. His tuxedo fit him so well that he should have been in an ad for Tom Ford, his shoes gleamed to a mirror finish and he gave me a grin that showed off all those perfect white teeth again.

"Mrs. Morozov, greetings," he nodded politely to Ella. "Tania, might I steal you away for a moment?" Over his shoulder, I could see Yuri's eyes narrow as he detached himself from the other group.

Rising from the bench, I ignored the hand he offered to help me up and followed him to a quiet spot. "Quite a scene there when you popped up," I said flatly, watching him chuckle and hating him for it.

"Oh, yes," he agreed. "It's one of the things I've never understood about the families in organized crime. How the wife must be pure and virginal while the husband could be infested with the nine plagues of the apocalypse and no one would care."

"You're a true crusader," I drawled, "enacting social change. A modern-day feminist."

He didn't seem offended, he just nodded indulgently like I'd said something adorable. "I think you'll find my intervention just saved your life, but I'll let Yuri clear that up for you."

"Why did you do that?" I searched his handsome, deceptively pleasant face, "Why would you risk involving yourself in a situation as explosive as this?"

"Well…" he hummed thoughtfully. "I see promise in you. I did it for a favor."

"I beg your pardon?" Yuri was there now, turning slightly to block me from O'Rourke. "We certainly appreciate your intervention, but what is this favor?"

O'Rourke's eyes turned a chilly brown, like the color of frost on the earth. "Why, Yuri Morozov," he said coldly, "you yourself said, "We are in your debt, did you not?"

"I said, Nolan O'Rourke, that *I* am in your debt," Yuri corrected.

O'Rourke ignored him and looked at me again. "You know, in some cultures, when you save a life, that life is then owed to you. That seems a little extreme to me. You will simply owe me a favor. I don't know what I will ask of you yet. But when I ask for what is due to me, I expect you to honor the request. Are your life and the lives saved from open warfare with the Balabanov Bratva worth it?" He held out his hand.

Yuri tried to interrupt, but I shook O'Rourke's hand. His skin was cool and smooth, but his grip was borderline painful. I remembered a story about someone who made a deal with the devil and carried the brand of a pentacle on his palm for the rest of his life. Until the devil came for him. I tried not to shudder, but his sharp eyes caught the movement. "I won't kill anyone for you," I said sharply.

He shrugged. "I rarely need anyone murdered, and it doesn't fit your skill set, dear."

"Then I promise to honor your request." I felt chilled and nauseous, knowing that I just agreed to something terrible. A man like him didn't ask you to make a cigarette run to the corner bodega.

His gaze went from me to Yuri. "May good fortune follow you both."

He was off, and every man in the room, including Maksim, nodded respectfully as O'Rourke left.

Everything was quiet for a moment until Balabanov growled something at Maksim and stormed out.

"He's not going to hurt that poor girl, is he?" I wasn't sure to who I'd directed the question, but Yuri answered me.

"There is a loss of face on both sides. He will not be happy, we can't control how he treats his family. However, Ksenia is his only daughter, his Bratva desperately needs money, and I suspect there will be another offer for her hand very soon based on the testimony O'Rourke presented."

Turning awkwardly to look at him, the whole intensity of the afternoon hit me. I felt like I'd just walked in front of a delivery truck on 5th Avenue.

He loomed over me, beautiful, cold and remote. His blond hair was perfectly styled and his eyes were the shade of glacier ice.

"This wasn't exactly the reunion I was hoping for," I tried to smile but failed miserably, "apparently I didn't really think through the potential outcomes."

"You never do," he said indifferently.

Turning to his brother, he asked, "Have you spoken with the Archbishop?"

Maksim said, "He will not honor the interruption of a holy rite, but he will allow one of the priests to handle it in the narthex."

"Wait, narthex? Priest? What is-" They both ignored me as Maksim whispered something in Ella's ear. She sucked in a huge breath of air, staring at me while he spoke with her.

"Are you sure this is the right way to handle this?" She looked up at him with big worried eyes, then glanced at Yuri, who was speaking with one of his men. "He doesn't seem-"

"This *is* the only way, *Solnyshko*," he said grimly, "explain this to Tania. We have fifteen minutes. I'll break the news to Mother and the girls." He left without looking at me again, and I knew I was on Maksim's shit list for life.

"Ella, what the hell is going on? This is a disaster. I am so sorry. I'll get the first flight out of here and I'll never bother the Morozovs again. I fucked this up beyond belief. I don't know-"

"Shh! Look honey, you have to listen to me." She dragged me out into the hall and over to a smaller room that was in shambles. I had a suspicion that this had been the bride's area before the godawful end to her wedding plans and they had just cleared out. She pulled me down to sit next to her.

"Okay, I need you to hear me out and not yell or anything, okay?" Ella was freaking out a little, I could tell. "Apparently, Nolan O'Rourke had proof that Ksenia had been having an affair with her driver for years. She was also very popular in the underground party scene in Paris. This disqualified her as an eligible bride for the agreement between their Bratva and ours. Don't start!" She pointed a warning finger, "I know it's revolting and misogynistic and yeah, it sucks. But here's the deal, between her little revelation and you crashing the wedding…"

I cringed so hard that my head nearly disappeared into my shoulders like a turtle.

"This news allows both families to step away from the union and save face," she continued. "But here's where it all falls apart."

"It falls apart?" I said hoarsely, "Is it worse than putting a bullet in my head?"

She flinched and I felt bad. "Not exactly. Balabanov is a monster. The worst. He's never going to forgive you for stopping the wedding and losing all the money he intended to siphon off from Yuri. Everything's settled between the two Bratvas - really tense, but settled - but you, honey? Since you're outside the scope of the agreement, you're fair game. He will kill you or do something much worse…" she stopped for a moment, swallowing heavily. I knew she was thinking about what her own brother and that sociopath Sokolov witch wanted to do to her.

"The Russians are very imaginative," she said bitterly, "especially when it comes to revenge. The only way to keep you safe is to marry Yuri. Right now."

# CHAPTER THIRTEEN

*In which Tania is sweating like a sinner in church*

**Tania...**

"Oh, hell *no!*"

Okay, I might have said that a little too loud because the door opened and Ivan came in, gun raised.

"Ivan, we're fine," Ella said, rubbing her eyes, "thanks for brandishing your weapon, though. It brings back all those memories from my wedding."

Nodding, he backed out, pulling the door shut.

"Tan honey, I know this is not ideal, but-"

"Are you kidding me right now? Do they really think I'm going to marry Yuri when he clearly hates my guts in some ceremony in the- what hell was that? The narthex? Whatever I thought I was trying to do, I did it all so wrong," I groaned, putting my head in my hands.

She put her arm around me. "If you'd told me what you were planning, I still would have told you to do it. Maybe not at the wedding, but yeah."

"We ran out of time," I sighed.

"We?" She turned to look at me. "Who's we?"

I opened my mouth and then closed it again. Telling her would put her in the middle between Maksim and me, it wasn't fair to make her keep secrets from-

"Tania!" Ella said sharply, "You obviously didn't do this by yourself, sneaking into a Bratva wedding?"

"It was Patrick," I caved instantly. "He came to my apartment and showed me a letter and an engagement ring. Yuri was going to propose the evening when he got shot. He flew me out here and smuggled me in. If you tell Maksim…" I shuddered, "Patrick knew he was going against the family by helping me. He said it was the only way to save Yuri from giving up his life and his happiness. You can't tell them it was Patrick."

"I won't," she promised, "though I think after everything calms down they'll figure it out and it will be fine because it all worked out and Yuri is with the woman he's supposed to marry."

"How's that magical thinking working for you, bestie?" I asked, shaking my head. "This is a fucking disaster."

"Well, it's not great," she admitted, "Look, I know Yuri loves you. You love him. You're actually working with better raw material than Maksim and I started with." She bumped my shoulder with hers.

"I can't do this!" Standing up, I walked over to the window. Could I get it open? Jump out and make a run for it? "Yuri does *not* love me, and now he's forced to marry me to save my life? How is this any better than Bala- Baba- Balbon- that girl? I know mob marriages are for life, Els. So eventually he'll pick up a mistress or two because he hates my guts. This is complete bullshit."

"Hey, do you recall that big pep talk you gave me when we were hiding in the bathroom at my wedding?"

"Yeah?"

"I was pretty freaked out like you are now," she admitted, "so I don't remember all of it. However, here were the key points." Ella held up one finger. "You're not getting out of this. Two, I have never met a man whose will to live you couldn't break. You will own Yuri within two weeks, I know you! And three, you have me, your emotional support animal."

"The reality here is that you *are* getting what you want. Not exactly the way you want, but you're getting it." She smiled, trying to straighten my dress, "There's no point in trying to bolt because I'm pretty sure the priest would marry you two even if you said 'no,' so let's brush your hair and touch up your makeup because we probably have five minutes before Ivan's coming through that door again, okay?"

**Yuri…**

"Do you remember that time we were climbing trees in the forest around the estate and your branch broke? You fell and as I remember, landed on your head?"

I sighed, cracking my neck irritably. "Is this story going somewhere, brother?"

"Your expression right now is identical to the one you had then, flat on your back, lying in the pine needles," Maksim supplied helpfully.

"Thank you, that is very uplifting," I said dryly.

"You are quite welcome." He slapped my back.

We were standing in the narthex - the entryway to the cathedral - with my mother and sisters clustered together on one side and the frowning priest on the other. I knew he was not happy about being the one to marry us but at this point, I was incapable of caring.

There was a cautious jubilation rising in my chest, no matter how many times I tried to push it back down. I was going to marry Tania after all.

Patrick walked up to us, holding Tania's purse. "*Sovietnik*, Ella told me that there's a ring and a letter in here. She thought you would want to use the ring for the ceremony."

"Do not waste your time with the innocent act, *Obshchak*," I said coldly. "You are the only one who could have helped her pull this off. We will discuss that later."

Patrick's poker face was good, I had to give him that. He sighed and offered the purse again. I stared at it, suddenly furious. Why couldn't Tania just… behave? If O'Rourke had not popped up with that extremely helpful testimony, we would already be in a firefight with the Balabanov Bratva. Though I would give my life before I let anything happen to her, it was quite possible both of us would have been dead, or worse.

"I will use my signet ring," I brushed him off, "that will be good enough."

Maksim raised one brow, but he said nothing. Glancing at my sisters, I saw Ekaterina grin and give me a subtle thumbs-up. They both liked Tania immensely and were very unhappy with me when I announced my engagement to Ksenia.

I did not know how to process this. I was so angry with Tania for risking her life with such a ridiculously stupid stunt. I would never kill Patrick, but he might wish I had by the time I finished with him.

The priest cleared his throat. I looked up to see Ella gently dragging Tania into the room. "Let us begin," he intoned.

Tania took her place next to me. She was shaking and refused to look up. I could see her body angling toward the entryway, like she was seconds away from making a run for it.

"We will conduct the ceremony here," the priest said sourly, "because the sanctuary is a holy place and not appropriate for this."

I felt a surge of anger and narrowed my eyes at him. There was no reason to shame Tania. "Please continue," I said.

He got the hint and hastily began the ceremony.

*Tania...*

I was sweating like a sinner in church and well… I was a sinner and this was a church and I was marrying the love of my life who now apparently hated me and who could blame him?

If I'd been capable of paying attention, I would have remembered the movements and words from Ella's wedding. That had been done with much pomp and circumstance and here, the priest was rushing through the ceremony as quickly as possible like he was ready to throw up. Which he might be. I was pretty sure weddings in the awe-inspiring Kazan Cathedral weren't usually held in the entryway with a scowling groom and a bride in a wrinkled dress.

I jumped a little when Yuri took my hands, and tilted his head at the priest, who was leading us in circles. I tried to pay attention until the end, when he slipped his signet ring on my finger. My heart sank. I knew Patrick handed him the engagement ring he'd originally meant to give me, once upon a time. After reading that beautiful letter and knowing he'd gone to such lengths to find a diamond that matched my eyes, the ring's absence on my finger was even more painful.

*I deserve it,* I thought bitterly, *thinking I was charging in to save the day and nearly starting a Bratva war instead.*

Ella and Maksim tried to make the clusterfuck more of a celebration. "Let's go back to the house and have some champagne," she said, smiling brightly.

Mrs. Morozov - who hated me which I never took it personally because she hated everyone - asked, "What shall we do with the banquet and wedding cake at the Hotel Astoria?"

Ella and I winced together.

Yuri glanced down at me expressionlessly. "What would you like to do with it?"

"Isn't that… um, the other bride's… her thing?" I said weakly.

*Smooth, Tania.*

"I believe the family will be on their jet and halfway back to Moscow by now," Yuri said. "So the decision falls to you."

I still couldn't meet his gaze, so I focused on Mrs. Morozov, who looked like she was contemplating the most effective way to murder me and dispose of the body. "How many were expected for the wedding reception?"

Her left eyelid twitched. "Eight hundred guests."

My eyes bulged, "Eight hundred people? Uh… you have homeless shelters around here, right? Group homes for women and children?"

Mariya jumps in, "Oh, yes. Absolutely!" She grins spitefully at her brothers. "Everyone loves lobster and wedding cake, right? I'll bet the hotel would be thrilled to deliver the food."

Yuri and Maksim are both looking at her with chilly expressions, and it makes me love her even more. She was the family's youngest, tall and skinny. She looked like Yuri, with her blonde hair and bright blue eyes.

"Thank you, Mariya, you're a genius!" I gushed, just to irritate them. "Maybe send the flower arrangements to a retirement home? Six retirement homes? There might be enough here to cover a children's hospital, too." I knew this collection of wildly out-of-season flowers had to have cost over a hundred grand.

"I will," she saluted me cheekily. I winked back. Thank god not everyone hated me in this family.

Only the one I was married to.

The 'champagne soiree' at the Morozov mansion was about as

much fun as a root canal.

Not that I didn't appreciate the effort, though Mrs. Morozov didn't even bother to take a sip from her glass during Maksim's - pretty gracious, all things concerned - toast.

The miserable day finally dragged to an end. Ella hugged me hard, "Don't worry," she whispered. "I know this sucks, but my marriage turned out to be a gift that I probably don't deserve. Yours will, too. Though I'm *never* going to be sure if Yuri deserves you. He has a lot of groveling in his future."

I laughed a little to make her feel better. But I didn't believe my marriage is going to turn out the way Ella's had.

"My wing of the house is this way."

Yuri's voice made me jump. We were alone in their entryway, which was the size of a hotel lobby and so over the top. It swept up three stories with massive stained-glass windows, staircases flanking to the right and left, and a chilly granite floor.

"You have a *wing?*"

He didn't answer, holding out his hand to direct me to the sweeping staircase on the left side. We walked up in silence and it was painful.

One of the things I had loved about him was that we never ran out of things to talk about; anything and everything from Russian history to the periodic table of elements. We spent an entire evening in his huge bathtub at his Manhattan penthouse discussing when the US shifted from an agrarian to an industrial economy, and then the totally implausible time travel plotline in "The Umbrella Academy" as he rinsed the shampoo out of my hair.

This silence solidified the fact that I just married a stranger who was inhabiting Yuri's body.

He led me down a long hallway and paused outside a door, opening it. "Your bags were already brought up. Let the housekeeper know if you need anything."

"Are we going to talk about this?" I stood between him and the door, noting that he kept a grip on the doorknob like he could hardly wait to shut it in my face.

Finally, he looked into my eyes. When Yuri was happy, his eyes were a brilliant blue, the color of the Caribbean. Tonight, they were a polar shade, like a glacier. "Not tonight."

He shut the door and I listened to his footsteps heading down the hall.

*Yuri...*

While I knew Tania was hurt, and quite likely scared to death, I couldn't stand next to her for one second longer without throwing her on the bed and ripping her dress off. And spanking her. Spanking her round, luscious ass red and listening to her screech at me.

I had no idea how we ended this day without bloodshed.

Entering the master bedroom, I pulled off my tie and jacket with a sigh of relief. Anya, our housekeeper, had lit a cheerful blaze in the fireplace. Even with modern heating, this house was stone, and massive, so it was always chilly. I knew she didn't light a fire in the guest bedroom, and I felt a moment of guilt, picturing Tania sitting there alone.

I rolled my eyes, unbuttoning my dress shirt. Tania was not the type to be weeping softly in the corner. By now, she most likely had already tied the sheets on her bed together and was attempting an escape out her bedroom window, cursing me the entire time.

However, there was no reason she should be uncomfortable during her escape attempt.

I picked up the house phone. "Anya? Please light the fire in the second guest bedroom and bring up some food for Tania. Make sure she has what she needs."

"Of course, *Sovietnik*. Right away."

Stripping, I took a shower, bracing my hands against the marble tile and letting the hot water pound against my skin.

Married.

To Tania.

# CHAPTER FOURTEEN

*In which Tania finds that being married to Yuri is acutely uncomfortable.*

**Tania**...

I've always been one of those weird people who woke up in a good mood. Tired, hungover, it didn't matter. My eyes opened with a smile on my face and...

*Oh, fuck me what have I done?*

Burying my face in my hands, I wondered if it would be better to just disappear. I avidly read stories about people who had managed to drop out of society. Become someone else. Maybe I could work on a wind-powered chinchilla farm in New Zealand and change my name to something super bland. Mary. Mary Smith. Mary Smith-Jones.

I'd been too tired and upset last night to really pay attention to anything, but looking around the room, I was stunned. This was just a guest room? There were wonderful floor-to-ceiling windows that looked out on the boulevard and the Neva River with blue and green tapestry draperies. Two comfortable leather armchairs with a table piled with books between them were set in front of the fireplace. The bed was a beautiful four-poster with carved wooden posts, draped with pale green silk, matching a quilt so thick that it buried me halfway into the mattress. I was blissfully warm and really didn't want to leave it.

Eyeing the enormous fireplace across the room, I noticed that the coals were still glowing red. I could be out of bed, throwing more wood on the banked fire, and back in bed in thirty seconds. Maybe less.

It was as I was bending over to put more logs on the fire when there was a brief tap on the door and it opened to reveal Yuri, who was staring at my panty-clad ass, which was the only item of clothing I'd chosen to don for this engagement.

"Hey!" I awkwardly crossed my arms over my breasts. "Ever heard of waiting 'till someone says 'come in'?"

Damn him. Yuri's gaze was making a slow circuit of my body, my red face, my poorly concealed breasts that were now sporting very pert nipples thanks to this freezing room, and my legs, rapidly turning blue.

"You are welcome to turn up the thermostat if you are cold." He pointed to the little white box on the wall next to the bed.

"Helpful," I managed, my teeth ready to start chattering, "thanks." Could you… close the door?"

He had the nerve to look me over again, lingering on my breasts with an expression that screamed, *I've seen those before.*

Dick.

"As you wish. Can you find your way back downstairs for breakfast?"

"Yes," I nodded firmly, "got it. Shut the door, I can't feel my toes anymore and I'm getting back into bed until I'm sure they're not frostbitten."

However, when Yuri left I changed my mind and headed for the bathroom. There was a huge clawfoot tub with elegant antique fixtures that looked like it had been here since indoor plumbing was invented.

I turned on the water, it was wonderfully hot and there was a tray of little crystal bottles filled with differently scented bath oils. I threw in some lavender because I was going to need some serious soothing aromatherapy to get through the next few hours. There was another fireplace in the bathroom which was the coolest thing ever and since it was set up with kindling stacked just so, I found the matches on the mantel and lit that sucker and then sank into the bath.

For a moment, I wondered if Yuri has a fireplace in his master bathroom, too. The thought was painful. His master suite. Where I was not welcome. He dumped me into - admittedly a palatial - guest room and it looked like it was going to be a permanent stay.

I could see the open closet door from my vantage point in the tub and someone had put away my clothes, just the few things I managed to throw into my suitcase before Patrick picked me up to begin the stupidest, most appallingly idiotic 'rescue mission' ever contemplated. Sliding down in the tub until I was completely immersed, I wished I could go back in time to three days ago and kick my own ass.

***Yuri…***

"Where's your lovely bride?"

"Good morning, Mother. She is no doubt preparing herself to face the inquisition." I seated myself at the table. Because my mother was in residence, even a meal as humble as breakfast had to be served in the formal dining room.

Looking around the table, I smothered my impatience. "It appears everyone is looking forward to live entertainment this morning?"

My sisters were both in attendance, eyes wide and excited to see the upcoming drama. A sleepy Ella was possibly dozing over her blinis and Maksim had a hand on her arm, keeping her from falling face-first into her breakfast.

He looked disappointed in me. "Between the two of us, you are the gentleman in this family and yet even I know that one escorts one's wife to breakfast. Particularly when she doesn't know her way around the house."

"Gentlemen? When, precisely, were we trained to be gentlemen?" I was edging on disrespect, but I was too tired to care.

"I raised you to be gentlemen," Mother interjected.

"You sent us to ballroom dance lessons," I said crisply, "it is not quite the same."

"Uh, good morning?"

While I knew Tania had always battled her own demons of insecurity and self-worth, she didn't give an inch here. She stood in the doorway, dressed in a fire-engine red sweater and black leggings.

"Good morning!" the entire table chorused - aside from Mother, whose lips were pressed tightly together. I pinched the bridge of my nose, trying to stave off another headache.

Rising, I walked over to where she stood, her feet planted like she did not plan on coming any closer. "Will you join us?"

She eyed me cautiously. Unlike yesterday, at least she could look me in the eye this morning. Clearing her throat, she nodded. "Yes, thank you."

There was silence for a moment until Ella pointedly started a conversation about Ekaterina's college exams, giving us a chance to get seated without the entire table staring at Tania.

"Miss Tania, I meant, Mrs. Morozov, would you like some coffee or tea?" Anya was stumbling over exactly what to call her, and given that there were three Mrs. Morozov's at the table, I had sympathy for her.

So did Tania.

"Oh, please call me Tania, all right? There's no need to get fancy.

Coffee would be great, Anya. Thanks."

I silently passed her the bacon which she loved, and then the blinis. I had made her the little pancakes for breakfast one morning in Manhattan and she was instantly enamored. I glance up to see Ella watching with a sly smile.

Mariya and Ekaterina did their best to make Tania feel at ease, talking about St. Petersburg and some of their favorite places.

"There is one spot, it's like the Seahorse Carousel that you and Ella took us to in New York. I think you would love it," Ekaterina said happily. She was always the sweetest and most gentle of us. She's willowy and tall, and while she may have Maksim's coloring, she was the polar opposite in personality.

"I wish we could take her to the cat cafe on Fontanka River Boulevard," Mariya said, munching on the last of her bacon. "I'll bet it's as cute as the one in New York."

I frowned, "But Maksim and Mother are both allergic to cats."

Maksim narrowed his eyes at an innocent-looking Ella. "Did you take the girls to a cat cafe on their last visit?"

"Hey, could I have another blini?" Tania hastily interrupted.

"Definitely!" Ella passed the platter over. "And we should definitely go sailing on Lake Ladoga, and…"

I ran my finger over my lower lip, hiding my smile and watching all four girls dominate the conversation while my brother glowered.

*Tania…*

"We're going into my favorite room in this ridiculously huge mansion," Ella said, linking arms, "the library." She sighed happily.

"This is going to be library porn, isn't it?" I teased her. "I'm surprised you haven't moved your bedroom set down here by now."

The library was a thing of beauty; two stories tall, floor-to-ceiling bookshelves with rolling ladders, another massive fireplace and built-in window seats in front of the lovely, old leaded glass windows meant for curling up with a book in the sun. Ella happily settled on one of the big leather couches and patted the spot next to her.

It was just the four of us, Yuri and Maksim took the armchairs facing the couch. They stared at me sternly and Ella put a protective arm around my shoulders.

"Now that the immediate threat of your death is over, we have to establish what comes next." Maksim went into full *Pakhan* mode, stern expression, tapping the tips of his fingers together.

"What's to stop the bride's family from coming after me, single or married?"

"They do not want the truth about their daughter and their desperate financial situation leaking out. It would destabilize their Bratva's position," Yuri explained. "And they know that anyone suicidal enough to attempt to harm someone from a family as powerful as ours means that we will burn them, their organization, and everyone in it to the ground. The only thing left would be ashes."

"Really? How would they know that?" I asked.

Maksim spoke, and his tone was like a polar chill. "Because we have done it before." He shifted in his chair, rubbing his eyes and for the first time, I noticed how exhausted both brothers looked. Did this mess keep them up all night?

*Great. A little guilt to add to my acceptance that I'm a complete moron, so that's good.*

"What happens now?" Ella asked, squeezing me.

Yuri's flat blue gaze shifted to me. "As my wife, Tania will live here with me in St. Petersburg."

Reminding me that I did not think this through. At all.

"W- what are you talking about?" I wheeze, "My job is in New York. My apartment. My life."

Maksim was looking at me with something close to contempt. "What did you think would happen when you barged into his wedding to someone else?"

"You don't have to be nasty," Ella defended me. "This whole situation is a mess and Yuri kicked it off with his little disappearing act."

I ran a hand through my hair, which was already falling out of its tidy ponytail. "I didn't think. Obviously. I hoped to keep Yuri from making a mistake he would regret for a lifetime. I thought there was something to salvage between us."

Forcing myself to look at him, I saw… nothing. No expression on his beautiful, scarred face. No light in his eyes, none of the tenderness he used to let me see.

Granted, I had only "seen" Yuri the *Sovietnik* a handful of times, his stern expression when taking a business call or when we were out and ran into one of his "work" buddies. They always looked me up and down and then quickly away when he gave them the look. He was always just my Yuri. Funny, charming, kind.

He was none of those things now. He and Maksim were wearing identical expressions during this disastrous talk, cold, focused, set expressions that gave nothing away. No warmth in his eyes. He treated me with the same courteous indifference he would use on unwelcome people trying to get his attention. Women, especially.

I took a deep breath and held it. Suddenly, all I wanted was to be back home. Alone. I've been alone before and I was just fine with it. I will live the rest of my life single if it keeps me from feeling this burning humiliation ever again.

"I was wrong. However, this is an unusual situation and not a real gangster alliance… union… thing. I'm sure you can get this annulled quietly. There must be dozens of pretty Russian princesses waiting for their shot at you."

"My marriage to Ella was not an alliance," Maksim said, "and I assure you, your union is just as permanent as the one Yuri would have made with the Balabanov girl."

"My place is here in St. Petersburg," Yuri added. "I asked for this. I wanted it. *You* may not have wanted this, but it is done and we must be here together."

My skin was burning, and I was so angry and scared that I couldn't even think of anything to say. My mouth opened and closed a few times while they watched impassively.

"Okay, wait," Ella to the rescue. "Why can't we go back to the old system where you both kept your home base in New York and traveled back and forth from here?"

Yuri shook his head. "We are still rebuilding after all the destruction from the Sokolov attacks. And even without the Balabanov alliance, I have made several new agreements with organizations in Moscow designed to strengthen our position here. My focus is here in Russia."

He looked at me. Coldly. The *Sovietnik.* "And this means that your place is here, too."

# CHAPTER FIFTEEN

*In which wedding cake and girl talk keeps Tania from bolting back to Manhattan.*

**Tania...**

No one stopped me when I left the library, barely stopping myself from barreling down the hallway and up the stairs. On the left-hand side up to Yuri's *wing. His own wing. Not our* wing because I was getting out of here and this pathetic period in my life would be gone and I would never think about it again.

Taking the stairs two at a time, I returned to my guest room and shut the door, leaning against it with my palms and forehead pressed against the wood.

*Well, wasn't that a punch to the heart?*

I can't fucking stay here. I just can't.

**Yuri...**

"That could not have gone any worse. Thanks, guys." Ella's acidic comment made me refocus on her instead of the door my new bride had just disappeared through.

"You knew how this conversation was going to go," Maksim said calmly. "Tania can't be that naive to our way of life after all this time."

"It's not about that," she argued, "it's you two sitting in judgment as the Bratva Death Twins. We're all trying to recover from yesterday, you could have been kinder." She pointed at me accusingly. "You didn't really want to marry Ksenia anyway. Admit it."

I shrugged, "I did not intend to spend much time with her, particularly since she stole my watch at our first meeting. I was not sure if it was her family's uncertain financial position or if she was a kleptomaniac."

"Oh my god," Ella groaned as Maksim tried to hide his laughter. She stood up, glaring at both of us. "Yuri, you can't fool us. We know you love her. We know you're struggling with everything that happened to you-"

"Which is why we will not rest until we wipe the entire O'Connell clan off the face of the earth," snarled Maksim.

It showed how much she had grown into her role as the *Pakhan's* wife when Ella didn't even flinch at his statement. "Hopefully, that will give you peace. Please, don't take this out on Tania. She risked her life for you. Give her room to process this. You could use some of that, too. Don't drive her away by being a cold-hearted bastard."

Her eyes darted to Maksim and I could see a sheen of tears she refused to let fall. "There are some things you can't come back from. Think about that."

She marched out the door, leaving us alone in the library.

Maksim gave me a moment to think, and I rubbed my forehead.

"Are you still getting the migraines?" he asked.

"Not so much," I lied. "I am glad Mariya and Ekaterina are here, they will keep Tania busy and out of trouble. This weapons deal in Moscow is right on the edge of an agreement that will bring in another $85 million a year. I would like to ask you to fly out with me and sign the deal. The Fedorov's will be happy to see the powerful Morozov *Pakhan* come in person to meet with them."

"Of course," he nodded. "I have five days before I need to be back home, just schedule it when you can."

"You called New York home," I observed. "When did that change? You have always insisted that St. Petersburg will always be your true home."

Maksim smiled, an oddly gentle expression I rarely saw. "I believe it's home because Ella is there. She is my home."

*"Let's take off his arm…"*

I rubbed my scar, which felt like a burning brand on my face.

*I am not a captive. I am alive, and I am strong. They have no power over me.*

"Brother?" Maksim looked at me, concerned. "Should I call Ella?"

Forcing a smile, I shook my head, casting about for something else to talk about. Something to distract him from staring at me so closely. "There is one thing about yesterday that still bothers me."

"What's that?"

"Nolan O'Rourke. He is a bastard," I said. "He seems to enjoy watching people suffer. Do you remember when he bought out the land under the youth home in Italy and evicted them because he wanted more parking space for his soccer arena? Why would he step forward to save the day?"

"He demanded we grant a favor whenever he decides to request it," Maksim mused, frowning. "But it was only after he discredited the girl."

"The man is known for playing games," I said, "but he also told Tania specifically that *she* will owe him a favor. Why her?"

He sighs, stretching his legs toward the fire. "I don't know. However, we have enough to deal with right now without worrying about the future. It - and all its accompanying problems - will be here soon enough."

"Why brother," I said in the tone I knew drove him mad, "I had no idea you were a master philosopher."

"You are healed enough that I could break your nose and not feel bad about it," he said casually, "do keep that in mind, *brother*."

An unfamiliar warmth spread through my chest. I never would have imagined that Maksim threatening to beat the hell out of me would be a good thing. It meant he did not see me as fragile. He did not see me as a victim.

*Tania…*

Ella showed up halfway through my efforts to find my suitcase. Everything from it was neatly hung in the closet or folded into drawers, but the actual item to carry my stuff the hell back out of here was gone.

She held up a covered plate. "I brought some of the wedding cake because this is amazing. Marzipan and chocolate ganache and a cream cake studded with golden raspberries that is so good you'll never eat cake again without a deep sense of disappointment." She settled happily on the bed, peeling the cover off.

"You and your filthy love of cake," I shook my head and tried to smile.

"Hey, I'm just making up for the fact that I was too upset to eat any of mine, remember?" She offered me a fork.

Taking it, I joined her on the bed. "I did tell you to take a huge chunk with you on your honeymoon, remember?" I swallowed the first bite. "Oh, damn that's good."

"Their choice for a baker fell through, so the Balabanovs wanted me to select a wedding cake," she said, taking another bite, "so technically, this is more my cake than theirs and I am happy to share it with you."

"I appreciate that because I know you would snatch it off my fork with the speed of a striking cobra if I tried to steal it from you." I took another bite and sighed deeply. This cake was made of chocolate clouds and angel wings or something.

"That would be after I pinned your hand to the table with my fork for having the audacity to come between me and my cake," she said primly, stuffing her mouth with a huge bite.

Laughing, I said, "That reminds me, we took one of the layers of your wedding cake up to the honeymoon suite and Yuri spent half the night licking it off my…" My smile died and I scraped the fork along the plate.

"I can't stay here, I just can't." I shoved another piece of cake in my mouth so she wouldn't hear my voice quiver. "I have to leave," I said through a mouthful of chocolate ganache. "I don't know this Yuri, but he wants nothing to do with me. This is nuts-"

"Okay, hold up!" Ella pointed her fork at me accusingly. "You know who I don't recognize? You! Who is this fragile flower? What happened to my Tania, who beat the shit out of that mugger who tried to rob us outside of the Callin Bodega? Or the girl who threw that sixth grader into the dumpster because he was making fun of me?"

"Or…" her voice softened, "the woman who graduated with honors from NYU on a full scholarship because she's brilliant? The Tania who stapled her resignation letter to her sleazebag boss's chest when he tried to grope her? I know Yuri's a closed-in mess right now. I think he's barely holding himself together and he's terrified that the slightest hint of softness could unravel him. If there's anyone who can get this man to heal and become Yuri again, it's you, Tan."

"I don't think I can do this." Damnit, my voice was wobbling pathetically.

Ella took my hands, "You have never given up on what you wanted. And you *want* this future with Yuri."

We hugged tightly, and went back to eating the cake. "You know the worst part about this?" I said.

"Hmm?" Her mouth was full of frosting.

I put down my fork, appetite gone. "I have to call my mother and tell her that not only did I get married, it was without her, it was in Russia and I'm staying here."

She swallowed the cake with a gulp. "She is going to freak. Be grateful that you're a full continent away from her."

The next five days were wonderful, mainly because the men were gone for three of them. I don't have to look at Yuri and have the galactic stupidity of what I've done smack me in the back of the head again and again.

We spent two days from opening to closing at the glorious Hermitage Museum. The girls dragged me through John Lennon Street, which was a tiny passageway that opened up into a courtyard filled with tokens, art, and sculpture dedicated to the Beatles. Mariya was a huge fan of the Beatles and refused to leave until she read every terrible bit of poetry that people had scribbled on the walls.

Ella insisted on a trip to the Literary Cafe, where writers like Fyodor Dostoyevsky wrote brilliant stories and dined on baked apples in puff pastry. We browsed the shelves filled with battered books from legendary writers who'd sat in these chairs, drank vodka and pondered their next masterpiece until Ekaterina begged to be fed. We sat at a table under the unnerving stare of the Cafe's seven-foot stuffed bear which made finishing my lunch impossible, that was a shame because the dried tomato carpaccio was freaking delicious.

On the last day, we joined Lucya and Alexi Turgenev and their family to go sailing on Lake Ladoga. I liked Lucya, we'd hung out together after she took Ella under her wing to help her navigate the weirdness of being a Bratva bride. It hit me as we were saying hello that I was one now, too.

"Tania!" she beamed, kissing me three times, left cheek, right cheek, left cheek. I was never a big social kisser, but I clumsily returned her greeting and smiled uneasily at her scary as fuck husband Alexi, who was staring at me intently.

"It's so cool you're here in St. Petersburg, too!" I said happily, "I didn't know I'd get a chance to see you."

"Oh," she exchanged glances with Alexi, "we were here for the… ah… the wedding, you see."

"Oh, yeah, of course." I nodded a little too fast.

*So, this is mortifying.*

I was saved from severe social awkwardness when Mariya and their son Konstantin started bickering over the rigging on the sailboat.

"Have you ever sailed before?" she snarked, "This mess won't even get us out of the harbor."

"No, it won't, the motor will," he sneered, "do you even understand how this works?"

"Yeah, that's young love right there," I murmured to Lucya.

"Oh, quite," she sighed, "it is customary to arrange marriages at a young age, but betrothing my son to your little sister-in-law still infuriates me."

"Ella told me Mariya was cool with it?"

"They were both raised in the Bratva, they understand their roles," she said. "As did I. It doesn't make it easier to watch. With this, at least, I am very happy that our two families will be connected. The Morozov family have always been our friends, they're loyal and honorable."

Lucya was beautiful, blonde and she had a perfect figure that would make me hate her, but the fact that she was extremely kind and had a wicked sense of humor made it impossible. Her warm brown eyes were so sad. "It doesn't always turn out that way," she murmured.

She sucked in a deep breath and smiled at me. "While yours may not be an arranged marriage, I cannot tell you how happy we are that you are married to Yuri and not Ksenia Balabanov."

"Thanks for the vote of confidence," I sighed, "all the Morozov women are okay with it, aside from Yuri's mom. She hates everyone so I don't take it personally."

Laughing, she gave me a side hug. "You are completely correct."

The day on Lake Ladoga was perfect. It was unseasonably warm and the sun made the wind feel welcome on my sweaty skin. Maryia's snarky comments aside, Konstantin was an excellent sailor and his father watched him proudly. Turning my head to look behind us, I grinned, seeing two boats following at a polite distance.

No body of water was safe as far as this group was concerned since a sniper tried to kill Ella by sending her under the ice of the Neva River.

Unfortunately, Lucya and Alexi's youngest daughter Yana was the one who was hit and fell through the ice until Ella nearly gave up her own life to save her. Watching the two of them whisper and giggle about Konstantin made me so happy. Ella was going to be an amazing mother.

"You needn't be concerned; they are well-protected."

*This time,* I thought.

Oh, *shit* Alexi Turgenev was *talking to me*. I had a mild freakout. The man was known as The Angel of Death, for fuck's sake. He was the guy that would make you go all Old Testament and paint your front door with lamb's blood to have him pass over your house.

"After what happened last winter? I'm surprised they're not in full scuba suits or like one of those inflatable hamster balls, or-"

I was babbling. And he was staring at me, one brow raised.

"One of those boats is Morozov security," he said. He had a scary deep voice and a very precise way of speaking that was unnerving.

"Oh, that makes sense," I smiled awkwardly.

"And the drone above us…" he pointed upwards and my jaw dropped, there was a huge, military-looking drone hovering over the boat, "transmits data to the security team back at the marina."

"I was about to call this overkill until I realized that was the wrong choice of words," I tried to make a little joke. Alexi was not amused. So naturally, I had to make it worse. "So, um, is the lake a big dumping ground for people the Bratva wants to disappear?"

He actually seemed to consider my idiotic question. "It is possible, though I, of course, wouldn't know for certain."

"Of course…" I echo nervously.

"But Lake Baikal in Siberia…" Alexi, who looked like the offspring of a supermodel and a serial killer, was warming up. "That's the deepest one in the world. It's an ancient lake with massive underwater caverns and fissures in the bedrock that are impossible to map. Bodies thrown into Lake Baikal will never surface again."

He paused, apparently enjoying my bulging eyes and terrified expression. If he'd said "boo!" at that moment I would have jumped, screaming, the hell out of the sailboat. I would have taken my chances swimming back to shore.

I was deeply relieved when he moved up to speak to his son.

Then Yuri and Maksim returned from Moscow. Ella and Maksim had to head back to New York. Ekaterina went back to college, and Mariya back to the family estate with her mother.

"I'm sorry, I wish we could stay longer," Ella whispered, hugging me tight enough to cut off the circulation in my arms.

"Hey, you've got important medical stuff to do. Aren't you assisting on surgery rotations with Dr. Gulianos next week?" I forced a smile; it wasn't fair to expect her to stay just to be here for me. And if I'm honest, clinging to Ella is also a convenient excuse to keep me from having to interact with the man I married.

Yuri and I stood on the enormous front steps of the Morozov mansion, waving goodbye to everyone. When the cars pulled away from the curb and everything was quiet, he looked down at me.

"I have some work to attend to. I will see you at dinner." He waited, I guess to see if I was going to answer.

So, I forced another smile, I was getting good at those. "Sure. See you then." I headed back down the hall, refusing to look back.

# CHAPTER SIXTEEN

*In which Tania and Yuri try to navigate their painful inability to connect.*

***Tania...***

***One week later...***

The only time I saw Yuri is at dinner, which we have in the obnoxiously huge dining room with the ten-foot table. He sat at one end. I sat at the other. He asked me some polite questions about my day, I asked him some. I ate the unfamiliar food that was magnificently prepared but I always wished there was just one meal where I recognized everything on my plate. The day I stopped putting off the inevitable and sent in my resignation - effective immediately - to Papachristodoulopoulos Equities, I didn't come down to eat at all.

After an hour or so, I heard Yuri's voice. "May I come in?"

I was lying in bed, staring out the window with my lovely, heavy quilt pulled up to my nose. "Sure," I croaked.

"Are you ill?" He came closer. "Do you need anything?"

"Yeah," I chuckled bitterly, "my life back." He sighed, and I sat up, angry. "Oh, I know this is my fault. I know this is the consequence of my rash behavior. My responsibility for charging in and trying to save the day like a complete and utter asshole."

He stood next to the bed, legs spread and hands in his pockets, wearing the custom-tailored suit that matched his eyes perfectly. He had a bland, careful expression, with a little furrow between his brows.

"I do not think that about you," he said. "I know this is a difficult thing to handle, changing everything in your life to be here."

I ran my hands through my hair, wincing at how tangled it was. "What I am supposed to do here? Wander around your ridiculously huge mansion all day?" A mean little laugh escapes me, "Start screwing some hot guy on the side? What do the other Bratva wives-"

"Stop!" Yuri's hands were like manacles, gripping my upper arms and pulling me off the bed. "You will *not* speak to me like that."

"I don't even know who you are!" I shouted, yanking my arms away. "I see your disappointment every time you look at me. I screwed up your master plan for Bratva domination. Sorry about that. Believe me," I hissed, "I'm disappointed every time I look at you, too. Disappointed that I gave up my life for the alien currently inhabiting Yuri's body. So we're even. I suppose I can't tell you to get out because this is your *wing*. I'm going into the bathroom until you feel like leaving."

Locking myself in the bathroom, I sat in the tub, freezing my ass off and staring up at the shadows on the ceiling. I pulled one of the towels down from the rack and covered myself up, shivering, and huddled in the grandeur of my bathroom in a house where I was not welcome and where I did not want to be until I heard the door to my room close.

*Yuri...*

"We will not be requiring dinner tonight, Anya. That will be all, thank you." I passed by our housekeeper, who was holding a large platter of prime rib roast, fingerling potatoes, and asparagus.

"Mr. Morozov, would you like me to keep the food warm for later?" Anya called after me.

I wanted a glass of very cold vodka that I could press against the scar throbbing on my forehead. "Not necessary," I said, still heading toward the library.

"Should- should I bring a plate up to Tan- to Mrs. Morozov?"

Pausing for a moment, I rubbed the back of my neck. Anya had made an American-style meal and I knew it was meant to make Tania happy. "That would be fine, thank you."

"Thank you, sir, I'll do it immediately."

Ignoring her relieved voice, I headed into the library and shut the door.

"Any updates on the O'Connell's, *Obshchak?*" I was on my daily call with Patrick and my voice sounded as cold as I felt toward him for his part in the wedding fiasco and he replied formally.

"There's a cluster of activity in Dublin at the high-end whiskey distillery they're upgrading. The O'Connell brand is rolling out next month, and by all accounts, it's meant to look like the family's going legit when the real plan is to use the distillery for laundering money. The distribution plan is worldwide, so they're already sending out discreet offers of their services to other organizations."

"What about in New York?" I asked.

"They've been lying low since we raided their warehouse near Elizabethport," he said with satisfaction. "We killed at least three of their lieutenants there, along with the four you hunted down, that took out most of their power structure, stateside at least."

I forced my clenched fist to loosen up. "The next step is targeting the distillery, come up with a couple of plans before you and Maksim arrive next week." My frustration about the distance between Tania and me morphed into spite. "After all, you're a genius with daring plans, *Obshchak.*"

The sound of Patrick's grinding teeth was audible. "Very well, *Sovietnik*."

*Tania...*

*Two weeks later...*

I was ready to see fire to this mausoleum and run screaming through the streets when Lucya came for a visit, bringing her two girls.

"You have no idea how happy I am to see you," I said, gratefully accepting her hug.

"Oh, I had a feeling," she said.

"You've been talking to Ella, haven't you?" I accused.

"Yes, and the fact that you haven't been showing up for yoga classes."

When I first became the extremely unwelcome Mrs. Yuri Morozov, Lucya, bless her, immediately invited me to go to yoga with her at a super bougie spa. I was grateful to get out of the mansion and see other human beings. But when she returned to the states, I realized no one else in the class had any interest in speaking to me, much less going out for coffee.

Shrugging, I admitted, "It wasn't the same without you."

She linked arms with me, directing the girls out into the really spectacular garden at the back of the house. It was one of my favorite places, with curved iron arbors and a pond, with lush lily pads. The girls ran through the sprawling storksbill geraniums, and I brushed my hand over the wall of Virginia creeper already turning a vivid red. It was only the end of August, but apparently, autumn came early in St. Petersburg.

We moved to the beautifully carved wooden pergola, Lucya kicked off her heels and relaxed into one of the squishy cushioned wicker chairs. "This is heaven," she sighed happily.

"It will be even more heavenly now that Anya is bringing out the little frosted cakes for the girls and cocktails for us," I promised. The housekeeper gave me a wink as she put the big tray down.

We toasted each other with our mimosas. "Do you spend a lot of time out here?" Lucya asked, happily taking another sip.

"Even when it rains," I said, trying not to sound pathetic. "The mansion is really beautiful, but it's so…"

"Dark? Grim?" she teased, "In desperate need of more modernization?"

"It's too easy to get lost in my thoughts and it gets harder and harder to pull back out," I said. "I feel as useless here as tits on a bull."

Lucya almost spat out her drink.

"I haven't heard that one before anywhere outside of Texas," she wheezed.

"One of my stepmothers was Texan," I admitted. "I learned all the really good Texanism's from her."

"One of them?" Lucya probed.

"Eh," I shrugged, "Dad got married more as… a hobby, I guess? He's on wife number six. After wife number five left him, he turned to me in all seriousness and said, 'Tania, I'm beginning to think it's me'."

She looked at me nervously, wondering if it was okay to laugh, so I did first, the awful half-snorting chortle I get when something is really funny and she joined in.

We calmed down after a couple of minutes, and she asked, "So that probably impacted your ideas about marriage."

"Yeah," I shrugged, "it means that most people think it's a disposable feature in life. I never planned on getting married until Yuri…"

*Until he was forced to marry me to save my life?*

I flinched, "Well, until Yuri anyway."

"I don't know you as well as I do Ella, but I'm certain you're not the kind to give up. And honestly, drifting around that - admittedly magnificent - mansion like an extremely sad little ghost doesn't seem like your thing."

She smiled a bit to take away the sting, but it was true, and it made me feel even more pathetic. I've never been a sit around the house person who waited for someone else to make my life interesting. What was happening to me?

"Let's start small," she continued. "You have some time right now, what's something you've been wanting to do but haven't had the time before?"

I remembered the evening I had waited for Yuri to come over, to dance with me, to have the most intimate sex of my life, and then throw me out like leftovers from the fridge. As I'd listened to "Satin Birds," I had missed playing the violin, and my fingers had unconsciously moved along with the melody. So much went wrong that night, but I wanted to salvage one or two good memories from it.

"I used to play the violin as a teenager," I admitted, "I've been missing it."

"There you go!" Lucya said approvingly, "Take up the violin again. While I'm in town, we'll go visit a couple of other yoga studios and find one that isn't so… snobbish?"

Squeezing her hand, I felt a rush of gratitude so strong that it was almost embarrassing.

Yuri walked through the huge double doors from the house to the garden and my smile died. My small steps toward having a friend here, reclaiming bits and pieces of myself seemed insignificant now, watching the man who apparently despised me approach us.

"Lucya Turgenev? How nice to see you."

He leaned over to kiss my cheek and then hers. I appreciated that he had the courtesy to kiss me so it wouldn't be pathetically obvious that he hadn't touched me since saying "I do."

He smelled so good; like pine trees, salt air, and warm cotton. I missed burying my face into the little hollow between his neck and shoulder. He used to pull me on top of him after sex and I'd breathe in the wonderful scent of him and we'd fall asleep together.

Looking up, I caught Lucya's concerned expression and pushed away the memories.

"...Will you and Alexi be attending?" Yuri asked.

"I hope we can. This year, we could take Yana as her debut of sorts into Russian society now that she is fifteen. It depends on Alexi's business in Moscow."

Smiling to myself, I heard her slight lilt that put quotation marks around the word 'business.'

Lucya turned to me, "We'll have our stylist come over and she can dress both of us for the ball."

Shrugging awkwardly, I looked between her and Yuri. "A ball?"

"*The* ball," she corrected, "the biggest social event of the year here in St. Petersburg."

"And you will need a gown," Yuri said, "something magnificent, a…" he smiled, "what you call a fairy princess dress."

Yuri hitched up his impeccably pressed trousers and sat with us. I guess the buffer of Lucya made it easier for us to circle around each other. Feeling his kiss on my cheek made my ovaries wake up and start shrieking like circus monkeys. I hadn't been with anyone since Yuri left me and… well, shit. How pathetic was it that all it took to turn me into a needy mess was a kiss on the cheek?

Yana trotted over when she heard her mother talking about her.

"This is the year, Mama?" she asked eagerly, "I finally get to come?"

"Yes, *sladkaya kartoshka*, it is," Lucya said fondly.

*She calls her sweet potato?* I thought, *that's freaking adorable.*

"But," she continued, "you'll need dance lessons first, you'll have to learn to dance the waltz. It's much more formal." She looked slyly between Yuri and me. "You know, Ella tells me that these two are amazing dancers. They always stand out because they move so well together."

"Oh, that was just Yuri," I said hastily, "he had all those lessons as a kid."

"No, you both dance so beautifully," Lucya persisted, "Would you show her how a waltz is done?"

"Yes!" Yana said, pulling me up from my seat, "Show me!"

He rose, looking for a moment like my Yuri, with a wicked little smile, and stepped closer. I almost took a step back, then planted my feet.

*Hold your ground, you're not afraid of him.*

"You hold your arms like so," he instructed Yana while he lifted my hand with his, sliding his other arm around my waist. "See the position? Tania has her head raised high, elegantly…"

From the corner of my eye, I could see Lucya lean forward, seeing Yuri's sudden warmth the way I did. His hand flattened against my back and the warmth of it seared through my dress. I have missed how warm he always was, how he could burn off the chill from the coldest day.

"Once you have your position, move your right foot as your partner moves their left, and…" His conversational tone faded away along with the little lesson as he gazed down at me. I could see conflict in his eyes - so close to Caribbean blue - then regret, and... fear? It couldn't be fear. That was ridiculous.

Smoothly pulling away from me, Yuri glanced down at his phone. "Ladies, please excuse me, I'm running late for a meeting." He slipped away before I could ask him if he would be home for dinner.

**Yuri...**

*Pitiful. You are pathetic, you cannot dance with your wife, you cannot touch her without cracking wide open? Is this all the self-control you can manage?*

My father's voice mocked me, but the fear was all mine.

Heading swiftly through the hall toward the front door, I cursed myself. I could not touch Tania; I couldn't dance with her and hold back the avalanche of emotion I felt. Feeling her silky skin again, her rosemary and jasmine scent made my bones ache with the need to hold her. But the need made me weak. I could not risk being soft. Missing what we had together was tied up somehow with my memories of the kidnapping. I could not feel one without feeling both.

I couldn't feel much of anything without crumbling, I needed to stay away from my wife as much as possible until I was stronger. I walked out the front door and away from the garden, where every part of me wanted to be, with Tania on my lap, holding her head with my fingers buried in her hair, kissing her until she was breathless.

Still, after overhearing her talking about music, I made a phone call to the best musical instrument store in St. Petersburg and took their suggestion for a 1923 John Juzek Master Art violin and bow. It was sitting on her chair in the dining room so she would find it when she came down for breakfast. Tania could continue to make music, even if it was no longer with me.

During the week leading up to the Imperial Ball, I found Tania was researching Russian history and the background behind the event. At dinner one night, she asked, "Why is this particular ball such a big deal?"

"The First Imperial Ball was a concoction by the nobles from Russia and Austria in the 1800s," I said, "the Austeris Group reintroduced the Ball for the first time since 1903. This is an important night for introducing you to St. Petersburg society."

"Okay, so I've been researching Catherine Palace since I found out that's where the ball's being held." Tania's beautiful face was alight with excitement. "Do we get to see the Amber Room? The Eighth freaking Wonder of the World?"

"I believe you are more excited about the Amber Room than the most prestigious event in St. Petersburg," I said, enjoying her smile.

"Balls, schmalls," she waved her hand impatiently. "That's rich people dressing up and getting drunk. The Amber Room, though…" she sighed reverently. "Even though the Nazis stole the original room, I know the recreation will be magical."

"I never fail to be impressed by the depth and breadth of your knowledge," I mused.

She settles herself, facing me with folded arms. "So, here's the important question."

"I am bracing myself," I said wryly.

"Do you think that the dismantled original was destroyed when the Royal Air Force shelled the shit out of Königsberg Castle, or do you think it was on board the *Wilhelm Gustloff* when it was torpedoed by the Soviet submarine?"

This was the Tania I adored, who could become utterly enraptured by both the mysterious and the mundane, and her enthusiasm would bring everyone in her orbit along for the ride. Her beautiful eyes glowed and she waved her hands wildly as she delved into her theory. How could this woman be so full of life?

"I mean, if the Nazis had the specialized team all ready to go to dismantle an entire room filled with ancient amber within thirty-six hours," she argued, "they had to have a bulletproof plan for it, right?"

It took me a moment to realize she was expecting an answer, this felt so good, the memory of all the animated conversations we had warming the cold, broken places in me.

"I must admit," I said, "that I am surprised that you are focusing on the Amber Room and not on what I thought you would target first."

"Which is?" she prompted.

"That Catherine Palace was the summer home of Catherine the Great."

"Oh, you thought I would go for the easy joke, right? Maybe wondering if it's possible to sneak off and take a roll in the hay in her bedroom? Get it?" Tania giggled helplessly, "Roll in the hay? Catherine the Great? Horses?"

"Now *there* is the Tania I know," I chuckled. "You will have Gavrill as your personal bodyguard. This is our first public outing and I am taking no chances with your security."

"The poor man definitely drew the short straw with having to shadow me," she cackled heartlessly.

"Tania." I pointed my fork at her, "You will not torture him and try to sneak away. He has pledged his life to keep you safe. Do you understand?"

"Well, when you say it like that…" She narrowed her eyes at me. "*Fine.*"

# CHAPTER SEVENTEEN

*In which there is a magnificent ball, sinister machinations, and Catherine the Great's horse.*

**Yuri...**

On the night of the ball, I knocked on my wife's door.

"Come in!" Tania sang out.

"Hey Anya, thanks for bringing up the-" I smothered a chuckle. She was lifting and settling "the girls," as she called then, into the highly structured cups of her strapless gown.

"Oh!" She fussed with the neckline of the dress for a moment before facing me. "Just um... just getting everything squeezed into where they're supposed to go in this dress."

She was exquisite.

I have seen Tania dressed up, naked, and everything in between, but with her hair pinned up in glossy curls and this gown... no one could be more lovely.

"You are beautiful," I blurted.

She flushed, smoothing the skirt. "Yeah? Well, thanks."

The dress was the darkest shade of green with black and gold beadwork on the hem and the corset top. The beading lit her eyes to a brilliant shade of golden yellow. Her breasts- *bozhe moy,* my god, her satiny skin glowed and they swelled against the tight fit of the dress. My hands twitched, wanting to pull them back out of the cups and suck and bite on them until she begged me to fuck her.

Clearing my throat, I held out a slim velvet box to her. "I thought these would go well with your dress."

Tania opened the box and blurted, "Oh, fuck are you kidding?" I smothered my chuckle. She lifted the necklace reverently, watching it sparkle in the light.

Stepping behind her, I took the necklace, fastening it around her neck. "This is Baltic Amber, forty million years old."

She touched the pendant gently. "What's this in the stone?"

"It is a flower," I explained, "almost perfectly preserved. To find one in this condition is unheard of. I thought you might like something you could wear every day, but it is certainly elegant enough for the Imperial Ball."

"I'll never take it off," she said, "thank you. It's… wow. It's gorgeous."

My fingertips slid down her back after fastening the necklace. Tania gave a little shudder and sighed, and I barely swallowed down a groan in time. I used to spend hours running my hands over every inch of her skin, loving the silky texture.

"Allow me," I said, taking the bracelet and fastening it around her wrist. "Perfect," I praised her, lifting her hand to kiss her knuckles, noticing that my plain signet ring clashed with her extravagant new jewelry. She swayed slightly toward me, and I turned her hand, kissing the thin skin on the inside of her wrist, feeling her speedy pulse against my lips. "You are so very beautiful, darling."

It was the closest I had been to her since our last night together, her lips were pink and slightly parted. I remembered how she tasted, how she would slide her tongue along my lower lip…

"Miss Tania, here's your-" Anya bustled in with a shoe box. "Oh, excuse me, Master Yuri, I didn't mean to interrupt."

"Not at all," I said, "Tania, I will see you downstairs in ten minutes?"

"Uh, yeah," she mumbled, sounding as disappointed as I felt.

I could tell that my beautiful wife was trying very hard not to bounce in her seat as the limo passed through the colossal gold and blue gates of Catherine Palace. Spotlights flashed in a dizzying array, and as the car stopped at the row of uniformed guards at the entrance, I took her hand.

"There is a line of paparazzi to pass on your way up the stairs," I murmured in her ear, enjoying the little shiver she could not control. "Keep your eyes lowered so they do not disorient you and give a small smile. Your Mona Lisa smile would be excellent here."

She eyed me curiously, "You have names for my smiles?"

"Well, of course," I said slowly. "There is the 'this is too ridiculous smile' you wear when you are dealing with fools, the huge 'here comes Ella and we are going to tear it up' smile, the…"

My door opened, the driver looking uncertain. "Did you wish for me to circle the drive again, sir?"

"This is fine," I answered, still staring into Tania's wide golden eyes. Getting out and moving around the limo, I brushed away Gavrill, her bodyguard, and opened her door myself. Holding out my hand to her, I nodded reassuringly, and she smiled back.

*How long has it been since she smiled at me?*

After kissing her hand slowly for the photographer's benefit, I guided my wife up the red-carpeted stairs to greet our first host, the Governor of St. Petersburg. Looking over his shoulder, I see a group of Bratva princesses clustered like a school of piranha, staring avidly at us.

A smile curved the corner of my mouth. I was going to enjoy watching Tania win them over - or terrorize them - no matter how jealous or catty they might be.

*Tania...*

Oh, sweet baby Jesus and all the Saints never in my life did I think I would be standing at the massive golden entrance to Catherine the Great's Palace, my hand on Yuri's arm. We were announced by a man who looks like he should be doing this 300 years ago, because he has the uniform for it and a voice like a bullhorn.

"Presenting Mr. and Mrs. Yuri Morozov of St. Petersburg," he intoned, and it took everything in me not to giggle like a schoolgirl.

"Keep up that smile, darling," Yuri murmured out of the corner of his mouth, "you're doing beautifully."

With that praise, I felt like I could float down the stairs.

I was trying so hard to look regal, like the wife of the Morozov *Sovietnik* should but oh, *my god* I wanted to run around like an over-caffeinated tourist, trying to see everything about this palace! The exquisite blue exterior with all the embellishments slathered in gold leaf, the magnificent golden chandeliers, and mirrors in the Grand Hall... I leaned a bit closer to look at a throne-like chair and slapped a hand over my mouth. Giving my full-out witch cackle would not help my image.

Naturally, Yuri caught the movement. "What is so humorous?"

"Um..." I stifled another cackle, "the chair inlay- it's covered in pearls. You were right about Russian royalty."

He gave me a slow, dangerous smile that was doing very bad things to my body. "I must show you her bedroom before we leave tonight."

"Does the horse cost extra?" I whispered.

As we entered the Grand Ballroom, we passed by one of the huge, ornate mirrors and I caught our reflection. We looked… amazing. Yuri was ridiculously hot in his perfectly-fitted tuxedo. His obsessive workouts to recover from his injuries had turned him into a mountain of a man.

In my dress… I felt like Catherine the Great. My posture was spectacular. Shoulders thrown back; head held high. Primarily because this dress was not only heavy, it was also strapless and my boobs were the only thing holding it up.

I could hear half a dozen languages spoken around me, Russian, obviously, and English. But there was also French, and German. Norwegian, I think, Ukrainian and some others I couldn't pick out yet. I was good with languages; I already spoke Spanish, French and Japanese before I met Yuri, so picking up Russian was going faster than I'd expected.

This massive ballroom with every available surface slathered in gold leaf and crystal vases exploding with exotic flowers was something out of a movie. An insanely huge, big-budget movie filled with beautiful, obscenely wealthy people. The gowns the women were wearing made anything on the runway during New York Fashion Week look like dishrags.

*"Privet, Yuriy, eto bylo slishkom dolgo."*

We turned and he nodded politely to the spectacular-looking princess who was eyeing him like he was carrying her future children's chromosomes. I was pretty sure she actually was a princess because the woman had an honest to god tiara perching in her blonde hair. The tiara was slightly bigger than my first car and I couldn't take my eyes off it, so it took me a minute to recognize her. Yuri's date. At Marcel's, back in Manhattan. After he broke my fucking heart.

"Mila Lenkov, it has indeed been too long," Yuri said. "Allow me to introduce my lovely bride, Tania Morozov. Tania, Mila's father and mine were close friends."

Knowing what I did about what a sick fuck Yuri and Maksim's father had been, I was already questioning what kind of man wanted to be friends with him, but… "It's nice to meet you, Mila."

She nodded slightly, not taking her eyes off Yuri. I was used to this. It happened constantly when we were out together. He was always very good about peeling them off him in the shortest amount of time and re-devoting himself to me. But she was as persistent as a remora attaching to a shark.

"Now that I am back in town, we must have lunch and catch up," Mila purred.

"I'm sure Tania and I can find some time to meet for lunch next month or so," Yuri said in his most bland and pleasant tone.

That ironed a patch over a corner of my broken heart.

We made a quick escape, and he drew my hand through the crook of his arm. "You need to know that the night- that night-" he paused and took a breath, "it was not a date. I was meant to meet her father for a business dinner, and he had her show up instead. I sent her home in one car and left in another."

"Thank you for telling me. It… helps to know that."

"Thank you for being willing to let me explain," he said, kissing my hand again with just the slightest bit of tongue touching my skin.

Smooth bastard.

I was flying high when I excused myself to go to the ladies' room and a tuxedoed Gavrill followed silently behind me. He was one of my favorites from Yuri's sinister legion of security guards, so I gave him a thumbs-up as I headed into the bathroom.

"Be right out."

"Of course, Mrs. Morozov," he nodded respectfully.

"Hey, just call me Tania, Mrs. Morozov is Yuri and Maksim's mom. Let's not piss her off by stealing the title, okay?"

He looked pained. "I do not think the *Sovietnik* would like that."

I sighed. "How about 'Miss Tania'?"

Gavrill looks like the very thought of using my first name guarantees him a spot in Hell's waiting room, just waiting for his ticket to get punched.

"We'll work on it," I promised, shutting the door.

After spending a good ten minutes trying to hitch up the huge skirt of my ball gown, I managed to hover over the toilet without peeing on my shoes. "So much easier to be a guy," I muttered, readjusting my dress and opening the door to the main area, "one zipper and they're just fine."

"Excuse me?" A cultured, courteous voice speaks up from behind me.

I closed my eyes, groaning silently. *Smooth. Very Catherine the Great-like.*

Attempting my best regal expression, I sailed over and washed my hands, smiling pleasantly at the woman standing there. She was drying her hands with a fancy pink towel. The attendant was hovering at my elbow, waiting to give me one as I finished.

"Hello, I'm Oksana Kuznetsov. And you are Yuri's new bride Tania," she said, offering her hand to shake.

I hated shaking with a wet hand but it's not like I could wipe it on my zillion-dollar dress so we shared a damp handshake and her smile never wavered.

"Nice to meet you, Oksana. I'm guessing you know Yuri?"

She nodded, "We attended the Ares Academy together, he was my brother's best friend there."

My brow furrowed, "Is that a boarding school?"

"You could call it that," she shrugs.

Giving her my best suspicious stare, I asked, "Are you getting all mysterious on me?"

"Yes, I am," she smiled impishly, "It will likely not surprise you that Yuri was always the life of the party. He ran a very successful side business, smuggling alcohol and other forbidden items to sell to the underclassmen. But as to what the Academy is, that is a long explanation and better suited to a conversation over lunch sometime."

My heart warmed a bit, a possible friend? "I'd love to."

We were swapping contact info when the door opened and Mila swept by majestically, refusing to look at either of us.

"I take it you've already met her?" Oksana said. "She chased Yuri relentlessly for five years or so. She must be furious that he slipped through her fingers."

"Yeah, I did meet her," I said. "She looks incredible. Satan did a good job when he created her."

Oksana opened the door for me, her face was almost purple from holding in her laughter. "He also did a fine job with her personality."

"The people who have to tolerate that woman on a daily basis are the real heroes," I said. "Shall we sail gracefully back into the ballroom?"

"We shall," she agreed.

Yuri caught sight of us and he had a genuine grin for Oksana. *"Pchelka,"* he said, kissing her cheeks, "how good to see you! Is Ruslan with you?"

"*Nyet,* he's designing a new cyber security system for the Lloyd's banking group right now," she squeezed his hands. "I don't seem to recall an invitation to your wedding for my brother and me in my mailbox?"

Yuri's jaw tightened, just slightly but I caught it. "As you see, that wedding invitation was for the wrong woman. Now I have the pleasure of introducing you to Tania, my bride." He smiled down at me and I was mildly disgusted at myself for how grateful I felt for his words and for slipping his arm around my waist.

"So Oksana, why does Yuri call you *Pchelka,* that means little bee, right?"

She looked mildly mortified. "When I was sent to the Academy, I brought a very sharp switchblade with me. Whenever a boy would hit on me or act like a creep in some way, I'd just give him a little poke in the butt to teach him some manners."

Yuri was laughing. "Osip Agapov needed sixty-three stitches!"

She shrugged, "He *really* needed some help with his behavior."

It was quite possible that she was going to be my favorite new person here in St. Petersburg.

Oksana eventually excused herself and went back to her date, and Yuri held out his hand.

"Shall we dance?"

*Yuri...*

What was I doing? Did I not walk away from her in the garden that day because I was not strong enough? Now, in a crowd where any weakness could prove fatal?

For one moment, I did not want to have to calculate the risk/benefit ratio of every action. I just wanted to dance with my wife.

Tania's eyes were wide, "Um... Sure, I guess." It wasn't the delighted "yes!" she'd always given me before, but I would take it. A clear lack of enthusiasm was what I deserved.

The crowd parted for us like the Red Sea, with all the little fish - and the occasional shark - staring at us. Some of the whispers were audible.

*"I'm surprised he brought her out of hiding…"*

*"She's not even Russian! And her family isn't important enough for a Morozov to marry an American…"*

*"He dumped a woman from one of the Bratva Six families for her?"*

Tania's jaw tightened, but she gave no sign she heard them, keeping her head high.

Staring down the loudest gossips, I raised her hands to my lips, kissing each one gently. My lips moved to her neck, breathing her in. "This is nothing, I believe, for a girl from Jersey. Isn't that what you always told me?"

She chuckled softly. "Let's blow these bitches right out of the water." The orchestra lifted their bows for the next song as I slid my hand around her waist, and the strains of a Mikhail Glinka tune began the dance.

If I closed my eyes, we would be back in my living room in Manhattan, teaching her how to dance the waltz as she laughed giddily on every spin. It would be before the kidnapping and if I just stayed in that moment, surely, everything would be as it was and we would be allowed to be happy.

"Oh! It's the "Masquerade Waltz!" Tania said, "I love this one!"

Chuckling, I spun her in wider and wider circles around the dance floor.

My wife danced like a queen; in perfect form with her long, elegant neck and shoulders thrown back. The long skirt of her gown swept around us and she wore her mysterious Mona Lisa smile, looking like royalty. A *printsessa*.

"Look!" Tania whispered happily as she spotted Alexi dancing with his daughter Yana. Winking at the thrilled girl, she gave her a thumb's up.

"She is doing very well," I murmured.

"Yana's a natural," she said, "but we practiced in the garden for six hours or so to make sure she perfected it. Look how well she's doing!"

"You gave her the debut of a lifetime, I am impressed."

"Hey, this is important!" Tania insisted, "This is such a huge moment for her. She has to look cool." I spun her again in a looping series of circles, admiring her ability to care so much for a girl that she had met perhaps twice before.

"I've missed this," I murmured.

She chewed absently on her lower lip. "So have I," she admitted reluctantly. My gaze moved to the huge, gilded doors that opened to the gardens outside and I spun her in that direction, her footwork still flawless going backward and in high heels.

Once we were out in the night air, Tania took a deep, rapturous breath. "Oh, this is so amazing… I…" She eagerly stepped forward and nearly fell down the granite steps, flanked by the fountains leading down to the formal gardens.

"Hold on," I grabbed her arm, bringing her upright. "This is a very bad time to break your neck, just as I'm about to sneak you into Catherine the Great's bedroom."

"*What?*" It came out in a shriek and she slapped her own hand over her mouth. "Seriously?"

I loved this woman. I loved her excitement for every new experience, I loved her enthusiasm for life, even while thrust abruptly into a new world with so few friends. "Yes," I whispered, running my hands up and down her arms. "Catch your breath. I will arrange this."

"*Sovietnik?*" It was Fedor, one of my new *Brigadiers*. "May I borrow you for a moment? There is a call from New York, a question…" he hesitated, looking at her.

"Go ahead," she waved, "I'll just wait here, rub my feet and quietly freak out with excitement."

I kissed her hand again, loving the feel of her warm skin on my lips. "The Dutch Garden is right in front of you, but do not wander too far. I will be right back." I nodded to Gavrill to follow her as she took off her high heels, holding up her skirt to keep from dragging it through the grass.

*Tania…*

This was turning out to be one hell of a night.

I looked amazing.

I made a friend. I think.

Yana launched into that waltz like a winner on Dancing with the Stars.

I danced with Yuri and it was even better than I remembered.

And my husband - shit have I ever even called him that? My husband has touched me more tonight than he has in the entire time we've been married.

So, something had to go wrong.

The Formal Dutch Garden outside the palace was lush, with perfectly spaced circles of green, hedges trimmed to a precise geometric edge, and trees that were still flowering, even in late summer. I could smell the crisp scent of freshly cut grass and traces of lavender on the breeze as I breathed in happily… which were then obliterated by the tang of men's cologne. Creed Spice & Wood, in fact. I knew because Ezio used to drench himself in the stuff before coming into the office.

However, this wasn't my old boss.

"Ah, lovely to see you again, darling. Are you still deep in wedded bliss?" Nolan O'Rourke moved into my personal space, smiling with his shiny white teeth all on display.

"Life is good," I said, noticing with rising anxiety that Gavrill was stepping up behind him, and the man following O'Rourke - who looked like a bull moose who had learned to walk on his hind legs - was sliding his hand into his jacket.

"Hey, Gavrill, stand down." I could feel sweat beading on my forehead, even in the cool night air. *There really have to be guns waved, even at the goddamn Imperial Ball?*

"Nolan, you want to tell your man this is not a 'shoot 'em up' situation?"

He gave a faint nod, and the hairy giant stood still with his hands folded politely. "You must forgive him," O'Rourke said, "he is understandably concerned with my continued good health. It has been a dramatic few weeks."

"You're not getting any blowback from standing up for me at the wedding, are you?" I felt guilty. Really? Guilty about this handsome sociopath getting heat because of me? "Although, that can't be. The wedding was only a flyspeck on the Lamborghini windshield of your life, right?"

Naturally, he laughed. "Oh dear, no. No… blowback." Eyeing me in all my ball-gowned glory, he said, "But if you wish to thank me above and beyond the favor you owe me, a kiss would do."

*I really, really should have pinned him down about that mysterious favor right there at the Cathedral instead of letting it hang over my head,* I thought gloomily. *Thank you, hindsight.*

"Kiss you? Yeah, I already know what disappointment tastes like."

Nolan O'Rourke was too rich and good-looking to be offended, so he just chuckled indulgently.

"Tell me, Nolan, what's been happening these last few weeks that has your guy there so trigger-happy?"

Now he sobered up. "Ah, plans are in play. People, businesses, goods, and services traded and sold. It can be a delicate balance."

"Yeah, I can imagine world domination is a tad time-consuming," I said, watching him with a frown. "What particular part of the planet are you conquering right now?"

"One that might interest you and your husband," he said, enjoying my reluctant curiosity. "Ireland, to be specific."

"With the O'Connell mob, by any chance?" I snarled.

"One must have connections everywhere, my dear Tania. But not necessarily allies." His eyes narrowed, looking at something over my shoulder. Leaning quickly to kiss my cheek, he whispered, "I have always wanted to be a master distiller." He slid into the pathway by the hedges, his tuxedo helping him blend in with the night.

"Was that O'Rourke?" Yuri said sharply.

I yelped, "Will you stop sneaking up on me like that? God, make some noise like a normal human!"

"I'm sorry, darling," he soothed, "I didn't mean to startle you." He put a possessive arm around my waist, an action I noticed with a great deal of satisfaction.

"Yes, it was Nolan. God, he's so irritating! He must have that silver spoon jammed so far up his ass that it's a miracle he can sit down," I said crossly. "He was infuriatingly inscrutable. Which is getting annoying."

"What did he say to you?" Yuri's calloused fingertips slid up my bare arm, making me shiver.

"Um…" that touch felt so good… "He did all this rich bastard mumbo jumbo about putting plans into action and moving people and around and how he was trading and selling goods and services. So, nothing that made any sense of course." My eyes fluttered shut for a moment as his fingertips made their way across my collarbones, delicately tracing one and then the other.

Regretfully, I held his wrist still. "But then he dropped this nugget of information. He's planning something in Ireland. He said that he could associate with the O'Connell's without becoming allies."

"Really," Yuri's expression was hard as stone. "What else did he share with you?"

"He said…" my brows furrowed, "he said he always wanted to be a master distiller. Is that some pompous way of saying he wants to be king of the planet or something?"

He was staring at me in a mix of admiration and deep frustration. "That son of a bitch just gave you more information in your garden chat than we have gotten out of him in months. My clever, delightful wife."

Yuri's hand went to my throat, his thumb pushing my chin up. His mouth landed on mine and his full lips pushed mine apart as his tongue slid between them, delicately sucking on mine as his other hand moved to my ass and pressed me against him. Hard.

Hard, as in *he* was hard. My entire front was squished against his broad, firm chest and his hand pushed my hips into his. If I wiggled just right, I bet I could feel those evil beads in his cock pressing against me.

When Yuri pulled back, his eyes were electric blue and he was panting harshly. "Would you like to see Catherine the Great's bedroom?"

My skin felt like it was burning and my nipples were hard enough to cut glass. "Is- is that a euphemism?" It was a weak joke, but I was dying with desperation to have him inside of me again, and I was scared if I showed it, he'd back away.

My husband gave me the filthiest grin. "Possibly." Swinging me up in his arms and ignoring my yelp, he strode into a more secluded entrance to the palace.

# CHAPTER EIGHTEEN

*In which nothing strengthens a marriage like going at it in a dead queen's bedroom.*

**Tania...**

"Where are we?" I whispered. Yuri had me by the hand and was moving so quickly that I was one stumble away from losing these stupid high heels and face-planting right on some magnificent bazillion-year-old rug.

"We are taking one of the servant's passages to the bedroom," he said, "they run all through the palace."

"That makes sense," I agreed breathlessly, yelping as he swept me up in his arms - gigantic dress and all - and made an abrupt right turn into what looked like another corridor. He pressed an indent in the wallpaper with his elbow and a hidden door swung open to… it was not enough to call it the royal bedchamber. This was a room where some of the greatest rulers in Russian history had slept and dreamed and plotted their next move.

A massive, stately blue bed and the gilded headboard dominated the room with a canopy overhang of tasseled tapestries and Yuri pulled me toward it.

"Oh, no no no, we are not doing it on Catherine the Great's bed!" I hissed fiercely, "That's sacrilege!"

His intent stare was directed at my cleavage and I wasn't sure he was listening. With a growl, he swept me off my feet and onto my back on the thick Turkish rug in front of the massive gold-framed mirror. Kneeling over me, he looked feral, ripping off his tuxedo jacket and the last thing I saw was his wicked smile as he flipped my skirt up, covering my face but leaving my lower half bare, except for my frilly undies.

"Mmmm... *Printsessa.* Such a fancy little scrap of lace."

My eyes rolled back in my head; Yuri was using the Voice. The Voice was a deadly weapon; his deepest, most filthy, guttural-sounding tone that meant I would be leaving here walking bowlegged.

His hands slid up my thighs, pressing them open and his mouth was against me, his hot breath warming me through my undies. I heard a little 'snick!' and the touch of a chilly blade right where he'd just kissed me. I bleated like a startled sheep, as every muscle froze in position.

"Y- Yuri."

"Hmmm?" The sharp tip of the knife was very lightly stroking down the thin skin of my inner thigh.

"Where did the switchblade come from?" My voice was pitched high enough to sound like I'd been sucking helium from a balloon.

He moved closer, shoving my legs wider with his shoulders. "You know I never travel unarmed."

I might have had more to say but my hips yanked upward as Yuri roughly pulled the lace up, rubbing harshly against my clit. He grunted, then cut through the fabric. Then his mouth was on me and my head dropped back against Catherine the Great's bedroom floor with a thud, my fingers mindlessly sliding into his thick hair, pulling on the longer strands.

*He's greedy tonight...* I thought, deeply pleased with this realization.

Yuri slid his hands under my ass and gripped it tightly, lifting me up closer to his mouth. He alternated long, tiger-like licks on my pussy with sucking my overwhelmed clit between his lips and batting at it with his tongue. His fingers flexed on my soft skin and his growl vibrated against my clitoris, still held by his lush lips and my heels pressed into his back as I came. I slid my hands into his thick hair, and pulled it as my back arched, "Oh, my god I've missed this!" I moaned. I could feel his shoulders shaking as his laughter was smothered by his mouth still pressed against me. The diabolical fiend kept licking to extend all the sparks flying through my lower half.

"Don't judge," I wheezed like air escaping a punctured tire, "it's been a while!" Clawing at my voluminous skirt, I pull it off my face enough to be able to look down.

I felt Yuri grin, his face still buried between my legs. His sharp teeth pressed against my left cheek before he bit. Ignoring my startled shriek, he bit the other cheek too, and pressed his lips against my pussy in a filthy open-mouthed kiss.

"I understand, *Printsessa,* it has been just as long for me."

"Wait- wait!" I grab his head between my hands and make my husband look at me. "Didn't you… you know, with your fiancée?" It felt like taking a slice out of my own heart, just asking this but surely he didn't mean he hadn't been with *anyone…*

"I have not," Yuri's beautiful face was solemn. "I have not touched another woman since I was foolish enough to leave you. I only saw Ksenia once before the wedding."

It felt like my entire being was radiating sunshine and I felt light. And alive. And grateful for another chance with this man.

"You are no *printsessa,*" he said, hovering over me, his hand coming up to cup my cheek, "you are my *Koroleva*. My Queen."

Yuri pulled me up enough to flip my dress up from behind to give me something between my skin and the ancient rug and pulled my breasts free from the bodice, squeezing each one with his big, rough hands. "I have missed you," he crooned, pushing them together and kissing each nipple.

"I've missed you too," I agreed breathlessly, and he stopped mauling my girls long enough to raise a haughty brow.

"I was talking to *them*," he said, angling his head toward my breasts and attacking them again as I laughed.

Bringing my knees up, I clench them around his hips. "Well, I've missed *my* magical bedazzled dick." I pulled his face up to kiss his wonderful, lush mouth. "So, give it to me."

He nearly rips his pants open, tapping the thick head of his cock against my extremely sensitive clit twice, making me jump and my stomach muscles tighten in anticipation. My nails dug into his jacket. There was something insanely erotic about him needing me so much that he was still fully dressed, his pants unzipped just enough to get his cock out.

"Are you sure?" Yuri purred in my ear, making me want to slap the back of his head.

"Yes," I hissed. I could feel it, the heated, broad tip of his cock pushing just up inside me. If he pushed in one more inch, I would feel the first of the pearls embedded in his perfect-

"Ask nicely," he prompted between gritted teeth. I could see the clear blue of his eyes disappearing as his pupils expanded, making him look darker, more savage and it was a testament to my husband's self-control that he wasn't already ramming into me.

"*Please,* darling," I said between gritted teeth, "I will set you on fire as revenge for my frustration, if you don't *please* put that cock in me right-"

I let out a shriek as my husband shoved half his shaft inside me in one push, my startled pussy trying to squeeze it back out.

"*Blyat',*" he groaned, "I thought I had just imagined how snug you are but..." his head dropped to rest against my chest for a moment, both of us strung tight as piano wires, vibrating together. Bracing his knees against the carpet, he slid out an inch or two, then pushed back inside me. "I can feel all your sweet muscles flutter against me. Halfway there, doesn't that feel good?"

"Yeh… wha?" I gabbled, no longer able to string enough sounds together to make an actual word.

Yuri's accent had thickened, as much as his gorgeous cock, and it was just as hot. "I imagine it stings a bit, doesn't it? But I think you like that, don't you? Do you like how much you have to stretch for me?"

His thick fingers moved between us, bracketing his shaft buried halfway inside me, feeling how my pussy was straining around him.

"Not the Voice," I whined, "I can't handle you and the Voice at the same time."

He chuckled softly against my ear, licking it and blowing on the goosebumps that sprang up on the thin skin of my throat. "You're on fire inside, I feel like my dick is melting into you. Just a few inches more, just a few inches more and I'll let you rest and get used to me inside this fiery little cunt. Lean in, put those delicious breasts against me."

The guttural sound of his voice, his accent, his very clear and present need for me was setting every nerve ending in me on fire, like he'd just struck a match to me. I could feel the first pearl nudge my clit on the way inside me, then the second, then the…

"Oh, my god! You just-" I bit mindlessly into his neck. Yuri was so thick, was he always this thick? And the pearls were rubbing relentlessly against all those soft, sensitive places inside me and it hurt in the best way. I have never felt so full, full to bursting and it was so wildly… "Fuck!" I came, writhing and squeezing him and clenching down hard enough that he almost slipped out again. He rocked against me greedily as he kissed me, all lips and tongue and teeth like he used to.

"My *Koroleva*," he whispered, "you're going to give me another one before I finish."

Sliding his hands back to my shoulder blades, Yuri hoisted me upward and I straddled him, still impaled halfway on to his cock and I stifled another shriek as I finally felt him come to the top of me- nowhere else to go. As we both looked down, he smiled in an utterly depraved fashion as he saw two inches still outside my pussy. Spreading his knees, he leaned back on his heels, settling me against his groin.

"Oh, darling..." his disappointment was clear. "You can't take all of me? Well, we can fix that. Slide up... good... now down again, move those hips. Ahhhh- God! There we are. See? You did have a bit more room in your cunt to take me, didn't you?"

Yuri began thrusting his hips up strongly, nearly knocking me off his cock at one point before I found my balance with a startled yelp. Biting down hard on my lower lip to keep quiet, I began to move again, more confidently as the burning sting began to fade. My slick began eagerly assisting the pull and slide of that wonderful, hard shaft inside me.

"Mmmm..." he purred. "Look down." I did, seeing my clit rubbing against the hairy base of him. "You've taken all of me inside you, such a good girl."

The combination of the sin and sex dripping from that deep voice and the increasing throbbing of him inside made me move against him again, scooping my pelvis in on the downstroke to grind against him, then arching out on the up to rub his thick head and all those pearls against my G-spot. Yuri - damn him - continued to compliment me, purring depraved thoughts into my ear as his hips snapped up sharply to help me.

As I felt my walls begin to spasm and that tight coil in my belly violently unravel, I grabbed his face between my hands. "You have to come with me. I need you to."

Yuri grinned. Like a pirate. Like an outlaw. Like the most delicious, nastiest man in Russia. "Come all over my cock, now," he ordered, "Make me wet. *Now!*"

I jumped slightly, then bit into his shoulder to keep from screaming as I heard his groans leaking through clenched teeth as the coil of my pussy against his swelling cock forced him to finish, flooding me with the searing heat of his come.

We swayed together, gripping each other tightly with arms and legs and our mouths fused together and I had never been so happy in my entire life.

# CHAPTER NINETEEN

*In which Yuri and Tania introduce themselves to each other.*

**Tania...**

I was not clear on how we got from half-naked on the floor of Catherine the Great's bedroom to the back of the limo but the privacy screen was up and I was straddling Yuri as he slid in and out of me. Slowly, because I was really sore.

Not that it would have stopped him.

"I am sorry that I could not give you the full experience," he said, using his best falsely sincere tone, pulling me down hard enough on his cock to make me gasp.

"Huh?" I answered intelligently.

One of his hands gripped my ass, making me move faster while the other was around the front of my neck his thumb pushing up my chin and keeping us face to face. "That I could not get a stallion on such short notice for the full Catherine the Great experience."

"Oh, that's okay," I said, bouncing up and down on him, "my husband is hung like one."

His laughter shakes me hard into another orgasm.

**Yuri...**

When the limo stopped in front of the mansion, I helped my wife attempt to tidy up, smoothing her hair and gently tucking her breasts back in her dress.

Tania gave me a shy smile. "Now that we're back at the house, are you going to turn back into heartless, frozen Yuri?"

Sighing, I stroked her cheek. I could see the anxiety behind the smile, and her fear. Her shoulders were tilted away from me like she was preparing to make a run for it. How could I make her feel this way? Why did I let my fear of looking weak hurt her so much? "I am sorry. You never deserved how I have treated you. But I would like to try to make it up to you now. Shall we start again?" Holding out my hand, I said, "Hello, I'm Yuri Morozov, your husband."

She shook it, "Nice to meet you, I'm Tania Morozov, your wife."

"A pleasure," I answered, kissing her hand.

Helping her out of the car, I kept hold of her hand as we walked into the house, lingering in the entryway.

"Are you hungry?" I asked, "I could have Anya make something."

Tania was uncharacteristically silent, simply shaking her head.

Squeezing her hand, I asked, "Shall we go to bed?" She nodded, allowing me to pull her to the left-hand stairway. "I recall something I should have done the first time we walked up these stairs together," I said.

Sweeping her up in my arms, I enjoyed her little yelp as I carried her up the stairs, down the hall, passing her guest room, and pausing in front of mine.

Ours.

"Will you move into the master suite with me," I asked, "or will there be a period of revenge-based torture for my behavior that you will inflict upon me first?"

She cocked her head, thinking about it. "No, I can get my revenge and live with you at the same time."

Opening the door, I carried her inside. "I have every faith you will send me through all nine circles of hell before you're finished with me." She laughed, which was not reassuring.

I sat in one of the huge chairs by the fireplace, settling Tania on my lap. "I will say this first. I am sorry for the grief and hurt I caused you. I am sorry for my coldness since we have been married, well, even before, back in New York. I did not know how… how to handle any of this."

Her arms went around my shoulders and squeezed. "I am so sorry for my insane rescue plan. For nearly torpedoing your Bratva, for all the pressure I put on you and Maksim." She thought about it, "Well, not for stressing out Maksim, but definitely sorry about making things so difficult for you." Resting her forehead against mine, she asked, "Please promise me that you will talk to me about this. About all of it. When you're ready."

I did not deserve this woman. But I would thank the god I no longer believed in for her every day. "I promise, my *Koroleva*."

Holding her tighter, I let myself enjoy one perfect, crystalline moment with my wife.

*Tania…*

When I opened my eyes the next morning, I was alone in Yuri's bed. There was one moment of crushing disappointment until I heard him talking on the phone in his dressing room. *Dressing room,* the immature part of me giggled, *who the hell has a dressing room?*

It was the size of your average apartment in Manhattan, with beautifully carved walnut shelves and drawers and three floor-to-ceiling armoires with ancient, silvered mirrors on the doors. With Yuri's custom-made business wear hanging up and displayed so perfectly, it was basically suit porn.

Getting out of bed was trickier than I expected. My thighs were on fire, and my girl parts felt red and swollen. Not that I was complaining, but… if that man keeps pounding me like he did last night, I was going to develop some kind of sex-related disability.

Finally, out of bed and limping toward the bathroom, I overheard Yuri, talking to Maksim, I thought.

"There's something off about O'Rourke's interest in Tania."

"Yes, I know he enjoys playing the game, but why would he seek her out last night? I know my wife has a way of bringing a man to his knees before he knows what hit him, but he offered her more information in a five-minute chat than we have gotten out of him in the last two months…

"I know the news is extremely helpful. But I don't like Tania being drawn into this…" He walked out of the dressing room, buttoning his dress shirt. Seeing him casually perform a minor task that had taken him an endless amount of effort and considerable pain after being kidnapped made me want to sing with joy. Or jump his bones. He had come so far.

He looked up from his shirt, giving me a filthy smile as he stared at me. Which was when I remembered I was naked.

"Brother, I must go. Something has just come up." Yuri dropped his phone on a chair and backed me up against the bed.

"No, no no no!" I was laughing too hard to sound serious, but when he threw me on my back and spread my legs, my laughter choked off into a groan. "Yuri baby, I am so sore!"

He was running his thumbs up and down my pussy, spreading my lips gently. "I have some numbing cream."

Then he put his mouth on me and it was much better than numbing cream.

"Maybe I'm not so sore…" I said, staring blissfully up at the ceiling.

**Much later...**

"So, what did you and Maksim deduce from O'Rourke's weird info dump last night?"

I was slumped against Yuri's broad chest, sitting on the blue tile bench in his shower, which was big enough to clean him and maybe twenty-seven of his friends at the same time. I was already emotionally attached to the rainfall showerhead currently cascading over us and was considering moving a fridge and my laptop in here and never leaving again.

His hand, which was currently spreading body wash over my breasts - for the fifth time - paused for a moment. "You have never asked about the family business before."

"True, but it wasn't my family then and didn't have weird billionaires turning up and sharing random information with me," I pointed out, and he nodded reluctantly. "Also, you have been washing my right breast long enough that the left one is getting jealous."

He gave me his filthiest grin. "Then I must rectify the situation."

Yuri's lips fastened onto my nipple - the left one - and the strength left my legs. "D- don't think this gets you out of explaining," I wheezed.

The sun is slanting low over the master bedroom when my insatiable husband and I woke up. We were on the floor in front of the fireplace and I was lying on top of him, his cock was still in me.

Yuri puts his arm behind his head, looking up at the lengthening shadows on the ceiling. "The O'Connell mob bought the most prestigious whiskey distillery in Dublin. The clan wants it to look like a bid to gain legitimacy as a reputable business, but it's a front for a huge money-laundering system. They can make millions from other crime families."

"Other mobsters will let those mobsters launder their money?" I asked, perplexed, "That seems like it would involve a lot of trust."

He shrugged, "It is all solid numbers, what goes in, what goes out. The real problem is this gives the O'Connell Mafia a place at the table, so to speak."

"How so?"

"Filtering hundreds of millions of dollars for other families means developing a relationship with them. Then, an alliance. The more families that choose to ally with the O'Connell mob, the more dangerous they become." While Yuri's expression was blank, the scar on his face throbbed an angry red.

"I hate those fuckers," I said bitterly. "There has to be a way to knock them down." Lifting myself off my husband with a groan as his cock slipped from me, I sat up with my back against a chair. "How does this circle round to O'Rourke and what he said last night?"

He frowned, "He made it clear that he's doing business with the O'Connell's, but not allied with them."

"Part of my position at Papachristodoulopoulos was vetting potential investors," I said, "O'Rourke came up squeaky clean. Rich as hell, which means he isn't; because no one has that much money without getting his hands dirty. But he's definitely not a mobster. So, what kind of business is he doing with them?"

"O'Rourke is at an Oligarch-level of wealth," he said, "it could be anything. But what is most useful is the last thing he said to you."

"That he's always wanted to be a master distiller?" I asked. "So… is this a hint that he wants to take over their business? And since he's sharing it with us, is he hinting that he wants your involvement? And if so, why doesn't this asshole just *say* it?"

Yuri gave me a look that was *so* Russian. World-weary, cynical, stoic. "Because he enjoys his games. Because once one has amassed that level of wealth and power, playing with the lives of men is the only game left to play."

"Well, that's depressing," I scowled. "You should probably feed me and cheer me up."

**Yuri...**

"What are your thoughts, brother?"

I was watching Tania dozing on a lounge by the pond, face tilted happily up to the indecisive sunshine, trying to soak up the rays before the inevitable clouds covered the sky again.

"Every scrap of intelligence Patrick gathered points to the clan gathering to celebrate the opening of the distillery," Maksim's voice was calm, but I could sense his eagerness to tear into the O'Connell's. "This is a once-in-a-lifetime opportunity to take them down for good."

"Do we have the manpower?" I asked, watching my wife look around to make sure she was alone and pulling off her shirt, basking in her sports bra and some tight little shorts. Our men patrolled the entire estate, but they all knew better than to get close enough to bother Tania. Or worse, get engaged in friendly conversation with her. Last week I walked in on a poker game in the kitchen where my wife was cheerfully winning four of my guard's wages for the week.

"Yes," he said, "Thomas has offered the Corporation security force to assist us, and Alexi and the Toscano brothers are sending soldiers as well. But the final piece is still that bastard O'Rourke."

"Ekaterina and Mariya's arranged marriages with the Toscano

and Turgenev families have been highly advantageous," I said dryly.

"Don't taunt me. They are both good matches to good men," he said sharply.

Rubbing my forehead, I realized my scar had not been troubling me as much these last few days, it didn't wake me up with the vicious, heated pulsing I had endured since the kidnapping.

"If what he said to Tania is accurate," I said, "then he's indicating that he wants the distillery, which seems ridiculous."

"Not necessarily," Maksim said, "this is a 200-year-old operation, and its whiskey is legendary. For the O'Connell's to buy up the entire company with all its global reach and prestige, it's a worthy prize. O'Rourke is doing business with them, he has insider knowledge of the clan event that would remove most of the variables we can't predict. But," he hissed, "he is not returning my calls."

I whistled, in part to taunt my brother, but also because I was surprised there was anyone in power who did not leap to take his call.

"However, we do have another option," he said.

"Which is?"

"O'Rourke's odd fondness for your wife."

"We are not using Tania to gain information," I said sharply, "every encounter she has with him concerns me more."

"Has he ever said anything inappropriate to her? Anything sexual?" Maksim was pursuing this and I was not happy.

"You are implying that if O'Rourke has not actually propositioned my wife, then she is safe with him," I snapped. "Have you forgotten that he has manipulated all of this? Telling her about my wedding, knowing that she would be brave enough to attempt to stop me from making the worst mistake of my life… showing up at the wedding with information that absolves us and frees me to marry Tania?"

"I know this, but-"

I interrupted Maksim for the first time that I can remember. "He demanded a favor from her, brother. Not just from us. A separate favor owed by her. They shook hands on it. She is part of his game and I will not allow her to be used, by O'Rourke, or by *us*."

He was silent for a moment, likely controlling his anger. "Has it occurred to you that you're doing Tania a disservice? Don't you see that she wants the O'Connell's to pay for what they did to you as much as we do? I have learned," he said wryly, "to not underestimate my wife. You shouldn't either."

Now my scar was throbbing. Rubbing the heel of my hand against it, I said, "I will contact O'Rourke myself."

"Very well," Maksim said, "good luck."

# CHAPTER TWENTY

*In which we discover a violin is the best foreplay ever.*

**Yuri...**

That prick.

That son of a bitch.

Nolan O'Rourke does not return my calls.

We have a general idea of when the grand unveiling of the O'Connell distillery will be, and we need to be there first. Patrick flew back to Dublin to try to pick up more information, but this would all be so much simpler if that irritating Irish prick would call me back.

Maksim gave me a week before pushing me again.

"You're infantilizing Tania."

"Where did you come up with that?" I scoffed, "Because I don't want my wife interacting with an unstable disruptor like O'Rourke, I'm treating her like a child?"

"Ella wanted to train to be a doctor," he said patiently, "she's saved the lives of several of our men. I had to learn to trust that she knew what she was doing and that she had the right to be part of this dynasty. Are you telling me that Tania is less worthy? That she can't handle this man?"

I irritably tapped my fingers on the desk. "Did Ella help you write this speech?"

Now his tone was frosty. "We need this information. We need it now, *Sovietnik*."

My jaw tightened. I had never questioned an order from Maksim as *Pakhan* before. But this order was for my wife. "Very well. I will ask her today."

*Tania…*

I was sitting on our bed, playing my new violin when Yuri came in. He leaned against the wall, hands in his suit pockets, and watched me with a faint smile.

"That song is beautiful," he said, "one of Abel Korzeniowski's, isn't it?"

"Mm-hmm," I agreed, "I love it, it's so mournful and beautiful at the same time." My eyes narrowed as his lit up with a devilish gleam.

Kneeling in front of me, he pushed my legs apart. "Keep playing," he ordered, and I did, shakily putting the bow back on the strings. He slowly pushed my skirt up as I tried to get back into the flow of the music, but my bow slipped with a discordant screech when his thumbs ran up my inner thighs and moved in slow circles over the silk underwear covering me.

"Yuri…"

"Keep playing," he reminded me, before lowering his head and putting my legs over his shoulders. When he blew hot air onto the wet fabric, I hit the wrong note again. He pinched my thigh - hard - and I yelped, trying to remember where I was in the song. Forcing my fingers into the correct position, I kept playing as he yanked my undies aside and I felt his tongue drive up inside me before pulling out and swiping a long lick through my wet lips. My bow slowed and he gave me a warning hum as he put his mouth against my center in a kiss so filthy I almost flopped backward.

I awkwardly segued into the song again, but when he slid two thick fingers inside of me, I wheezed, "Baby, I'm-"

My whining cut off in a shriek when he bit me. There. Not gently.

This time, his voice was a little muffled since his mouth was attached to my pussy, but it was dark and gravelly. "I said. Keep playing, my *Koroleva*."

I fumbled through the last half of the song, sawing absentmindedly, every now and then my bow against the strings gave a screech that almost covered up some of my yelps and moans. My core muscles were shaking with the effort of keeping me upright. Damn it! I was so wet that I could see a slick spot on the expensive silk quilt below me, and Yuri's grin just got filthier.

On the last few notes, I leaned into it, trying to eke the music out until he pursed his lips around my clit and the nails on his two fingers inside me very carefully scratched my G-spot as his teeth scraped against my pearl. The violin flew across the bed and the bow to the floor and my fingers were digging into that smug bastard's lovely, thick hair… and he did it all one more time, just to show he could.

When I was the consistency of a boneless chicken, sweaty and moaning, he crawled up my body, stopping to kiss each breast before tapping his cock against me, sliding the thick head through the mess he's made before pushing it inside me. He chuckled cruelly when my hips lifted up, trying to meet him halfway.

"What do you want?" Yuri taunted me.

He was *right there,* the heated head of his cock, already stretching me wide, those pearls ready to pop into me. "Don't be mean," I moaned, "you know…"

"Say 'I want your cock in me,'" he instructed.

"*Nyet!*" I snarled. What a dick!

"Say it, *ty plokhaya devochtka*," he warned.

*Bad girl?* I thought, *He's calling me bad?*

"*Nein!*" I snapped back, wiggling my hips again. The tip was inside me now so if I could just angle the right-

Yuri leaned back, slapping my clit briskly.

*Oh, my god what is that-* The sting from the slap turned into a spread of heat that made my wet center prickle and throb.

"Ow! Yuri!"

"Say, 'I want your cock in me' or I am taking it away from you for a week," he warned. Oh, no. This was Edging Yuri. Edging Yuri had kept me right on the brink of madness before.

In furious Spanish, I snapped, "*Quiero tu polla en mi!*"

He rotated his hips slowly once, twice, to really make sure I knew he was right there, just inside me and all it would take would be one push and… He put his lips to my ear and whispered, "Not in Spanish, you bad girl, in Russian."

I thought of all the ways I wanted to murder him. But as he was about to pull out of me, I hissed, "*YA khochu tvoy chlen vo mne!*"

Yuri sank in, hard, and we groaned together. Every time with him stings. Every time the tip of his cock pushes against my cervix and the tingle it causes zaps through me and down to my toes. And every time everything inside collides and reforms and I come out better for it. His arm snaked under me, lifting me up to meet his kiss.

The muscles in his thighs coiled and moved as he thrust harder and his other hand shoved up under my shirt, running a hot trail between my breasts and then lightly cupping my throat.

He leaned up as he slammed in and out of me, squeezing his fingers around my throat just slightly. Yuri was the only man I'd ever trusted enough to do this, but now, with his face in shadow and his eyes half closed and looking like a darker twin, it was shockingly erotic. I groaned, feeling the danger as his fingers tightened again, the burn, and a certainty that he knew just how much I could take.

"H- h- how can you be getting harder?" I wheezed, trying to get the words out between his thrusts.

"Because nothing else will ever feel like this; your pretty cunt gripping me like a fist, your pulse under my thumb-" his head dropped as I drew my heels up against his flexing ass. Squeezing my throat one more time to get my attention, he growled, "Come with me, *Koroleva*."

It felt electric; like a spark tearing through my nervous system and flaring violently inside me where Yuri was coming too, the heat from him sending up another flare of pleasure mixed with pain inside me.

*Yuri…*

"Initially, I had a reason for seeking you out," my voice was muffled because my face was buried between Tania's breasts, my cock still inside her.

"Oh yeah?" she slurred. I loved my wife's sweet, loopy smile when she had just come, sounding cock drunk.

"I must ask you to do something for me," I said, hating myself. Hating Maksim. Specifically and especially hating Nolan fucking O'Rourke.

She giggled, "I'm not really in the shape for it right now, but gimme a minute…"

"No, love," I soothed, kissing her forehead. "Nothing so pleasant, sadly. Let me get a cloth and…"

Her legs tightened around my hips. "Stay. Stay in me for a minute."

Sinking against her again, I cupped her breast. "This request was in no way connected with buttering you up through sex."

Her laughter pushed her hard pink nipples against my chest. "This was an accidental buttering me up?"

"Precisely, so you must save it for a later request of mine," I said.

"All right," Tania said, flexing one leg, "one buttering me up through sex credit for later. What do you need?"

Taking in a deep breath and letting it out, I attempted to not sound bitter. "Nolan O'Rourke has the information we need on the O'Connell gathering for the whiskey distillery opening. He is not taking Maksim's calls. Nor mine." Gritting my teeth, I said, "We believe if you leave a message, he will contact you."

"Okay."

I balanced on my elbows, looking down at her. "I know he makes you uncomfortable. I do not like asking this."

Casually waving a hand, she kissed me and looked around. "Where did my violin go?"

*Tania...*

I was lying through my teeth.

The thought of talking to Nolan O'Rourke again opened up a bottomless pit in my stomach and anything I threw in to appease it - cake, glasses of wine, another orgasm - wasn't enough to fill it up and stop the anxiety. I didn't want to remember I owed this man a favor that he could cash in at any time. But I dialed the number Yuri gave me and left a message.

In less than thirty minutes, Nolan Facetimed me back.

I picked up on the first ring. "Hello?"

"I had a feeling you'd be hovering over your phone, Tania dear," he said.

"Just like a fourteen-year-old waiting for her first crush to call," I agreed flatly, watching Yuri's fists tighten.

"Flattered, I'm sure," he said, "though I imagine you're interested in the comings and goings of a certain Irish Mob? I'm surprised the Morozov brothers didn't figure it out on their own, they have several skilled spies infesting the streets of Dublin as we speak."

"Apparently not that skilled," I sighed, "so, what do you think? This is important. I know you're already waist-deep and you know the Morozov Bratva will give you what you want."

"True," he allowed, "but even when you're in bed with someone, a little extra courting never hurts."

Rubbing my eyes to stave off the headache that was blooming, I impatiently said, "Oh, Nolan you're my hero. You are the best, Nolan. What a guy. You have great hair. And I like your shoes."

Yuri's expression was thunderous.

"So gracious darling, thank you," O'Rourke said, grinning as if he knew Yuri was sitting right across from me. "I suppose we are close enough to the grand event to coordinate our plans. Go ahead and give the phone to your husband."

"Thank you Nolan," I dutifully recited, ready to roll my eyes hard enough to see the back of my skull after I handed my phone to Yuri.

"Tania?"

I pulled the phone back to look at the screen. "Yes?"

He gave me a huge smile, every one of his perfectly straight, white teeth on display. "I will be calling your favor due, very soon."

The cold sweat on my forehead and the back of my neck made me nauseous. "Yeah, I'll be mainlining antacids until I know what you want." Handing the phone to Yuri with relief, I ran my hand over my face. I really wish he hadn't smiled at me. I shuddered, getting up to go change my silk shirt before I ruined it.

Yuri found me outside, tucked in one of the big wicker seats.

"Thank you, I didn't want you speaking with him," he grumbled, giving me a kiss.

"Did you get what you needed?" I asked.

"I did," he admitted, not looking at all happy about it. "I do not like him taunting you about this favor. You need to let me know right away when he tells you what he wants from you. You should not *owe* him anything."

"Well, I do. Owe him something, I mean," I said seriously, "I could have screwed up things so badly between you and the other Bratva that people would have died because of my selfishness in wanting you back. I do owe him a debt and I will pay it."

Kissing me, Yuri stroked my cheekbone with one thumb. "Whatever he asks, you and I will face it together."

*Yuri…*

*Two days later…*

"Ella and Maksim are arriving today."

Tania was attempting to fasten her dress, and I stepped behind her, trailing my knuckles on the soft skin of her back as I pulled the zipper up and enjoyed her little shiver.

"I'm so glad," she said happily. "Ella and I talked last night but she wasn't sure when they were flying in."

"It's important to have the two of you here, safe and together," I said, resting my chin on the top of her head.

She stilled, looking at me in the mirror with her wide, golden eyes. "Does that mean your… uh… your mission to Dublin is on and you're… what, consolidating us to coordinate security?"

Squeezing her arms gently, I said, "We leave tomorrow."

"Are you going to be okay, babe?" She leaned against me. "This is... so much to deal with."

I placed a kiss on her neck, and then one just under her ear.

*"Let's cut off his arm..."*

Stepping back, I unbuttoned my shirt again and pulled it off.

"On the third day of my captivity - I think it was the third day, time moved differently in the warehouse - one of the old man O'Connell's sons, Colm, came in to see me. The men torturing me were angry because I would not give them anything. It was bad. Very bad, but my father had beaten, stabbed, and burned Maksim and me since we were children, so I knew I could handle it."

Tania stared up at me, lips pressed together. "You should *never* have had to 'get used to it.' I'm so glad your dad is dead. What did he want?"

"He said it was time to, 'mix it up.' He pulled out the chainsaw and started it up, revving the engine right by my head, over and over. I remember the smell of the diesel fuel, and their laughter..."

I placed her shaking hand on the thick red scar on my shoulder. She was warm, fingers stroking gently over the healed gash.

"I remember the blade cutting through skin and muscle," I said, "I pulled myself into a memory, back when you and I were making my driver loop around the park over and over while I defiled you in the back seat?"

Her eyes brimming, Tania laughed, "That is a very good memory."

"Colm O'Connell was not getting the response he wanted, so he turned the chainsaw off and told me he'd be back for my eyes if I didn't tell them what they wanted to know. My torturers glued the skin on my shoulder back together, but…" I stopped; my throat too tight to go on.

Her mouth pressed softly on the top of my scar, her kiss was cool and tentative, when I leaned in slightly against the pressure of her lips and nodded, she continued kissing along the ugly length of it. "You go take what you need to, my sweet husband. Go to Dublin and take it all, if it keeps you from going back into that dark place again. Okay?"

Pressing my forehead against hers, I pulled in a deep, shaky breath. "I love you."

"I love you, too," she whispered, eyes still wet. "If you go into the dark again, I will come to find you and pull you back out. I will. Just… please don't push me away."

She wrapped her arms around my waist, squeezing me tightly.

*Tania…*

"Is it time?"

It was past midnight but I couldn't sleep, not when my time with Yuri was ticking away. I was in my favorite spot, sprawled on top of him, kissing along the scar on his shoulder. His spent cock was still between my legs, both of us still wet from making love as many times as we could manage.

His sigh told me what I needed to know, and my knees tightened around his waist. "I want to be a tough Bratva wife," I whispered, "I do. But I'm so scared for you."

Putting his arm under his head, my sweet husband smiled down at me. "I will not take any unnecessary risks, my *Koroleva*. I have someone to come home to."

"Good." Running my fingers over his beautiful, lush mouth, I yelped when he playfully bit the tip of one finger.

"Ah," Yuri gently rolled me off him and stood up, stretching, "I have something for you." I rolled to my side to appreciate the gorgeous play of all that muscle moving under the skin of his back. There were more scars there, many hidden under elaborate scrolls of tattoos. There was a clear bite mark on his ass and I tried to smother my laughter.

"Are you looking at your bite mark, you little vampire?" He grinned lecherously. "Don't look so pleased with yourself, you have a matching set on that juicy little ass of yours."

"It's not that little," I drawled, rolling over on to my stomach. He *did* love my ass, maybe if I wiggled a bit, he'd forget about getting ready to leave and I could keep him inside of me.

He was digging something out of his bedside table drawer, "Oh, it is definitely juicy, darling." Turning back, he slapped my left cheek as I screeched.

"Ow! What was that for?"

"Because this gorgeous, pert bottom of yours looks best when it's all pink," he said, unrepentantly slapping my right cheek for emphasis.

I was seconds away from smacking his gorgeous butt in retaliation when Yuri got on one knee.

Naked.

"My beautiful *Koroleva,* there is nothing I would not give if I could go back in time to that day. If I could stop the O'Connell mob and have our night together. I had planned a speech in my head… I even wrote a letter to you in case I forgot everything I was planning to say."

"I read it," I confessed, I was shaking and a little lightheaded.

Yuri's brow rose. "Patrick?"

"Yes."

"I am going to have to give that pushy little bastard a raise," he murmured. "But I have nothing smooth to say tonight. No brilliant way to propose that would guarantee you would say yes. But I love you. You would have always been the love of my life, but I no longer believed I deserved you after that night. I can promise to love you till the end of my days. Only you. It was always you, my Tania."

He sucked in a breath, like he was trying to pull together his courage for this. As if he even needed it.

"Will you marry me?"

Crawling off the bed, I settled myself in his lap. "We're already married, babe." I ran my fingers through his thick, silky hair.

"The right way," he said, kissing me tenderly. "The way you deserve."

"Yes, my gorgeous and lovely husband, I'm saying yes. I only need you, though. Nothing fancy. Just you."

"Oh," he said in his stupid tone of false innocence. "Then I will just return this ring to-"

"Don't you dare!" I gasped, frowning when he burst into laughter.

He slipped it on my finger, the ring with the beautiful yellow diamond. Kissing my knuckles, he lifted my hand up. "It matches your eyes perfectly," he said with great satisfaction. "I knew it."

I put my hands on either side of his face, kissing him and trying to pour all my feelings into the movement of my lips against his. "I love you too, my beautiful, bedazzled man. I'll love you forever."

Ella and I stood on the huge stone steps in the front of the mansion, watching our men drive away in a limo bristling with bodyguards, more in an SUV in front of them, and two more cars making up the rear of the caravan to the airport.

Yuri had kissed me deeply, cradling my face in his big, rough hands. "Give me one of my favorite smiles," he said.

"Which one?" I sniffled.

"Your brave, take no prisoners smile," he said, so kindly.

"This one?" I straightened up, smiling at him radiantly, trying to look like a stone-cold, hardcore Bratva bride.

His grin illuminated me, making me feel powerful and beloved. "That's the one."

As if on cue, as the cars turned the corner of the boulevard and out of sight, I started sobbing. A look over at Ella told me she wasn't much better.

"C'mon," she put her arm over my shoulders. "Let's go in and find the most fattening thing in Anya's fridge and eat it all."

# CHAPTER TWENTY-ONE

*In which O'Rourke claims his favor.*

**Tania...**

My phone rang a couple of hours after Yuri left and my hand shook when I saw the number on my screen.

"Hello?"

"Hello, Tania dear. How are you?"

I sucked in a silent breath. "Nolan O'Rourke. You just checking in? Want to chat? Exchange some recipes? Girl talk?"

He chuckled delightedly as if I was just the cutest thing ever. "It's time."

"Time?" I echoed stupidly.

"I'm calling in my favor."

"What do you want me to do?" I asked, proud that I kept my voice steady.

"At 10pm, there will be a car waiting for you, one block down from your home. I'm sure you can find a way to slip out unnoticed by your bodyguard and the lovely Ella." This man sounded so *smug*. "Your driver's name is Marcus, he will take you to a private airport and put you on my jet."

"Where am I going?"

"Is it really important, dear?" O'Rourke chided me, "I will have you home before your husband returns."

"It sounds like you don't want me telling Yuri about my favor coming due," I said.

"Your husband and the Morozov Bratva have a full schedule for these next couple of days. You wouldn't want to distract him, would you? Distracted men become dead men."

"Are you threatening Yuri?" I hissed.

"No." I could practically hear him shrug. "I can have you do your part and be safely back home in no time. Then, you're welcome to speak all you like about it to him afterward."

Rubbing my forehead, I thought about how stupid this was. How risky. "All right. I'll be there."

"Excellent!" He sounded genuinely delighted, like we were about to go play polo or something. And then hung up without saying goodbye, as if that last extra word was beneath him.

At nine-thirty, Ella and I were sitting in the library, saying nothing useful because we were both thinking about what was about to happen in Dublin. I pleaded exhaustion and said goodnight.

"Are you sure?" she asked, "We can binge-watch something. I know where Anya's hiding the rest of the *Medovik* honey cake from dinner."

"No…" I could barely look at her, I felt so guilty. "It's been a week of long days and sleepless nights. If I can sleep tonight, I'll be functional again, you know?"

"I do," she sighed. "Okay. Come find me later if you can't sleep, okay?"

"Will do," I hugged her before standing up.

*Yes,* I thought, cringing, *I so am going to hell for lying to Ella.*

The helpful part about living in a crime lord's lair is that there are multiple ways to get out of it. I'd been briefed early on about the Panic Room on the third floor, the escape door through the wine cellar, and a nearly invisible panel in the garden wall that could open directly into a hidden section of the massive garage behind the house. The wine cellar option seemed like the best one.

*What do you take for a stealth assignment by a mysterious and probably unhinged billionaire?* I thought, packing my laptop, a change of clothes, my passport, and a fistful of cash in my messenger bag.

It was almost too easy, sneaking down the servant's stairway, hiding in a bathroom on the first floor till the guard walked by, and then down to the basement and through the wine cellar. Wiping my sweaty palms on my jeans, I speed-walked to the corner where, sure enough, there was a ubiquitous SUV with blacked-out windows waiting for me.

The biggest man I had ever seen stepped out of the car, wearing a proper black suit with his giant, mutton-like fists folded in front of him, his dark face expressionless. He was so large that the streetlight behind him made him cast a shadow that stretched halfway down the block.

"Mrs. Morozov, may I take your bag for you?" He had a well-bred English accent and a voice so deep that it was a wonder the cobblestones didn't rattle when he spoke.

"Nope, I'm good," I grinned nervously.

*I wonder what Yuri calls my stupid nervous grin?*

"Very well," he opened the back door and as my stomach twisted inside out, I got in.

We were almost at the airport when I called Ella.

"Hey girl, you could have just come over to my wing," she chuckled.

"The wings…" I shook my head. "These men and their wings. Who else has a house with their own wing?"

"Accept that we will never understand it," she counseled, "you want to come over and watch something?"

"Here's the thing…" my skin was prickling and I was pretty sure I was going to projectile vomit from anxiety the minute the car door opened. "I'm not in the house."

Ella was instantly sober. "What did you just say?"

"O'Rourke called in his favor," I gulped. "I'm flying out on his jet, we're just pulling up to it."

"Why didn't you tell me!" she exploded, "I would have come with you! This is dangerous and I know you're calling me because you won't tell Yuri."

"You are correct," I said, "I'm not going to risk letting Yuri get distracted. Look, I know it sounds so trusting that it's pathetic, but I don't think I'm in danger here. Whatever the favor is-" I shuddered, feeling sick again, "-it's not going to kill me. He's helped us with the O'Connell thing, I can do this."

"Where are you going?" Ella asked plaintively.

"I don't know," I confessed, "he's not telling me.

The SUV pulled up to a Boeing 767-33A ER jet and my gigantic minder got out, opening my door. "I have to go. I'll call you as soon as I can."

"This is wrong, honey," she fretted, "I should be with you."

"Trust me, I got this. Now, love your guts."

"Love yours more," Ella said, "be safe."

I wasn't proud of it, but I'd definitely been spoiled by being married to a billionaire. Any luxuries I've enjoyed with Yuri paled in comparison to O'Rouke's private jet.

An impeccably beautiful flight attendant named Kimber showed me around, to the huge bathroom with a jacuzzi tub, a palatial bedroom with a king-sized bed with silk blankets, and the "theater room" with a TV that stretched the width of the cabin and leather recliners. When we got to the main cabin and I viewed the magnificent throne-like seat, slightly elevated over the surrounding ones, I started laughing. "So what do you think O'Rourke would do if I sat in his throne chair?"

She smiled anxiously. "Can I show you to a comfortable corner Mrs. Morozov? It will make setting up your workstation a little easier."

I was so tempted to sit in the ridiculous throne chair but I didn't want the poor woman to have an aneurysm, so I followed her to a corner where a large and extremely expensive laptop was already set up. After fluttering around me, adjusting the heat, and offering me blankets, snacks, champagne - that one I accepted - Kimber told me that she'd be back with my cocktail and that O'Rourke would be calling in shortly.

I shifted uneasily, looking around the cabin, too nervous to settle in.

Sure enough, a buzz came from the open laptop and his face appeared on the screen. "Hello, Tania. I knew a woman with your cunning would have no trouble outwitting her bodyguards."

"What's the plan here, Nolan?" I asked flatly.

"Your flight is about three and a half hours, and I thought I might keep you busy."

"Nothing better to do, what's on your mind," I said, trying to look like this whole thing wasn't freaking me out. Like I was used to traveling on weird billionaire's planes for mysterious errands that would no doubt be horrible in some way.

"You are quite good with numbers, darling. My cybersecurity head notified me when you were poking around my finances when Papachristodoulopoulos approached me about investing in the Lincoln Street project."

"He did?"

*Well damn, I thought I had gotten in and out without a ripple!*

"Yes, I didn't take offense. I did fire him for not catching you more quickly."

Now I felt guilty.

"But I find myself thinking you could help me do a little digging," he continued.

"Sounds like you fired your cybersecurity guy a little too soon?"

"My cybersecurity staff numbers at over 200, along with several excellent freelance hackers," he chuckled condescendingly, "but I thought you might enjoy this since my system's ability to crack a firewall is unparalleled."

"Some people might think you're showing off right now," I said sourly, "but okay. What am I doing?"

He went to a split screen and I watched a waterfall of numbers pour down the monitor. "The O'Connell Mob have been storing their funds in various offshore banks and legitimate business concerns. This is money they must use to continue to function in other areas while they build their distillery business. It would be a terrible shame if the funds evaporated, right when they needed them the most, wouldn't it?"

"Can I just say that I find your spiteful nature to be your most attractive quality?" I asked, then wincing when I remembered I'd been on the receiving end of it.

"Thank you, I am very proud of it. I thought you'd enjoy this," he said magnanimously.

"You would be correct," I said, cracking my knuckles. "Because fuck those guys."

"Eloquently said, dear. Well, I shall leave you to it." The connection was closed before I could ask any more questions, but it was fine. He'd left me a trail of breadcrumbs. A few soft targets to start with, some O'Connell assets to chase.

I've always had a relationship with numbers. Spend as much time as I have going over them and it's understandable. Seven, for instance. Seven is an all-star number, you can count on seven. Four, too, but four is more likely to be plagued by division and complication. One hundred is not to be trusted. It's one of those numbers liars use when they're trying to make things look better than they are.

Diving in and out of random accounts and tracking country codes on transfer histories was fun. In fact, the possibility that I could strip those Irish pricks of their money was making this a positively Zen moment for me. In fact, when Kimber came back in to tell me we were landing, I was startled.

"Really? Already?" I asked, then thought about it. "Where are we landing, by the way?"

She smiled as if she was used to flying around people for her boss who had no idea where they were going.

"Dublin, Mrs. Morozov."

It felt like someone had just punched me hard in the solar plexus. It took me a minute to get my breath back. If I was being honest with myself, I knew all along that O'Rourke was going to throw me into the O'Connell mess. But if he put me in a position where I could distract Yuri, I will gut that man like a fish.

As the wheels touched the tarmac, I noticed something interesting in my search results. "Can I take the laptop with me?"

Kimber nodded, "It was meant for you. As a gift, I believe."

Marcus helped me out of the jet and into another expensive SUV with blacked-out windows. "Where are we headed?" I asked.

He looked at me in the rearview mirror, his expression impassive. In fact, I don't think I'd seen him have any other look than inscrutable so far. "To Mr. O'Rourke's home. He thought you would be more comfortable there than in a hotel."

*And completely under his thumb...* I thought crossly. It hit me that I was so close to Yuri right now. Mere miles from wherever he was and the need for him was painful. Was he all right? Was this plan to overturn the O'Connell's forcing all those horrible memories back into his brain? Without thinking about it, my phone was in my hand.

"You're not calling him, you idiot," I whispered.


The Range Rover was blazing along a ribbon of a road by the ocean, Marcus turned a corner and there it was…

"Oh for- are you serious right now?"

"Ma'am?" Marcus enquired politely.

I had to laugh because of course this man would have a castle. "That is a castle. Nolan has a castle."

"Yes," he agreed, "the castle was originally constructed in 1270. Since then, numerous improvements have…"

I sat back and let Marcus' history lesson wash over me. Only twelve months ago I had never heard of the Morozov Bratva. Ella had not been kidnapped by Maksim. I had not yet encountered the glory of Yuri's bedazzled cock. And now, I'm driving up to a castle and trying to figure out what exactly this sociopathic billionaire is going to expect of me.

My mother's stern voice from when I finally worked up the

courage to call and tell her I was married came back to me. "I knew you'd never have a normal life. But it's going to be an interesting one. So, you just keep it together, little missy! You remember who you are and where you came from and you'll be fine. Also, send me some of those Russian nesting dolls because they are adorable."

*Keep it together, girl*, I think as we pull up in front of the massive front doors. *I got this.*

There was a proper English butler with enormous gravitas in Nolan's castle, who led me to a guest suite. I passed suits of armor nestling suspiciously in alcoves, looking like they wanted to lunge out at me. And I thought Yuri's mansion was drafty? I'm freezing by the time the butler - whose name was James, not Jeeves which would have been the best thing ever - had instructed me on every possible amenity in my suite and finally shut the door.

The ancient bed was so high that I had to make a running start to hop up on it, which was ungainly enough that I was grateful no one was there to witness it.

Dialing Ella, I wondered if the room was bugged. Oh, well.

"Omigod Tan I'm so glad you called; I haven't been able to sleep!"

I cringed, feeling guilty. "It's okay, honey. I'm in Dublin, which should not have surprised me, huh?"

"I don't like how this man is manipulating the situation," she sounds furious. "Maksim and Yuri are placing a lot of faith in his intel and now he's got you there? I hate this!"

Rubbing my forehead, I looked out one of the four-hundred-year-old windows at the surf crashing against the beach below the castle. "I know there's a lot riding on this, Els. Maybe everything is riding on this. But even an oligarch with a narcissistic personality disorder isn't insane enough to go against the Morozov Bratva."

"And the Turgenev Bratva, and The Corporation, and the Toscano Mafia," she added.

"Exactly. Nolan set me up with one of their spy programs to look into the O'Connell clan's finances. They're strapped for cash after buying and building up this distillery. If we can find their hidden money reserves, that could finish them off after Yuri and Maksim take over the distillery."

"That doesn't make sense," she pondered, "you could have done that here. He didn't need to fly you to Dublin and in the middle of whatever is about to happen. There's got to be more to this favor."

"Yeah," I said uncomfortably, "that had occurred to me. But once the guys take over the distillery, leaving the O'Connell mob broke is the best 'fuck you' ever, right?"

"Honey… you don't think that they're just going to… take the distillery, right?" Ella says.

It feels like my body temperature just dropped twenty degrees. "What?"

I hear her sigh softly, that anxious little sound she makes when she's really stressed out. "They're going to kill the leaders of the clan. Between what happened to you and me, and what happened to Yuri? Their father sounds like a complete bastard to me, but he taught both of them that when someone hits you, you beat them to death. Any strike against the Bratva must be met with ten times the violence."

"How do you know that?" I said, trying to make my numb tongue work properly.

"I've been… aware of the inner workings of the Bratva longer than you have, Tan. You need to be ready for this, okay?"

I thought about what the O'Connell's had done to Yuri. What they had done to Ella. "I'll be ready."

We do our "love your guts" sign-off and I hang up, putting my head between my knees and trying to catch a full breath. Who gets used to this? How does anyone get used to this?

The laptop 'pings!' helpfully and I see that the thread I'd been pulling on from one of the O'Connell accounts has unraveled. I pushed away the thoughts of death and fear and concentrated on something I know how to control, my numbers.

It's 2 am when O'Rourke's image pops up on the laptop screen, making me yelp. "It's quite late, Tania dear. You should be asleep."

"You're the one who gave me all these leads to follow," I reminded him. "By the way, the O'Connell's aren't even trying to hide all the mining shares in New Zealand, and their accounts in the Cayman Island banks are unsecured."

"I am very pleased with your progress. However, you have more work to do today, so get some rest." He looked perfectly put together, from what I could see, still in a suit and tie.

"Do you ever sleep, Nolan, or just hang upside down like a bat?"

He chuckled indulgently, "I do just fine. Now, to bed with you. There's much yet to do."

"Yeah…" I said, "do you want to share what's next with me?"

He gave me a smile that, had he been in the room with me, I would have punched right off his mouth. So smug, enjoying the anxiety and uncertainty he was causing me. All part of his little game.

"Not tonight," he said gently, "go to sleep, Tania."

# CHAPTER TWENTY-TWO

*In which Tania learns about single pot stills and third-best jets.*

*Yuri…*

Maksim was stretched out on the couch in the house Thomas had considerately provided for us; a large stone cottage that he and his wife, Lauren used occasionally when business took them to Dublin.

"Let's go over the plan again," he said, rubbing his eyes.

"Men from The Corporation and the Toscano's will be dressed as waiters, busboys, and parking attendants at the distillery's event center," Patrick said. "We're making sure to plant men that the O'Connell clan wouldn't have seen around before."

"The chemist who helped us compound the gas that Ella isolated has the dosages ready for the whiskey tasting," I added. "The drug is odorless and tasteless. On an average 200-pound man, it takes effect within three minutes. Specialty dosing the bigger men is problematic, so we will have men stationed closer to them if they have to be taken out quickly."

"And O'Rourke?" Maksim asked in the same tone he would use to enquire about a flesh-eating bacteria.

I scowled, "Following through as promised. He will be making the third toast and will give the signal."

"Where is he now?"

Shrugging tiredly, I said, "When I spoke to him this morning, he was at his castle in Malahide."

*Tania…*

A genteel tap on my door dragged me kicking and screaming out of my exhausted sleep, and I was about to shout, "Go away!" until I remembered that I was currently enjoying the "hospitality" of Nolan O'Rourke. I rolled on my back, groaning. I used to be happy when I woke up. Now there's this life-sized cloud of doom the minute I open my eyes.

Checking my phone, I groaned. It was almost 10 am here in rainy Dublin and my exhaustion was completely my own fault for staying up for another three hours after my bedtime call from my host.

But I'd isolated so many juicy little money caches! The O'Connell Mob may be vicious, murderous pricks, but they sucked at hiding money. It made me wonder how they were going to pull off something as detail-oriented as money laundering.

There was a second knock on my door, less genteel than the first and I called out, "Come in!" in my most pleasant guest voice.

This was a mistake.

A parade of women marched through, the first carrying a big breakfast tray - yay! - followed by others pushing a dress rack and hauling bags and cases.

"Uh, what's up, ladies?" I croaked.

"Good morning, Mrs. Morozov," the woman carrying the tray placed it on my lap. "I'm Mrs. Walsh, the housekeeper of Malahide Castle and these are your stylists. They are here to get you ready."

I was silently thankful I had fallen asleep in my clothes last night. Naked and in a room full of strange women was more than I was ready for this morning. "Okay, thank you, Mrs. Walsh. What um… am I getting ready for?"

One of the women wearing a black smock seated herself comfortably on a pretty silk-covered chair next to the bed while the housekeeper poured me coffee. "Hi, I'm Marie, and Mr. O'Rourke has given us quite a lot to do in a very short time, so if you could just hurry breakfast along, I'll debrief you on the assignment, all right?"

Clutching a muffin in one hand and my coffee in the other, I nodded a little too fast. "Sure, debriefing." I looked down at the exquisite china cup Mrs. Walsh had used for my coffee. It was delicate Limoges porcelain and I was afraid to hold it too tightly. I would *not* be the one who broke a cup and ruined a matching set of what was likely two-hundred-year-old castle china. Taking one tremulous sip, I moaned in delight at the perfectly roasted coffee with fresh cream. Realizing Marie was still seated stiffly next to me on her chair and looking a little uncomfortable with my flavor-gasm, I stuffed a piece of muffin in my mouth and nodded invitingly at her.

"You'll be impersonating Maureen Ryan, the Libation Historian at the O'Connell Distillery whiskey unveiling, so-"

"Libation Historian?" I tried not to spit out my muffin. "What would that be, exactly?"

"The Libation Historian joins the master distiller in celebrating the new O'Connell Collection by telling the story of the liquor's origin," Marie explained, "we will make you look exactly like Maureen and you will be hosting the new brand's unveiling at the O'Connell Distillery tonight."

I choked on my mouthful of coffee.

"T- tonight?" I wheezed.

"Mm-hmm," she nodded brightly, "and there's quite a bit of

information to absorb, since the Libation Historian is expected to be the expert on single pot still whiskey, and there will be questions, of course, about the triple distillation and heritage barley grain used in the process."

Seizing the fine linen napkin off the breakfast tray, I jammed it against my mouth until I was sure I wasn't going to throw up.

The other women, also sporting matching black smocks, were unpacking a trunk load of makeup, six wigs, and several outfits.

Marie was still talking. "...so as soon as you finish breakfast, we can get started."

"Could you give me a moment?" I squeaked out. "Mrs. Walsh, could I trouble you to take me to see Nolan? It seems I have some questions since my job description keeps… evolving."

She folded her hands, smiling pleasantly at me. "Mr. O'Rourke anticipated your response but wished me to impart that he is unavailable this morning but will meet with you this afternoon to examine you in character as Maureen Ryan."

My left eyelid twitched as I attempted to smile at her.

"I cannot do this in an Irish accent."

I was reading through the thick notebook of information I was expected to memorize before tonight, and the makeup artist kept clucking irritably as she blotted the sweat off my face.

"Fortunately, Maureen Ryan is American-born Irish, so your accent is acceptable," Marie said, trying one pair of glasses on me, and then another.

"We've been at this for six hours and I need another six days to pull this off. Or more like six weeks. I can't become a whiskey expert in six hours - I don't even like whiskey!" I was trying to keep calm because showing agitation just meant they would all go a little harder with their tasks; jamming wigs on my head, and aggressively blending foundation to the point the top layer of skin was gone from my cheeks and nose.

"Tell me about the process of distilling The O'Connell Collection again," she said, relentless and indifferent to my fear.

My head drops back as I groan, looking at the magnificent fresco painted on my bedroom ceiling. I think it's Aphrodite sailing onto land in her fancy clamshell. Gathering my scattered thoughts, I try to recall everything I'd memorized today.

"The O'Connell Collection is a thirty-year-old triple-distilled single malt whiskey," I recited dutifully, "the unique process of a single pot still gives the drink a singular blend of heritage Irish barley, both malted and green."

"It was important to the O'Connell Clan, the new owners of the Liberties District Distillery, to introduce a unique distillation that will reclaim the prestige that Irish whiskey has always been famous for on the international stage."

"Tell me more about the flavors," Marie prodded.

"The O'Connell Collection ultra-rare whiskey was taken from a single barrel, a 401 Pedro Ximénez cask. It is deep treacle in color, and-"

"Excellent!" There was applause from the doorway and we turned to find that elusive son of a bitch O'Rourke, smiling and clapping in a paternal fashion like I was a sixth grader at my ballet recital. "Well done, dear. And the resemblance to Maureen? Uncanny."

"Thank you, Nolan." I managed to keep my voice under a shriek. "May I speak with you for a moment?"

"Of course." He looked at me politely, hands folded. All the women in the room also looked at me.

"Um... somewhere else?"

He never took his eyes off me. "Ladies?" They all scooted out of the room instantly and silently. It was a little creepy.

Folding my arms stubbornly, I shook my head. "I'm not a master of international intrigue, like you, but you've been playing with me since I stepped on your magnificent, 'I'm such a billionaire' jet with the big throne chair."

Even his frown was pretty. "Are you unhappy because I didn't send my best jet?"

"What?"

"I was using my primary jet, so it wasn't available, I fear."

Now I was distracted. "You think I would be unhappy because I was using your second-best jet?"

"Well, my second-best jet was in France. I was craving some lovely little croissants made by a bakery in-"

"You sent your second-best jet to France for baked goods?" I might have been laughing a little too hard, but I was so wound up, it felt good to find something ridiculous instead of terrifying. "Hey, it's your world, we all just live in it. Please help me understand. What is the plan here? Do you really think I can pull off impersonating a whiskey expert? And why? What are you really expecting me to do tonight? Because it's not chattering about the 'slight tobacco backdrop and silky-smooth cherry notes.'"

O'Rourke's eyes had gone the color of frozen earth. "I expect you to play your role. I expect you to be convincing."

It felt like the room temperature just plunged fifty degrees.

"Do I really look like this Maureen Ryan?" I kept my voice steady; I wouldn't let this eccentric, rich creep intimidate me. "How is my taking her place benefitting you?"

"Because this will be a legendary night for the O'Connell Distillery," he said, his smile chilly enough that I really wish he hadn't bothered. "You need to be my eyes and ears. My toast will be the third, and after that, you have fulfilled your obligation to me."

He turned me briskly enough that I let out a yelp, looking into the mirror. It was over the top huge with a thick gold-leafed frame. "Look at yourself."

The red wig was cut in a long bob with heavy bangs, which matched the makeup spackled onto my face. "If I smile, I'm going to crack this foundation wide open," I mumbled. The stylist had tried to wedge blue contact lenses on my eyeballs, but I wrestled the case away from her and did it myself. They made my eyes water and itch.

"We'll use this pair," O'Rourke said, handing me some scholarly-looking glasses with black frames. "There is a camera in the eyewear so we can see what's happening and a mic in your lapel pin."

"What…" I shook my head, more confused than ever. "What am I looking and listening for?"

He smiled over my shoulder at our reflection. "I will know when you see it." He had his hands on my shoulders, long fingers and nicely manicured. I stepped away from him, which seemed more polite than swatting them off me.

"You're putting me in the middle of Yuri and Maksim's operation," I pushed a little harder for answers, "this could endanger my husband if he gets distracted."

O'Rourke shrugged. "You're unrecognizable, darling. He won't even know you're there. Play your part and I'll pluck you out before there's any unpleasantness."

"So something terrible *is* going to happen tonight," I said, my lips numb.

He tilts his handsome head, considering it. "Possibly."

"Are you bipolar?" I demanded, "Is that the real issue here?"

Even his shrug was elegant. "Oh, I'll be taking your phone and laptop. You won't need them."

"No!" My gaze darts over to my phone, sitting on the elaborate nightstand. "I'm here paying off my debt to you, Nolan. You're not my dad taking away my electronics because I missed curfew."

"Yes, but maybe…" he drew it out, likely to make me insane which was going to take very little effort at this point. "Maybe you will start getting a bit nervous? Wanting to chat with your best friend Ella about your concerns?" He strolled a little closer, deliberately looming over me, "Perhaps Ella would be worried enough to call Maksim? Then, these two men you seem so concerned about would be distracted? This is a complicated scenario tonight with many moving parts, dear."

My heart was thumping at just a touch under myocardial infarction level. "I won't call anyone," I managed, "but you're not taking away my ability to communicate."

How had I ever thought this conniving fuck was attractive? His smile downgraded to a frozen grin. "All the same, you will leave them here. I do hope you've memorized your script for tonight."

"I'll go over everything in the car," I tried to sound confident, but I'm pretty sure I looked ready to burst into tears. Which I was.

# CHAPTER TWENTY-THREE

*In which Tania discovers that when things are bad, they can still get so much worse.*

**Tania...**

I am going to fucking die.

I stepped out of the Range Rover, so terrified I was about to vomit on the front step of the distillery. What the hell was O'Rourke thinking? A six-hour crash course would make me sound like a... libation historian? I didn't even know that was a thing!

Remembering O'Rourke's nasty little smile, I straightened my shoulders and sucked in a deep breath. I cannot let these Irish assholes be suspicious of me. I can't become a risk to Yuri and the men poised to take over the new O'Connell Distillery.

So, when an older gent in a good suit with red hair fading to gray came bustling down the stairs, I held out my hand authoritatively. "Kenneth Byrne? A pleasure. I'm Maureen Ryan."

"So happy you could make it," he enthused, pumping my hand up and down vigorously in his. "While I certainly know our product as the distiller, I know your grasp of the history behind it will make the presentation so much more satisfying."

The history. Of whiskey. Oh, god I'm definitely going to die tonight.

Attempting to look wise, I pushed my glasses back up and nodded. "Indeed. I'm very much looking forward to seeing your process for the O'Connell Collection."

Byrne gave me an excited grin. "Shall we?" He extended his arm and I took it.

"We shall."

I'd been on a wine tour when Ella and I visited Napa Valley in California once and had loved it - how beautiful the vineyards were, the elegant stone houses, the mysterious caves where the wine was stored in massive casks.

I had not expected a distillery that was as uniquely beautiful.

The O'Connell Distillery was at the end of one of the most gorgeous old streets in Dublin. It was a massive brick building built a hundred and fifty years ago and it was magnificent, with the old paned windows, curved at the top to a point like a cathedral's and a slate roof. Inside, their designer wisely kept the ancient oak floors, the stone fireplaces, and even the modern updates, like the exposed silver duct work and heavy industrial-style lights blended together perfectly.

Byrne walked me through the exhibition space quickly with an apology and a promise to go through for a better look at the distillery later. "I'm a little nervous, and I'd really like to coordinate tonight's script with you now."

I tried to give an expression of well-bred surprise. "You? You've been the master distiller here for, what, twenty years? Surely you can't be nervous."

"These are new owners and they are not forgiving of mistakes." It was all he was willing to say and I certainly couldn't blame him.

"We'll go over it as many times as we need to make the evening flawless," I assured him, not mentioning that if anyone screwed up tonight, it would be me.

The event space was lovely, located on the second floor with a long deck area overlooking the gleaming copper pot stills and oak barrel fermenters. *At least I remember what they're called,* I thought, trying to build some confidence. The other side looked out on the old cobblestone street and thankfully, few people strolled on the sidewalk. I didn't know what the evening entailed, but I was pretty sure it included violence and the fewer innocent bystanders, the better. Two long mahogany bars flanked each side of the room and the center held a small raised platform with a podium and a mic.

"…So they'll roll the cask in and place it here…"

Oh, crap Byrne was talking. He was gesturing here and there, showing me the plan of action while waiters were setting up round tables with white linen and I tried to pay attention.

"How many people are we expecting tonight?" I asked.

"Around a hundred," he said distractedly, "the O'Connell's are bringing in all their most important… ah… family members."

Watching one of the waiters bringing in clean glasses, I couldn't help think he looked familiar. I could have sworn he was one of Thomas and Lauren's bodyguards from that disastrous New Year's Eve party last year when the enemies of the Morozov Bratva opened fire at the stroke of midnight. I still couldn't hear fireworks going off without jumping and shrieking. He looked up briefly and then away, and I did the same. Of course, Yuri and Maksim will have people infiltrating tonight. And here I am staring at one of them like a moron.

Trying to re-grasp my painstakingly memorized information from this morning, I asked, "Are we still planning for three formal toasts?"

"Yes," he consulted his iPad. "The first from the head of the clan,

Padraic, the second will be from his son Colm, and the third from their chief investor in this project, Nolan O'Rourke."

*You sneaky son of a bitch!* I thought. Of course, he'd be here. Was O'Rourke here to help Yuri and Maksim, or to totally fuck everything up? If it was the latter, maybe it was good that I was here. I would stop him in any way possible if he gets in my husband's way.

**One hour before the party...**

Byrne insisted that I try the sacred whiskey that we're rolling out tonight, the O'Connell Collection batch. He blathered on about the "smoked caramel on the back palate, which gives way to the vanilla cigar of the finish," and my brain felt like it was leaking out of my ears.

"I'll have what the lady is having," a deep Irish brogue pipes up from behind me.

*Well, I'm having an imminent panic attack and I'm not sure they have any more of those behind the bar, but go for it,* I thought.

"Mr. O'Connell, hello sir! I didn't know you were here already, I would have come out to greet you!" Poor Byrne was almost lobster red with anxiety and man, can I relate.

Forcing myself to turn around, I offer what I suspect is a terrible-looking smile, more like a grimace as he introduced me to the Underboss and second in command of the O'Connell mob.

"Sir, allow me to introduce the finest Libation Historian in the whiskey field, Maureen Ryan," he said, gesturing toward me as if hoping it would take the heat off of him.

Colm O'Connell had dark hair and a face like an angry bulldog, and his sharp blue eyes looked me over appraisingly. "Ah, I thought you were single."

My brow rose. *That's* the first thing he wants to know? Then I look down at my wedding ring and groan silently. "Uh, a newlywed," I said, raising my hand to show it off, fluttering my fingers nervously. "And how are you? You must be looking forward to tonight, after all these months of hard work."

"Years," he corrected coldly, "years. It's been a long road to bring the O'Connell family to the level we deserve."

This is the man that ordered the kidnapping and torture of my husband. This is the man who made my Yuri suffer so terribly that I'd wondered if he could ever climb out of the dark pit where they tried to bury him. I wanted to take the knife the bartender was using to cut limes and stab this motherfucker in the eye with it.

His eyes narrowed, watching me. Shit.

"Well, it sounds like it's been a long road, but here you are, the owners of the oldest and most prestigious whiskey distillery in Ireland and about to debut what will be the finest product introduced in decades," I said, trying to smile.

O'Connell took his glass from the terrified bartender and lifted it in a toast. *"Go dtí an méid atá tuillte againn."*

"To what we deserve," Byrne echoed, nervously sipping his whiskey.

*As a toast, that really sucks in this context*, I think, but I repeat it, then drink the fancy thirty-year-old whiskey.

"Ah, goddamn that's good," O'Connell groans.

"Can you taste the oak of the cask?" I offer, trying to keep my hand from shaking, "the age of the 401 Pedro-"

"I don't need to hear the fancy shite," he cut me off. "Just make it look good tonight, Maureen." To my horror, he reached out, running one of his stubby, tobacco-stained fingers down my neck. "We'll talk after."

"Of course," I assured him, "but if you'll excuse me, I have to go over some notes with Mr. Byrne, if you could spare him for a moment?"

I didn't like the way this creepy fuck was staring at me. It's not even the look of a man who found me attractive, more the expectation that he was going to fuck me. Like he did this a lot. Just… grabbed other human beings and expected them to drop to their knees and be grateful about it.

O'Connell waved his hand impatiently. "Go. But you better be ready to make this the biggest fuckin' night this dump has ever seen."

Byrne visibly stiffened at hearing his beloved distillery called a 'dump,' but he practically bows as he backs away.

*Yuri…*

I have had a persistent urge to call Tania all day. It is not possible; there is too much to do and we don't risk personal phone calls during a sensitive operation like this, but it's impossible to shake.

Maksim catches me, "Stop staring at your phone and get your focus back where it needs to be."

"Of course, you never think once about Ella," I retort, "not with the steely self-control of a Pakhan."

Scowling, he leaned in closer. "Of course, I do. I think about her far too much. But if we don't focus, we're not only risking our lives, we're risking the men from the three allies who are loyal enough to share their soldiers with us."

My scar was throbbing and I rubbed it. "You are right, brother. Patrick just checked in; his group of men are in place. Have you spoken with the Toscano's?"

We continue checking in with our allies, making certain everyone is where they are supposed to be, that the guns are positioned for instant distribution, but my mind is still on Tania. Some nagging little push in my brain, like there is a detail

I've forgotten.

*Tania...*

I didn't know if I was just losing it, or if the entire waitstaff are plants from Yuri and Maksim. I kept feeling flashes of recognition and just avoided looking at them at all. I heard the low buzz of people entering the reception area as the band started up with a traditional tune, I think it's "The Wren's Nest." The fiddle player sounded a little flat, though I really was not expert enough myself to judge him. I hid in the bathroom a little longer, wanting to splash some cold water on my face but I'm too worried that it would ruin the elaborate makeup job.

"Um, one, two, three? Can you hear me?" I spoke into my lapel mic and immediately felt like a complete idiot.

Who *does* this? I took deep breaths, trying to calm my racing heart. Although Nolan was the one to throw me into this, taking over the distillery and weakening the O'Connell clan was Yuri and Maksim's plan. My job as Yuri's wife is to help him, however I can. I will suck it up and just… handle it. Making the sign of the cross and murmuring a quick prayer, I straightened my spy glasses and told my reflection, "Get your ass back out there, Maureen Ryan."

There were already guests - a hundred or so - strolling around the reception area. I didn't see any wives or families here, for which I was grateful. It meant less chance of innocents getting caught in the crossfire. There didn't seem to be any media either, though this seemed like an ideal time to show off the newly remodeled distillery, and that was not a good sign. It was an odd crowd, even for being made men, they all seemed stone-cold sober, dressed well and no one was having any fun. Not in front of O'Connell Senior, anyway. I realized that this was a mob meeting, not a celebration

*Shiiit,* I groaned silently, *there's going to be guns everywhere tonight.*

"There you are, Maureen!" Poor Bryne, who's entire being was radiating anxiety, hustled me off to the stage.

The lights on the stage made it difficult to see anyone in the crowd, and I was fine with that. This wasn't a well-bred crowd here for an elite event, this was a herd of tightly buttoned up monsters who were here for their chief, and they were not listening to my careful speech about the perfection of the distillery's single pot still technique and the heritage grains locally sourced for the production and the triple distillation and… God, I'm even boring myself.

"The Macallan 1926 was described as the 'Holy Grail of whiskey' when the first bottle sold at auction for one point nine million pounds. Mr. Byrne and I firmly believe the O'Connell Collection will easily eclipse that price." There was a drunken cheer as I finish my history lesson and Byrne hastily steps to the mic.

"*Ceann Fine*, will you please join us for the presentation of the cask and the first toast?"

The floor shook under the stomping and cheers from the men as their lunatic chief stepped up. Padraic O'Connell was a giant barrel-shaped man with a shock of white hair. He took the mic away from a terrified Bryne and shouted, "Bring in the cask!"

A roar went up as the doors to the service area opened and a large wooden cask was rolled in. It was placed in a well-lit spot next to the stage and Padraic put a reverent hand on it. "This is the symbol of our new power. And a promise that we will not rest until we take back everything owed to us." His eyes looked blood red in the glare of the stage lighting and it was easy to picture this evil fuck as some kind of Celtic demon rising from Hell to celebrate.

He pulled open his shirt and with an eerie synchronicity, so did all the men in the room. They all had the same mark on their chests and I realized it was a brand. The same brand burned into the cask of whiskey.

Padriac's brand was hard and black and clearly there long enough to look almost fused into his chest, as was his son's. Some of the brands on the younger guys were red and swollen, like they were freshly burned into their skin. The brand is some variation of the Celtic Knot, but twisted and gnarled and it was *big.* How much must that have hurt, how much agony just to prove themselves?

*Don't you dare throw up,* I thought frantically, *don't you dare!*

The roar went up; "*Uí Chonaill go deo!*"

"O'Connells forever!" Padraic shouted again, the lights defining the ugly black burn on his chest. "Now lads, let's tap this bastard!"

Another huge cheer rose as Bryne deftly inserted the spigot and as the whiskey flowed, waiters filled the glasses and distributed them through the crowd.

My gaze darted to Padraic and he was looking at me, eyes narrowed. Maybe I wasn't hiding my horror well enough. The lights in the room were slowly dimming, gaining a reddish tinge like a nightclub's dance floor. The crimson glow terrified me, turning all these made men into monsters, lending a bloody tinge to their skin and eyes.

"Colm O'Connell will lead the next toast," Bryne intones, a sheen of sweat on his forehead and his shaking hands showing I'm not the only one scared half out of my mind.

The men were stirring and moving around like a pack of wolves, with more noises and grunts than speech and some hysterical part of my brain wondered if this thirty-year-old whiskey was really some horrible transformation potion that was turning them into the monsters they really are. Like their skin suits were being stripped away and showing the gnarled meat and bones and claws underneath.

Colm deliberately brushed against me, making his way to the podium and my skin tried to crawl right off my body. I could still feel his chest against my back like a film of slime.

"Brothers!" Colm roared, "We have spilled blood. We have shed our own. But this night begins a new era for our family. New allies." He nods at Nolan O'Rourke, who makes his way gracefully to the edge of the stage. He was wearing a perfectly cut blue suit with a green silk tie, and as I squinted closer, a pin of the O'Connell crest. Their *crest?* That seems pretty friendly.

*You bastard,* I thought, *you better not be fucking with Yuri and Maksim or I swear to god I will kill you myself.*

That demented freak Colm was still shouting. "We will kill every fekkin' piece of shite who crosses us - the Morozov's, The Corporation - any fucker who comes at us will be a rotting corpse, left in a pile with the rest of their family. Wife. Kids. Da and Ma - we will kill 'em all!" He raised the second glass of whiskey and downed it, his herd of killers doing the same.

I can't breathe. My chest was heaving in oxygen but I can't breathe and now I'm wondering if these brainsick *hijos de puta* have already murdered my Yuri. Is he even alive? Has Nolan been holding me and taking away my phone to hide it from me?

Someone touched my elbow and I jumped and just barely stifled the scream surging up my throat. "Hush now, lambkin. You look terrified and not at all professional." It was O'Rourke.

"Wh- what the hell is this?" I wheezed, "This isn't a party it's a fucking war council. What are you *doing?*"

I noticed Colm watching us and apparently, Nolan did too, because he gave me a brisk, impersonal pat and continued to the stage. O'Rourke straightened his already straight tie and clears his throat, smiling pleasantly. "My friends!" His voice carried perfectly through the room, his tone of paternal warmth in this setting was extra creepy. I watched as a few of the men in the audience shook their heads, as if they were confused. A couple of others rubbed their eyes.

The lights in the back of the room dimmed again, making it harder to see past the stage. O'Connell Senior and Junior were standing next to O'Rourke like they were all the best of buddies.

"My friends," he repeated, "this is indeed a magnificent day for the O'Connell Clan; for your family and your continued good fortune. This distillery represents more than just a legitimate and prestigious business concern, but even better, the beginning of the kind of power your ancestors fought for. You have made helpful and influential friends." He paused, smiling modestly at the ripple of laughter through the room, though most of the men stared at him blankly, waiting for the passing waiters to hand them their third drink.

Smoothing down the pristine lapel of his suit, O'Rourke continued. Slower, with longer pauses as he looked around the room. There were some rumbles of impatience, but this conniving dick was taking his sweet time. Even the two O'Connell's on stage were swaying with eagerness to take the last shot of whiskey.

I thought I heard a 'thud!' in the back of the room, and O'Rourke raised his voice. "To the most powerful family in this new world, the O'Connell family!" He drained his glass, as did Colm and Padraic. There was another 'thud!' and another… what the hell-

Then the shooting started and it was just like New Year's Eve all over again.

*Yuri…*

"Everything is going just the way we mapped it out," I murmured. I heard Maksim softly issue an order before he answered me in my earpiece.

"All clear here," he said, "you have eyes on O'Rourke?"

"Yes, his security is edging into a perimeter around him now, it looks like he is almost finished with the toast- wait, three of O'Connell's men just dropped like a bag of rocks. The drug is taking effect quicker than we expected."

I watched O'Rourke, who was talking louder to cover the sound of unconscious bodies hitting the floor. There are four gigantic bastards - the old man O'Connell's guards - who are barely swaying. They were within arm's reach of him and his son. "Patrick?" I whisper.

He answered back instantly, "I'm here, boss."

"The old man's security detail does not look even remotely affected by the drug. Move some men into position as quietly as you can. They need to be taken out the second O'Rourke's toast is done."

"On it."

O'Rourke was speaking slowly, and I knew he was dragging out his speech to give the drug time to take effect, but with three O'Connell soldiers down, we had seconds to get into place before they realized what was happening. The master distiller and the woman who gave a rousing speech about the history of the product were standing off to the side, but still too much in the spotlight.

*Who was supposed to cover them?* I thought, *they need to be pulled out of here immediately.*

"Dario, do you have eyes on the distiller and the redhead?"

"Of course, I do," he answered, "she's hot as hell and I'm going to comfort her after her traumatic experience tonight."

"Just make sure they're covered," I said, exasperated. Only Dario would try to hit on a woman during a shootout. Narrowing my eyes, I watched her move restlessly. She was very pretty... she subtly moved her palms against her skirt, obviously trying to dry them. Looking at her hands, my heart nearly stopped.

The woman - Maureen - was wearing a magnificent wedding ring. A brilliant yellow shade that flashed in the stage lighting. A ring identical to my wife's.

"*Blyat*'!" I hissed, "The redhead is Tania!"

Maksim's voice broke through the chatter. "There's no way."

"She's staring at that bastard O'Rourke like she knows exactly what he's doing and unless this Maureen somehow managed to snag an identical wedding ring to the one-of-a-kind gem I gave to Tania, that is my wife!" I was already moving to the left, slipping through one of the windows leading to the terrace, where thirty of our men were poised for their signal to start shooting.

The first round of gunfire blasted through the room and I watched Tania jump and shriek, putting her hands over her ears.

"Not yet!" I shouted, knowing it was too late. I had to get to her before a bullet did. The staccato bursts of automatic fire rattled through the room, blood sprayed over the pristine white of the tablecloths and O'Connell men were being mowed down like a grisly harvest and my wife was still lit up like the world's easiest target by the goddamned spotlights.

A man in front of me had gotten his gun out, firing unsteadily around him and hitting two of his own people before aiming at me. Staggering backward, it felt like someone had just hit my chest with a cricket bat. I was wearing a bulletproof vest but it still hurt like hell. I put a bullet in him before he could get off another lucky shot.

Tania was down, yanking the distiller down with her and crawling toward the edge of the platform. My smart girl. That bastard O'Rourke was standing casually behind his human wall of bodyguards, watching them shoot everyone who was not us.

*The old man and his son- where were they? They had been on the stage, right next to that Irish prick, where-*

I heard Tania scream, Colm O'Connell had abandoned his wounded father and wrapped his arm around her neck, his gun to her head as he dragged her toward an exit.

"Cover me, you fekkin' little-" Padraic O'Connell coughed up a gout of blood, trying to scream at his son to come back and save him.

"Maksim!" I shouted into the mic on my jacket, "Colm's got Tania! Kill the old man. I'm going after her."

"Wait-" I could barely hear him, "Yuri, wait for backup!"

I shot the reeling, staggering guard between me and the door they had disappeared through. There was no time.

# CHAPTER TWENTY-FOUR

*In which Tania and Yuri discover how much of a manipulative asshole a sociopathic billionaire can be.*

**Tania…**

"Drag your feet and I'll fekkin' shoot you right now!"

Colm was trying to yank me loose from my desperate grip on the doorway. O'Rourke had just *stood* there, smiling behind his impenetrable barrier of bodyguards while poor Byrne and I were dodging bullets. He'd just left us out there! Now this homicidal fuck was probably going to kill me as soon as my usefulness as a human shield was gone.

I'd seen Yuri. He was sprinting for the stage, eyes wide with horror. Did he know it was me? Did he recognize me, even in disguise? Oh, god he was distracted, they could shoot him oh god-

A red wave of pain slammed into my cheekbone as Colm hit me with his gun.

"Move, ya slag or I swear-"

"Drop the gun, O'Connell." Yuri was there, blocking the way out with his gun trained on this prick who had me in a chokehold. "Take your hands off of her and I'll let you live."

"You're full of shite, Morozov," he shouted, "I shoulda cut your fekkin arm off when-"

Yuri was looking at me, his gun steady and aimed at O'Connell's head. His eyes moved to the left briefly and he gave me a small nod. I dropped to my knees, falling to my left and away from the gun pressed to my head as I heard Yuri fire. I barely heard the thud through the ringing in my ears, I definitely felt the spray of something wet against my leg as I curled into a ball, shuddering. Gasping, I tried to suck more air into my lungs, but they weren't working. There were dead bodies everywhere in that room and the stench of smoke and gunpowder and-

Thick arms wrapped around me, holding me tightly. "I have you *moye serdtse*, my heart, shhh, you're safe." It took me a minute to realize it was Yuri. I wanted to be brave and tough. Instead, I started sobbing, wiping compulsively at O'Connell's blood on my arm.

"I'm sorry, I know this is hard," he soothed, "I need you to listen to me. Gavrill is here, he's going to take you to a safe place while we finish this-"

"Don't!" I clutched his shirt, "Don't go. Please just stay with me, okay?" Through my ringing ears, I could hear the gunfire slowing down to sporadic bursts now, and I buried my face in his neck.

"I have to go back, I have to make sure everyone is safe. I will only be a moment. Can you be strong for me, my *Koroleva?*" He tried to soothe me as I nodded my head mindlessly. He handed me over to Gavrill, gently pulling my fingers loose. There were two other guards covering us and he glared at them. "Keep my wife safe," he said. "Nothing else matters."

I was sobbing too hard to say anything else, and Gavrill took off, carrying me tightly. "It's okay, Miss Tania," he said, "he'll be okay. I'm going to get you out of here." I closed my eyes to block everything out and then it all faded to black.

After that, even when I woke up there were just... flashes. A word

here and there, a penlight shone in my eye, and my pulse taken. I was too tired to answer any questions.

*Yuri...*

The entire gunfight at the distillery took less than ten minutes. Ten minutes and a hundred O'Connell's dead. Even for men hardened and used to death, this was overwhelming. Most of our men were silent, but oddly, the Toscano soldiers were chuckling, sharing smokes and flasks of something that smelled a lot like rubbing alcohol.

"Is there anything that shakes the confidence of the *famiglia?*" I asked Giovanni, who was watching his troops with some amusement.

"We have seen worse," he said cryptically.

We were in a warehouse provided by Thomas, who was still impeccable in his suit and snowy white shirt, and gazing at a handcuffed and bloody Padraic. He had his hands in his pockets, thoughtfully looking over the last O'Connell as he struggled against his bonds and screamed obscenities from his bloody mouth.

"Fekkin' bastards, you're all gonna die for this!" He spat out blood and Thomas casually angled his stance so that it landed on the floor with a nauseating splash. "I'll have your families killed! Everyone from your sweet gran to the smallest baby, you-"

Thomas casually backhanded the old man, sending another spray of blood on to the wall. "You won't live long enough to issue any orders, and anyone who would take them is dead in that distillery." O'Connell howled in rage as Thomas walked away, chuckling.

Maksim put his hand on my shoulder. "Do you want to stay and finish him, or go to Tania?"

"What I want," I said, teeth clenched, "is O'Rourke. I want him to tell me why he put my wife in the line of fire before I beat him to death." All my fury and terror came back to me, the horror of realizing the redhead on stage was Tania and knowing he did this to her.

"We're overdue for a *very* long conversation with him," Maksim looked as furious as I felt. He offered his gun. "If you want to kill the old man, I will give you the pleasure."

My gaze moved to the old man, bleeding from bullet holes in his chest and leg, still shouting like a wounded bull.

I felt nothing. The memories did not rise up to swamp me, he was just another vicious bastard and the world would be better without him. "I killed Colm. If I had had more time, I would have drawn it out, he deserved it for putting a gun to my wife's head. I do not need to off the old man."

"Can I do it, then?" Dario Toscano asked. I was secretly grateful that his brother Giovanni was the Don for their *famiglia* and the man our sister would be marrying, not Dario. Gio, at least, was capable of self-control.

"Get in line," Maksim said coldly.

"I need to be with Tania," I told him quietly, and he gripped my shoulder.

"Go take care of your wife. This is finished."


"Oh, my sweet girl…"

Tania was huddled in the warehouse's small office, curled up in a chair, making herself as small as possible. Her red wig was halfway off and dark tracks of mascara ran down her face.

"I tried to help her clean up," Gavrill stammered, looking genuinely distressed, "she didn't want me to touch her. But the doc examined her and said there were no serious injuries, just some scrapes and bruises."

"Thank you, Gavrill, I have her now."

He nodded, looking worriedly at Tania before leaving, shutting the door gently behind him.

Scooping her up, I sat with her on my lap, rocking her gently.

"I'm sorry," she sobbed, "I saw you coming for me! You could have been shot!"

"My darling, *you* could have been killed. It was a miracle that you didn't catch a stray bullet up there on the stage." I kissed her forehead, squeezing her tighter. I was furious. Furious with her for putting herself in harm's way, for not telling me that O'Rourke called in his debt. I was enraged with that selfish, heartless prick for using Tania and risking her life.

When she stopped weeping, giving out the occasional gulp or hiccup, I lifted her chin with my finger. "I'll take you back to the safe house and clean you up, you will feel better."

"The doctor tried to give me medication, for shock or something but I wouldn't take it," her lovely gold eyes were filling with tears again, "I wouldn't, I had to see you first."

Cupping her face gently, I stroked my thumbs over her cheekbones. "I will take care of you, sweet girl. I will not leave again, all right? I am here." She rubbed her eyes with the back of her hands, an oddly childlike gesture that broke my heart.

### *At the cottage...*

When Tania needed soothing, a shower would not do. She wanted a bath, a hot bath with some kind of relaxing scent. My only experience with elaborate bath accessories was with the jar of bath bombs in her bathroom back in Manhattan. I would randomly pick one out and throw it in a tub full of warm water. It never failed to comfort her.

Seating her gently on the counter, I rolled up my sleeves and started the water in the bathtub, which fortunately was large and elaborately outfitted. There was an elegant little tray of bath salts and I lifted the stopper on the first bottle, holding it under her nose. "Do you like this one?" She shook her head silently, her gaze following me as if I might disappear.

"How about this one?" She nodded with a small smile, so I tapped out a bit into the bathtub and found body wash, a sponge, and a pitcher to wash and rinse her hair.

After I lifted her off the counter, Tania stood still, letting me take off her crooked wig and remove the hairpins. Her thick brown hair fell loose as she let out a groan of relief. Then, the serious, dowdy suit and shoes and her underwear came off. She was still strangely passive, simply letting me move her arms and legs as I undressed her and helped her into the hot water.

Kneeling next to the tub, I ran my knuckles across her cheek. "Hot enough?" She nodded, drawing her knees up and resting her head on them. "My sweet wife…" It was too much, it was all too much. I had grown up seeing this kind of violence, enduring it, committing it. But Tania was not ready for something like this. She should never have witnessed this kind of atrocity. I gently smoothed the body wash over her skin, washing away the blood and sweat, I could feel her muscles relax slowly.

"What happened to Bryne," she asked, "is he okay?"

I ran the sponge over her shoulders. "Yes, two of Turgenev's men were tasked with getting him out safely."

"Was that- tonight, was that always the plan?" She was watching me now and I set the sponge down.

"Yes."

Her head dropped to her knees again. "I see why you didn't tell me. Ella tried to…prepare me, I guess by telling me you and Maksim would take out the top players in their clan. But that was… that was so many people." Her chest hitched with another sob.

"You never should have been there," I said bitterly. "I'm going to kill O'Rourke for playing his sick game with you."

"No more killing," she said vehemently. "Not for me."

"This is part of our life in the Morozov Bratva. It will not change. Tonight? I do not feel remorse for any of those men. Not when they were instrumental in kidnapping you and Ella. Not when they tortured me. They have murdered and tortured hundreds of people, maybe thousands."

Tania took my hand, examining it. There was blood under my fingernails, I thought I had washed it all off. Pulling on it, she urged, "Get in with me, please? We'll just sit here. You know, for a little bit."

"Of course, love. Whatever you like." Stripping quickly, I slid in behind her, cradling her against my chest and wrapping my arms around her. "We can stay in here as long as you want."

*Tania...*

It took hours of arguing with Yuri and Maksim the next day to keep them from murdering O'Rourke. Not that I didn't think the rat bastard deserved it, because he did. But he was too rich. Too connected.

Too powerful.

"Trust me, there's better ways to handle him," I promised my scowling husband.

Patrick joined us for lunch. He looked exhausted and prepared to enjoy a liquid lunch of whiskey until I filled a plate for him, nagging until he gave in.

"Leave off, woman," he sighed, seating himself. "It's been a long week and that whiskey is my reward."

"I just realized that you're going gray," I said. "Already? Damn, these two are working you too hard."

He shrugged, stuffing another chip in his mouth. "Runs in the family, my Da was completely silver-haired by his mid-thirties."

"You've only got a couple of years to go then," I teased him, "though working as this family's *Obshchak* would turn anyone gray."

"Patrick here is getting a promotion," Maksim said. "We couldn't have pulled this off without our undercover Irishman. You were a menace last night, *Obshchak*."

Raising his glass in a toast, Patrick nodded but kept eating.

"Congratulations," I said, adding more fish and chips to his plate, "what's the promotion?"

The three men exchanged some sort of irritating, meaningful glance that told me absolutely nothing.

"It's less a promotion," Yuri said carefully, "as it is Patrick reclaiming what's his."

I looked between the three of them before sighing. "Okay, thank you for the eloquent pauses and the explanation that clarifies absolutely nothing. What is Patrick reclaiming?"

There was a wry twist to his mouth when Patrick said, "My family were the original kings of the Irish Mob. The Doyle's. The O'Connell's managed something similar to the bloodbath last night against my family. But they were more..." he swallowed and Yuri leaned forward, like he was trying to offer support.

"They were more thorough. They killed my parents. My uncles, aunts, and cousins. My grandparents. And..." Patrick's eyes were like ice chips and the funny, kind man I knew was buried under years of fury and hate. "They murdered my little sisters. But not before they... they hurt them."

"Oh, my god Patrick, I..." I took his hand, clenched in a fist and smoothed out his fingers. "I am so sorry. How long have you been suffering with this?"

He shrugged. "Ten years. I was shot three times but I lived. I'm sure Jimmy O'Connell would have been back to finish the job, but Yuri found me first. We met up at the Ares Academy when we were younger. He and Maksim took me into the Morozov Bratva. I've been here ever since."

Yuri stared at our clasped hands, and Patrick hastily withdrew his. "He found Jimmy O'Connell a couple of years later and took a very, very long time killing him. It sent quite the message." He smiled approvingly at Patrick.

"This is Patrick's territory now," Maksim said, making it sound like a formal proclamation. The Doyle family will take over O'Connell interests."

"And pay the Morozov Bratva a healthy percentage," Patrick added, sounding a bit more like his usual cheeky self.

"Of course," Maksim shrugged as if it was obvious. "The Doyle clan might be small, but Patrick will be growing it very soon." There was another look exchanged that I didn't understand, but before I could ask some prying questions, Gavrill stepped in.

"*Pakhan,* Nolan O'Rourke is here. He wishes to 'say hello'."

I could practically smell the hate in the room.


"Good morning!" O'Rourke said cheerfully as he strolled into the room, holding my messenger bag and laptop case. "I thought I'd drop off Tania's things, though of course, she is always welcome to stay at the castle."

A low growl came from behind me and it sounded like a rabid dog got loose in the cottage. When Yuri's heat radiated off my back, I realized that the growl came from him and he, apparently, was coming for O'Rourke.

"Hey, hey, hey hey hey, honey. Hold up!" I stepped in front of Yuri, "You can't kill the sociopathic billionaire. Not cool. Besides,

I'm pretty sure you met your kill quota last night so please…"

*Oh my god*, I thought, disgusted with myself, *I am joking about my husband's Bratva killing a hundred men. I am the worst person alive.*

Yuri clenched his fists, radiating fury and hate and scariness, his head was lowered like he was about to charge O'Rourke like a bull.

"Tania could have been killed because of your stupidity!" he roared, "There can be no excuse for putting her in the middle of this!"

"Yes, but you saved her," O'Rourke said, looking a little bored which was not helping his case. "So, all is well."

"You left her unprotected in a goddamned spotlight on stage while your bodyguards surrounded *you!*" Yuri shouted.

O'Rourke's eyes were turning that frozen earth color again. "You have what you want," he said coldly, "and without my assistance it is unlikely you could have overthrown the O'Connell mob. And I have what I want. Our business is concluded."

Maksim was no happier than Yuri was with this smug asshole, but he was apparently capable of more diplomacy. "Our business is concluded," he said coldly. "While we have kept our part of the bargain, you deliberately put my sister-in-law in harm's way. And for no reason we can find. I've seen a photo of Maureen Sullivan. Tania does not resemble her, even with the wig, makeup, and glasses. So, why?"

O'Rourke paused in the doorway, looking at me with an unkind little smile. "Do you remember, darling, when you shook my hand at the wedding, agreeing to repay my favor? You told me - quite nobly - that you would never kill anyone."

My brow furrowed, "I remember."

The midday sun came through the window, lighting his face oddly, one side in the sun, all handsome-looking, and the other half in shadow. It was jarring, and his little smile only made it worse.

"I wanted to prove to you that you *would* kill. That you would do anything I ask, steal, lie… Not quite so principled, are you, darling?"

"You had me hack those O'Connell accounts, dress up like that woman and watch those men be slaughtered just to- to-" I flailed, trying to finish the thought.

"You could have warned the O'Connell's," he said in his nasty, silky voice. "You knew these two were going to kill them. You could have saved over a hundred men, but you kept quiet, didn't you? You killed those men just as surely as if you were holding the gun."

My lunch was threatening to make a reappearance. He was a vicious, manipulative bastard. But he was right.

"You endangered my wife, just to show you could make her do these things to entertain you?" Yuri said viciously. "This was a game for you."

His hand reached into his jacket and I panicked, knowing he was going for his gun. Yuri was not reckless with weapons, he made it a point to use his gun or knife only as a last resort.

I grabbed his arm. "Babe, he is not worth it. He's not. Please."

Yuri breathed in deeply, jaw clenched, but he pulled his hand away from the holster.

"I believe it's time for you to leave," Maksim said, herding O'Rourke out the door. Before the door closed, he looked over his shoulder at me with a saucy wink.

"Hey, remember when we talked about this?" I said, smoothing Yuri's jacket with anxious hands, "Remember? You said, 'Once one has amassed that level of wealth and power, playing with the lives of men is the only game left to play.' He did all this, just to show he could. Because he was bored. Who knows? Please, let it go."

He was struggling, my sweet husband, his hands clenched into fists, but Yuri forced himself to relax and kissed me. "You are right, my *Koroleva.* But I will not forget."

I wish I could forget. I heard Nolan O'Rourke's voice in my head for weeks after that day, telling me that I was capable of lying, theft, and murder. He was right. And I hated him for it.

# CHAPTER TWENTY-FIVE

*In which there are revelations, a job offer, and happily ever after.*

**Yuri**

**A week later...**

I leaned against the French doors that led to the gardens, listening to my wife play her violin, lounging in one of the chairs by the pond.

She was so beautiful, the weak sunlight filtered through her hair and made her skin glow, swaying slightly with the music as her long, graceful fingers moved over the violin strings.

Tania was good at keeping a happy face for me, but I had heard her, locked up in the library, weeping and talking to Ella on her phone.

"Give her some time," Maksim had advised me. "They have been friends much longer than we've been husbands. There are things you and I speak of that no one else understands. It is the same for them."

What hit the hardest was that I walked away from that night in Dublin free. There is no miraculous cure for what happened to me during the kidnapping, but putting that entire family down like dogs took away my nightmares, and the moments when their laughing voices were too loud in my head to push away. But I felt tremendous guilt for it, as if I had traded my struggles for my wife to be burdened with hers.

Looking up at me with a smile as I approached, she put her violin aside. "Hey, gorgeous," she said, "how was your meeting?"

"Productive," I said, lifting her chin with my finger to kiss her. It was easy to forget everything else with Tania's lush mouth, her tongue tracing and curling with mine. I picked her up from the chair seating myself and then her on my lap, straddling me.

"How are *you* doing, my *Koroleva?*" I brushed a strand of hair off her cheek, tilting my head to get her to look at me.

"I'm fine," she shrugged with a false smile. Then, she sagged a bit, leaning her cheek against my hand. "I mean, I will be. I'll work this out in my head and make sense of it."

"Will you let me help?" I asked, "I want to take this pain from you."

"I know. I wanted to take yours, too. Just… you know. Just be here, okay?" She buried her face in my neck, taking in a long breath.

"Are you *sniffing* me?" I teased.

"You smell delicious." Her voice was muffled against my neck.

"Like one of Anya's honey cakes?" I chuckled.

"Nope. Like pine. And sea salt and warm cotton," she kissed the tight cord in my neck and I felt her warmth spread over my skin.

Biting her soft earlobe, I whispered, "You are heading for a very full afternoon if you keep this up."

Tania gave her hoarse little chuckle against my skin. "Is that a double entendre?"

Sliding my hands up under her skirt and grabbing the rounded cheeks of her ass, I squeezed them, enjoying her yelp. "We have run out of Catherine the Great horse jokes, we must find something new."

Now she really chortled, and it was so good to see her laugh again.

Standing up, I kept my hands on her ass as her legs wrapped around my waist. "We cannot walk into the house like this, Yuri!" Tania gasped, "Seriously-"

"I am not taking you into the mausoleum," I corrected her, heading in another direction. I grinned at her embarrassed expression. "You think you are the only one who likens this house to a mortuary?"

"No, it's really beautiful and-"

"Ah, ah. No lies, even if they are polite ones. I have plans for you." Taking a left at the arbor covered in roses, I headed for a little stone cottage almost hidden by the vines.

"What is this?" Tania stopped sucking on my neck long enough to notice the cottage.

"It was used by the guards for a while until we built them a new base of operations," I said, "I've kept it for a quieter spot to escape to when the house is full of people."

"I'll have to remember that," she kissed me again as I fumbled for the handle.

The instant the door was shut, I slammed her up against it, squeezing her ass as I lifted her higher to bury my face between her breasts. "Take this off," I pulled at her sweater with my teeth. She yanked it off and was left in her bra, a pretty black lace and silk one. I sucked her nipple harshly over the lace, feeling it pebble instantly, then groaned and moved to the other breast. Tania's nails scratched gently against my scalp, then she gripped handfuls of my hair as I bit the nipple I had just coaxed free from its cup.

Swinging her off me and over the arm of the couch, I yanked her leggings and panties down her legs and slapped her luscious-looking ass. The red imprint of my hand was gorgeous on her tanned skin, and I slapped the other cheek, just to be fair.

I pressed my hard cock against the curve of her body leaning over the couch, growling as I grabbed a handful of her hair, pulling her head up to kiss her. "What is the word?" I whispered into her ear.

"Schenectady," Tania moaned, feeling my cock rub against her, ready to rip free from my zipper.

"It will be impossible to ever forget that safe word," I bit her neck, a sharp nip that made her jump and gasp. Sliding my hands from her shoulders, up her arms and to her wrists, I put them on the middle couch cushion, forcing her to stretch to reach it. "Do not move your hands from here," I warned her, "I would hate to deny your orgasms for the next week."

My wife made an irritable sound that ended in a gasp as I sank to my knees, pressing my mouth against her perfect cunt.

*Tania…*

This man was going to kill me.

Yuri's hot mouth was against my pussy, his tongue and fingers spreading my wet lips and humming against me, setting off sparks that made me go up on my toes to push against him. His fingers tightened against my hips and he said, "Do not move. You will come twice before I will put my cock in you."

"Are you sure you're not intentionally torturing me?" I moaned, the tendons in my legs straining to hold my position. He pointed his tongue and drove it up me, chuckling when I shrieked. One of his thick, calloused fingers circled my opening and stabbed back inside me while another leisurely circled my clit. He put his knees between my feet, pushing my legs open wider as he ran the flat of his tongue over me, swiping between my wet, swelling lips. His head moved deeper between my legs so he could take my clit delicately between his teeth, batting it back and forth with his tongue and then sucking it hard enough to make me let out a scream as I came.

"One more…" he reminded me before sliding two fingers up inside me as his lips continued to suck against my already overworked clit. He scissored them inside me, "So tight. Even after all the times I have been inside you." Yuri groaned and the sound made me arch my back.

"Please, babe. Your dick is hard enough to qualify as a medical emergency!" I moaned, "Please put it in me."

He lightly slapped my ass. "You know what to do." His fingers inside me moved faster, rubbing against all those sensitive, secret spots I could never find on my own. I had a white-knuckled grip on the couch cushion, desperately trying to stay in place because I knew Yuri could be a complete bastard and would really hold me to that threat.

Kissing the base of my spine, my diabolical husband began murmuring filthy things to me in Russian. Anything that sounded dirty in English was positively filthy in his native language and I couldn't stop the next orgasm from taking me by surprise. He gave me another long lick before standing up.

I could hear his belt whipping through the loops on his pants and his zipper being yanked down. "You are doing so well for me, my *Koroleva,* don't move." He slid his belt around my hips and held the ends like reins. "I have waited all day to debauch you," he chuckled, his warm breath on my neck making me shiver.

He dragged his thick cock between my thighs, spreading my legs wider. My breath hitched as I felt the broad head against my opening. "Hold on…" he warned before jerking me backward with his belt and yanking me on to his cock.

"Babe… Yuri…" I wheezed, "I can feel you clear to my belly button." I have never felt so full, full to bursting and I panted, trying to catch my breath. He pulled out slowly, and then tugged me back again with his belt, I could feel the muscles in his abdomen clench as he slammed against me and I already felt that tight spiral, something that ran from my center and moved outwards, up my spine, down my legs and through my fingers and toes and when it started spiraling back in, I knew I would blow apart when it reached my pussy again. My entire focus narrowed down to that moment, moaning shamelessly as I waited for it, wanting it, craving the moment when-

Yuri leaned over my back, making me feel his weight as he pulled harder on his belt around my hips. "I can feel you tightening up, so close to coming. What would it take, coming against my cock, coming so hard you nearly squeeze me out? Because you are right there."

His hand reached around and slapped my swollen clit and I screamed. Like a banshee. Like a woman with no sense who did not care who heard her because *nothing* could feel this intense. The red heat of pain and the delicious stretch and then my porn star of a husband came too, his biceps bulging as he yanked on the belt ends one more time. I could feel the surging warmth from his finish all through me as my muscles turned to concrete, trapping him inside me as he groaned, still spurting his finish.

## *Yuri...*

I had to brace my elbows against the arm of the couch to keep some of my weight off Tania, my legs felt like water. Licking the sweat from her back, I said, "I fear we must cut this short. My brother and Ella are on their way from the airport."

I groaned as she stiffened, her cunt gripping me tightly as she tried to stand up. "Why didn't you tell me!" Tania gasped. "Also, there was nothing *short* about this, mister!"

Regretfully pulling my cock from her, I kissed the back of her neck. "Hang on, lovely. I will clean you up." Getting a wet washcloth, I wipe gently between her legs, enjoying my wife's little moan.

"You might have to carry me back to the house," she admitted,

"I'm a little shaky."

"Really?" I bit her earlobe, "I was intending to ask you to carry me back."

She cackled delightedly, as I knew she would.

My beautiful bride.

Ella kept the rest of us laughing uncontrollably at dinner with her descriptions of a TikTok influencer who showed up at the hospital with certain… items wedged up his ass.

"Toy cars!" she wheezed, slapping the table, "Six of them! He kept insisting it was a new trend out of Asia and he wanted to be the first one to try it in New York."

Tania tried to catch her breath, wiping her eyes. "I want to give him 'A' for effort but an 'F' for his crippling lack of emotional intelligence."

Maksim shook his head sourly. "My brilliant wife, wasting her skills on that man…"

The talk shifted to Dublin and the aftermath of the O'Connell Mob's demise.

"How is Patrick doing?" Ella asked, "Does he need more support?"

I exchanged a glance with Maksim. "He is doing well, though he does have quite a bit of rebuilding to do. O'Rourke," I added sourly, "has kept to his part of the bargain, though there is a matter of a huge amount of money missing from the O'Connell accounts, no doubt siphoned by O'Rourke."

"Really?" Tania said casually, "Like, around two hundred and twenty million pounds?"

Maksim leaned forward. "And how would you know about such a specific sum?"

Tania put three flash drives on the table. "This one is for the Cayman Island accounts. And the red one has the holdings from Suisse Bank. This little purple guy has the cash transfers from their prostitution and white trafficking business. I would really like you to use that money to support these women while they recover and get back on their feet."

For once, my brother, the mighty *Pakhan,* was speechless.

"You slinky little minx," I leaned over, kissing her hand. "What have you been up to?"

"I had a feeling O'Rourke was fucking with me when my job description went from financial hacker to undercover redhead. So I used his firewall program to breach the bank accounts and transfer the money."

Ella gave Tania a standing ovation and Maksim finally regained his power of speech. "You are a woman of many talents, sister. You're dangerous."

"Only to assholes," she said sweetly. "I had a feeling O'Rourke was going to strip all the money from the O'Connell businesses and make it impossible for Patrick to get everything moving again. This way, he's got some capital to work with and there's enough for the Bratva so that he won't have to pay tribute for a while."

I grin at Maksim and he nods.

"I had planned to offer you a job at the company here in St. Petersburg even before this genius stunt but now, Maksim and I are very enthusiastically inviting you to join the new construction and land development company we are opening." I kissed her hand. "No one could be a better CFO."

Tania thought about it. "This is an actual position where I have the power to make independent decisions?"

Maksim and I nod. "This is in your area of expertise, darling, not ours. You are far too skilled to be wasting the clever brain of yours," I said fondly.

"I'd like to look at the business plan," Tania said, "but you already know the answer is yes." She grinned, bouncing in her seat, *"Hell, yes."*

"To our brilliant and cunning brides," I toasted.

Maksim raised his glass. *"Vashe zdorov'ye!"*

"Cheers!" Ella said, and Tania echoed her. It occurred to me that this dining room rang with more laughter tonight than at any time in my memory. I raised my glass to Maksim silently, both of us toasting our very good fortune.

"When you said you were giving me a pearl necklace," Tania said lazily, "I kind of thought you meant the other kind."

We were lying on the rug in front of the fireplace in our bedroom, my wife sprawled on top of me. Hooking my finger under the golden Australian South Sea pearl necklace I had given her tonight; I pulled her closer. "I am always happy to fulfill all of my beautiful wife's wishes," I said, "but you might need to give me a moment to recover." She laughed, wrapping her arms and legs around me.

I spent some time kissing along her neck and shoulders before saying, "I am proud of you, finding a way to pull all that money right out from under O'Rourke's nose."

"I owed Patrick," Tania said, smoothing back my hair, "I never would have come here without him pushing me."

"I would have lost you forever," I sighed, resting my forehead against hers, "without you having the courage to come charging the rescue."

"Yeah…" she drawled. "Not my smoothest maneuver, babe, but here we are, right?"

"Forever," I promised, raising her hand and kissing her wedding ring.

"Now, there's just one last thing to do," she said.

Groaning, I sat up against the leather couch, stretching my back and resting her head in my lap. "What would that be, my *Koroleva?*"

The evilest smile spread across her sweet face. "Going back to New York and meeting my mother. You're going to have a lot of ass-kissing to do."

My jaw dropped and my bride cackled gleefully.

# EPILOGUE

*In which Patrick's plans for the Doyle dynasty include one extremely unwilling participant*

**Yuri…**

"Where is your wife?" Maksim asked as I entered the study.

"Blissfully unconscious," I said, rubbing my eyes and feeling my chapped, overworked cock twinge against my leg.

"Good," he said, putting in a call to Patrick.

When he appeared onscreen, he looked just as exhausted as I felt. "How are you, *Ceann Fine?*"

"Just pulling everything together," he said, "there's a lot of moving parts here. Just deciding what men I can trust is kicking my ass."

"Speaking of ass-kicking," I grinned a bit maliciously, "how is it going with sweet little Aisling O'Connell?"

As if on cue, we could hear shouting in the background. "Feck you, you fekkin' fecks! All of you can go straight to hell! *PÓG MO THÓIN!*"

"That means, 'you can kiss my ass,'" Patrick supplied helpfully. "Why does this feel less and less like a reward?"

"Becoming a leader is never simple, or easy," Maksim said, not without sympathy. "When is the wedding?"

"There's not gonna be any fekkin' wedding!" Aisling screamed.

Patrick sighed as he stood up and we were treated to the sounds of a fierce struggle until he handed her over to two of his guards and the door slammed shut. Returning to the call, he ran his hand through his hair.

"Is your hair whiter than it was last week?" I asked incredulously.

"Nothing will turn your hair white faster than an Irish woman on the rampage," he said. "I will set the wedding for next week if you can make it. It will make the big meeting of the new captains go more smoothly if the alliance is sealed and it's clear you stand behind it."

"We'll be there," Maksim nodded. "I hope all your limbs will still be intact."

Patrick didn't even bother to pretend to find that amusing and signed off quickly.

"This reeks of disaster," Maksim said.

"So did our marriages," I pointed out, "and look how ours have turned out."

He raised his glass of vodka, clinking it against mine. "The poor man won't even know what hit him."

"Probably not," I agreed.

# READ THE EXTENDED EPILOGUE!

What comes next after Happily Ever After? In the Morozov Bratva, nothing is simple. Yuri and Tania's story continues in the extended epilogue. Download your free copy here: dl.bookfunnel.com/sq26af4ws7

**Please review...**

If you enjoyed Yuri and Tania's story, can I trouble you to leave a review? Reviews are the lifeblood of an independently published book and can mean the difference between success or failure. Thank you for your time!

**Free books!**

Join my email list to keep up with new releases and giveaways - I'm too lazy to spam you, so the emails will pop up only when something interesting is about to happen. For instance, Book Three in the Morozov Bratva Saga, Patrick and Aisling's story, coming in May 2023.

I'll have a free book waiting for you to say thanks for joining us- download The Reluctant Spy here: dl.bookfunnel.com/6xud62rmg0

# AFTERWORD

If you've not read Maksim and Ella's story, Book One from the Morozov Bratva Saga - Mistaken - can be found here:

Are you curious about Thomas and Lauren's story in The Corporation series? Find the Reluctant Bride here:

# BOOKS BY THIS AUTHOR

## Mistaken - An Arranged Marriage Bratva Romance

What happens after a mistaken identity, a kidnapping, and a terrifying chase through the woods?
Something much worse. Marriage.

Maksim Morozov is the billionaire Bratva King of New York City. He takes what he wants. Unfortunately, that includes me. That's what happens when you're in the wrong place at the right time.

He thinks he will keep me locked up in his penthouse like a princess in a tower. He thinks I'm a commodity to be used, like the other women raised in his world.

What's worse? Maksim Morozov wants to own me, body and soul.

So, in the weeks between a Christmas wedding and Valentine's Day, he's about to find out that owning me is not going to be that easy.

Mistaken - An Arranged Marriage Bratva Romance contains dark themes and is for 18+ readers only.

## The Reluctant Bride - Dark Tales Of The Corporation Book One

Wait. What do you mean, my dad gave me to you?

I was ready for a fresh start in England, a career with the London Symphony Orchestra. But my father's "underperforming" company is bought out by The Corporation. Suddenly, I'm being told I'm marrying the tall and terrifying Thomas Williams, because dad would rather trade me to keep control of his company. Thomas tells me that it "looks better" to be a married man as his organized crime empire starts a partnership with the Russian Bratva Syndicate.

Really?

I'm a wife. I have a giant diamond ring to prove it... and a husband who can be kind in one moment and scary in the next. And there's car chases, and assassination attempts. There's a body in my cello case! Who has a marriage like this?

But by the time we're in St. Petersburg and surrounded by new friends and old enemies, my gorgeous, terrifying husband might just need me.

The Reluctant Bride is a Dark Mafia Romance and is 18+ only.

## The Reluctant Spy - Dark Tales Of The Corporation Book Two

Maura MacLaren - mousey, dowdy, and very, very good with technology - is a perfect Corporation employee. Brilliant at her job, smart enough to know to keep her head down, and in debt to the criminal enterprise that gave her a chance when her past left her with nowhere to turn. But this puts her under the watchful eye of the Corporation's diabolical, gorgeous, and utterly unforgiving Second in Command, James Pine.

Pine has been sent by the head office in London to be sure nothing will go wrong with the Corporation's largest deal to date. The last thing a man in his dangerous position needs are feelings, or surprises. Especially feelings for a nerdy underling who is turning out to be full of surprises, including a sensually submissive nature that Pine finds too compelling to resist. But Pine is as cold-hearted as he is handsome and he never denies himself what he wants.

But when Maura's darkest secret puts her life and Pine's deal in danger, they both find themselves shocked at the sensual depths he will drag her to for revenge. And the lengths he will go to in order to save her life.

The Reluctant Spy is a dark Mafia romance and for 18+ readers only.

## Mr. And Mrs. Ari Levinsky Invite You To... The Worst Wedding Ever

An Arranged Marriage Mafia Romance

Heather's given to Mafia King Ari Levinsky in an arranged marriage to create an alliance with her terrible mobster dad. She's supposed to be touring Europe after graduating from college, but before she can blink she's standing at the altar trying to read her vows in... Aramaic? Heather's new husband is gigantic; tall, muscled, terrifying, and loud. And she doesn't even get to pick out her own wedding dress! Then, it's on to a romantic beach honeymoon, with so much double-crossing, and she finds the only way to outsmart her scary, ridiculously hot husband... is to out-sex him.

Mr. and Mrs. Ari Levinsky Invite You to... the Worst Wedding Ever is for 18+ readers only.

## Blood Brothers - Captive Blood One

"It'll be good for you," he said. "The stalker will never find you there." My agent sends me to stay on an Oregon mountaintop, cared for by a surly handyman named Steve, who looks like a supermodel ... lumberjack ... Greek God sort of guy.
I'm supposed to feel safe here? I keep having all these dreams ... dreams where Lumberjack Steve is biting me. Now, I'm losing time. Losing blood.
And I think it's possible my stalker is closer than I thought.

## The Birdcage - Captive Blood Two

Black Heart keeps me in the Birdcage, high above the blasted remains of the earth after the Night Brethren plunged us into darkness. At the gate of his mansion, the Shadows wait to tear screaming humans into pieces of blood and bone. In the Birdcage, the vampire who keeps me is growing impatient. What does he want? My blood? My soul? I don't have long to decide whether to take my chances with the Shadows or find out what Black Heart intends to do.

To make it worse? He's not the only monster who wants me.
The Birdcage is a dark romance meant for 18+ readers only.

## I Love The Way You Lie - Loki, The God Of Lies And Mischief - A Dark Romance

A nameless princess: innocent, damaged and very lethal. A ruthless king with the power of a god. And trouble, lots of it.
When King Loki of Asgard takes the daughter of the Dark Elven Queen captive, he not only strips an enemy of a powerful weapon, but gains for himself a wife. Now the newly named and wed Queen Ingrid must learn to survive the perils of court

life, the wages of war, and most dangerous of all, her seductive husband's bed.

"I Love the Way You Lie" is a Dark Loki romance for 18+ readers only.

# ABOUT THE AUTHOR

## Arianna Fraser

Working as an entertainment reporter gives Arianna Fraser plenty of fuel for her imagination when writing tales about current-day romance-suspense stories and Norse Mythology - Loki in particular. There will always be an infuriatingly stubborn heroine, an unfairly handsome and cunning hero - or anti-hero - romance, shameless smut, danger, and something will explode or catch on fire. She is clearly a terrible firebug, and her husband has sixteen fire extinguishers stashed throughout the house.

When she's not interviewing superheroes and villains, Arianna lives in the western US with her twin boys, obstreperous little daughter, and sleep-deprived husband. She is also very fond of snakes.

Join her email newsletter to keep up with new releases and she'll bribe you shamelessly with a free book!
https://dl.bookfunnel.com/4cnao7l0mg

Have a thought? Wanna share? ariannafraser88@gmail.com

Find her on Tumblr: https://www.tumblr.com/blog/view/

ariannafraserwrites

On Goodreads: http://bit.ly/ariannafrasergoodreads

Printed in Great Britain
by Amazon